Praise

"*The Heroine's Labyrinth* offers something greatly needed in the world of storytelling, a key to the special conditions and unique logic of the Heroine's Journey that will be game-changing for writers. Through careful analysis of a multitude of popular stories featuring female protagonists, Douglas Burton has cracked the code and made it accessible. He shows convincingly that the Heroine's Journey is distinctly different, motivated by different needs and drives, but still compatible with the masculine-centered Hero's Journey. Especially useful are the summaries of his findings at the end of each chapter, giving solid principles for building emotionally satisfying adventures that put women in the driver's seat."

—**Christopher Vogler**, author of *The Writer's Journey: Mythic Structure for Writers*

"*The Heroine's Labyrinth* is filled with profound and unique observations on the topic of story structure, no matter what the gender of your protagonist. Burton closely analyzes a wide breadth of stories and proves his thesis that Joseph Campbell missed half the story."

—**Matt Bird**, author of *The Secrets of Story* and *The Secrets of Character*

"*The Heroine's Labyrinth* is a revolutionary book on storytelling from the feminine perspective. It provides a bold new framework for understanding the female Hero's Journey. But it is not new in its origin and is actually primordial. Douglas Burton has uncovered a hidden treasure that unveils how the great women's stories have always been told throughout the ages, if we had only seen it. The Heroine's Labyrinth is not just a journey into the depths of story structure, it is ultimately a deep dive into the nature of the soul itself."

—**Kamran Pasha**, author of *Mother of the Believers*

THE
HEROINE'S
LABYRINTH

ARCHETYPAL DESIGNS
IN HEROINE-LED
FICTION

DOUGLAS A. BURTON

SILENT
MUSIC·PRESS

Silent Music Press, LLC
8505 Jilbur Drive
Round Rock, TX 78681

Book cover and interior design by Monkey C Media
Edited by David Aretha
Author photo by Julia Crist Photography
Tarot cards work for hire artwork by
Mystic Muse (fiverr.com/mystic_muse)

First Edition
Printed in the United States of America

ISBN: 978-1-7330221-5-6 (trade paperback)
978-1-7330221-6-3 (ebook)
978-1-7330221-7-0 (hardcover)
978-1-7330221-8-7 (audiobook)

Library of Congress Control Number: 2023923260

This book is dedicated to storytellers everywhere.

ACT 1
ORIENTATION

 The Labyrinth

The Masked Minotaur

Claims the Sacred Fire

Captivity Bargain

The Black Swan

Call to Adventure

ACT 2
EXPLORATION

Cult of Deception

Chambers of Knowledge

Chamber Guardians

Beast as Ally

The Fragile Power

The Broken Truce

ACT 3
PERMUTATION

The Poisoned Apple

The Unmasking

Home as Battleground

The Shieldmaiden

The Broken Spell

Atonement

The Heroine's Labyrinth

START

The Masked Minotaur

Claims the Sacred Fire

Captivity Bargain

ACT II

ACT I

The Broken Truce

The Fragile Power

The Black Swan

(Heroic Partners)

Beast as Ally

The Poisoned Apple

(Center/Power Shift)

Call to Adventure

ACT III

The Unmasking

Chamber Guardians

Cult of Deception

Home as Battleground

Chambers of Knowledge

Atonement

The Shieldmaiden

FINISH

The Broken Spell

CONTENTS

PREFACE

he *Heroine's Labyrinth* is a book for writers—novelists, screenwriters, role players, memoirists—anyone who loves and cares about storytelling. The narrative concepts within this book are not variations of the hero's journey; they are not a response to any criticism of heroines, nor are they prescriptive notions of my own design. The heroine's labyrinth is a model of the archetypal power that **exists now**, **has always existed**, and **will continue to exist** for as long as there's still a heroine to write about.

In 2018, I was deep into writing my first novel, *Far Away Bird*. The historical fiction novel centered around the real life of Empress Theodora, arguably the most dynamic empress of the Byzantine Empire. Her tale included historical and biographical details that any novelist needed to follow to capture the truth and essence of her character. However, to help me organize Empress Theodora's story into a workable structure, like many writers, I turned to the hero's journey. You see, I had decades' worth of notes, Excel spreadsheets, hand-scribbled index cards, and countless analyses of individual stories, all centered around the hero's journey. I trained myself to spot patterns and themes in stories, similar to reading tarot cards or dreams, because the patterns are often intuitive and visual, symbolic and insightful, distinctive and psychological. The exhaustive effort prepared my instincts as a writer so that I could apply the archetypal themes to my own stories.

Like many writers, I trusted my novel to the time-tested hero's journey. But midway through the novel, I came to the most frustrating conclusion possible—that the life of my beloved empress and leading heroine *did not follow the hero's journey.* As a full believer in the hero's journey, this was a devastating realization. So, begrudgingly, I did what seemed to be the next and most logical step in the writing process.

I searched for the feminine equivalent of the hero's journey.

Dear writers, instead of finding a single version of the heroine's journey, I found a gazillion theories, blogs, articles, and books that covered feminine spirituality, treatises on womanhood, feminist critiques, advice for writing female characters, and literary criticisms. While all of these reads enlightened me to various degrees, none matched the clarity, magnitude, and usefulness the hero's journey offered me as a writer.

For those writers who don't yet know, the hero's journey is a unique narrative arc found in numerous stories across countless cultures, from the Bronze Age to the current date. Storytellers worldwide have told and still tell mythological tales about a hero who sets out on a journey to overcome a powerful villain. From the perspective of comparative mythology, these unrelated cultural heroes experienced eerily similar events, themes, and narrative arcs. You'll find the hero's journey in the esteemed company of stories like *The Epic of Gilgamesh*, The Book of Moses, The Bhagavad Gita, *The Iliad, Beowulf, The Lord of the Rings, Star Wars, The Lion King,* and *The Life of Pi.*

The academic and comparative mythologist Joseph Campbell identified a sequence of archetypal designs that recurred so often that he named each theme—the Call to Adventure, a Threshold Guardian, the Wise Guide, the Belly of the Beast, and so on. A hero leaves his home as an immature young man, masters skills and ethics, defeats a monstrous villain in combat, and returns home as a mature hero worthy of distinction and, often, a bride. The patterns of the story mirror a specific growth arc that consistently resonates with people around the world.

But *how* and *why* did these storytellers all tell such similar stories in the first place?

The answer: archetypes.

The word itself roughly translates to "primal models." These primal models seem embedded into the human psyche and may even be the very wellspring of human creativity, instinct, and dreams. Specific human experiences, when strung together, can form a recurring series of archetypal events or narrative arcs that we call a monomyth. One such monomyth is that of a soldier who leaves home for war.

I believe the hero's journey is an evolved version of the soldier's journey. Throughout history, regardless of historical era or geographical location, human societies have *always* needed people to fulfill the warrior role. Soldiers, even today, leave home, lose their youthful identity, master specific skills, and are prepared to confront a potential culture-annihilating militant enemy. The confrontation can be larger-than-life. The warrior role is fraught with the possibility of the warrior's destruction far from home. And hopefully, the warrior returns.

Fulfilling the warrior role is a stark and inevitable reality for human civilization. Therefore, the recurrent warrior experience comes with a pattern of events that doesn't change much through the generations. A wide range of people can fulfill the warrior role in a culture. However, since most soldiers in human history have been men, there's definitely a sense of male-centrism to the warrior-oriented hero's journey, which limits the narrative and often draws criticism.

But if storytellers of different cultures and periods had unconsciously created the hero's journey, wouldn't they also unconsciously create our heroine's journey? If true, then the heroine's narrative arc would also model individual growth using archetypal patterns and events.

So, what *about* the heroine?

I decided to take a second look at fictional heroines on my own. I reread many novels and rewatched hundreds of movies that featured a lead heroine. Everything was back on the table—from *Memoirs of a Geisha* to *Wonder Woman* (2017), from *Their Eyes Were Watching God* to *Jane Eyre*, from *Xena: Warrior Princess* to *Barbie*. What did all these heroines have in common? What events and patterns did they share in their tales? And what archetypes and symbols emerged in their stories, as if from a shared nightmare or dream?

The Feminine Monomyth: Conception

In *The Art of Storytelling: From Parents to Professionals*, Professor Hannah B. Harvey presents a lecture on fairy tales, where she discusses the origins and mythology of Little Red Riding Hood. The common ingredients for the story are an innocent girl, a masculine beast in disguise, and an attempt by the beast to eat the girl. Professor Harvey explains that Little Red Riding Hood is actually a fable about budding womanhood and a cautionary tale about the life choices of a young heroine. I immediately realized that this scenario had vast archetypal power because of its recurrent themes throughout a broad spectrum of stories. Suddenly, we spot Little Red Riding Hood reborn as Dorothy Gale, Buffy the Vampire Slayer, Clarice Starling, or Bella Swan. But the Little Red Riding Hood tropes and scenarios didn't appear *anywhere* in the hero's journey. Therefore, Professor Harvey's interpretation and analysis gave me the exact framework for the narrative model I searched for—a *heroine* with a thousand faces.

I decided to reorganize *all* my notes on heroines—not as a derivative of the hero's journey, not as a criticism of heroines, but as a distinctive stand-alone monomyth found in stories. What I found changed my perspective and understanding of our countless heroines. And so, my desire to unlock the heroine's secrets led me to write the one book I'd never found while writing my own heroine-centric novel.

The copious notes I collected during those years became the foundation of this book. If it helped me, then it can help you. *The Heroine's Labyrinth* is the final result of a life-long passion for storytelling, a personal fascination with archetypes, and an unexpected labor of love in understanding the journey of heroic women in our collective works of fiction. And dear writers, I can't wait to share it all with you.

The Heroine's Labyrinth differs from other books on the topic because of five storytelling guidelines.

1. The heroine is always sovereign, regardless of portrayal, historical period, or restrictive circumstances.
2. The primary focus is on the art of writing and storytelling.
3. The archetypal patterns and themes must be distinct and recurrent in heroine-centric stories.
4. We'll approach story structure as intuitive, semi-sequential, and flexible rather than formulaic, linear, and fixed.
5. The heroine's labyrinth does not invalidate nor diminish the hero's journey.

The combination of these five guidelines delivers a distinctive and original take on heroine-centric stories and the art of storytelling. Many books that studied heroines veered away from the craft of writing. Other books approached feminine stories critically, perhaps discussing heroines more *as they should be*. However, as you'll see, heroines *as they are* and, more importantly, heroines *as they have always been* are far more powerful, inspiring, and memorable.

Joseph Campbell himself said, **"For the symbols of mythology are not manufactured; they cannot be ordered, invented, or permanently suppressed. They are spontaneous productions of the psyche, and each bears within it, undamaged, the germ power of its source."**

In other words, we cannot devise by preference what the heroine does on her own. As writers, we cannot tell the heroine what to do, how to act, or which virtues to model. Instead, we must listen, observe, and learn from her actions and choices. There is a constant heroine across culture and history, through myth and story, and she brings unique solutions and timeless archetypal wisdom to life's challenges. **The heroine's story is *our* story. Her struggles are *our* struggles. And the wisdom she gains, she gains for us all.**

What to Expect

The heroine's labyrinth is one writer's deep dive into the human psyche, a splashdown into the hidden world of dreams and creativity surrounding our favorite heroines. The patterns and archetypes—the primal models—are there.

This book presents examples from the most popular stories in pop culture because they are the most recognizable. One of the problems I had while reading *The Hero with a Thousand Faces* was that most of the examples and references Joseph Campbell used were unknown to me. I had to take his word that an obscure folktale followed the hero's journey and that he accurately interpreted the events from one of a dozen versions of the same story. Older mythologies can often be relatively short, with only a handful of details and multiple versions of the story. The reason it took *Star Wars* for the hero's journey to finally break out is because the film served as a universal reference that everyone knew and understood. The movie had one version with enough details that people could recognize. Therefore, in this book, I'll avoid obscure references for the sake of relatability and clarity. There are over two hundred different stories referenced as examples throughout these pages. So, although some films and stories may be cited multiple times, I did my very best to spread examples across a vast landscape of recognizable heroines and their stories. Films often made for the best references due to their visual nature, permanent details, and the fact that other storytelling mediums, such as novels and comic books, have also been adapted into films.

Lastly, my goal is to stay focused on the heroine, her themes, and her story patterns. The hero's journey will be referenced from time to time, but mainly for the purpose of contrast. There are cases where the uniqueness and beauty of the heroine's labyrinth will be better appreciated when seen in contrast to the hero's journey.

Worth it?

Damn right, it's worth it! So, we must begin the arduous process of decoupling the heroine's journey from the hero's journey. Let's quickly examine the primary distinctions between the hero's journey and the heroine's labyrinth and familiarize ourselves with some of the core concepts.

A DIFFERENT KIND
OF JOURNEY

So, why a labyrinth?

While watching the film version of *The Shining*, I concluded that the story is actually about Wendy Torrance, the true heroine of the tale. The star power of Jack Nicholson misled me into thinking the story was about Jack Torrance. Once I rewatched the film as a story about a heroine, my entire understanding of the story shifted. Near the beginning of the film, Wendy tours the Overlook Hotel and comments, "I feel like I have to leave a trail of breadcrumbs." Her statement, which also references the cautionary folktale, Hansel and Gretel, struck me as an intriguing piece of story exposition. The tour showed Wendy the many hallways, chambers, and dead ends she'd soon have to navigate at the Overlook Hotel. Wendy Torrance was in a labyrinth. As if to further emphasize this thematic reality, a real labyrinth—the infamous hedge maze—lay just outside, a perfect literary complement to the symbolism of the heroine's setting.

This first and most basic orientation sets the tone for the entire story you plan on telling, whether it's fiction, a personal memoir, or even a roleplaying adventure. The nature of the journey determines the nature of the conflict, which often defines the villain. These are organic structures that emerge within a story. The hero's journey plots a linear course, traveling from point A to point B, ever onward, further from home and into unfamiliar environs before returning home. However, many heroines in fiction go on a different journey, one characterized by repetitive circles and often closer to home. Indeed, most heroines never leave the native culture. The adventure hides behind closed doors and interior spaces of otherwise familiar places. The journey travels inward and creates incredible friction while the heroine develops her sense of identity and self-realization. **So, many heroine-centric stories feature heroines in conflict with their native culture, and this conflict lays the groundwork for the entire narrative structure I call the "Heroine's Labyrinth."**

In India, the Chakra Vyuha is a specific type of labyrinth designed to be harmonious and even beautiful in its mathematical precision. From above, the shape has also been described as a "blooming lotus." The inward spiral also resembles the psychological complexity of the human brain.

The Chakra Vyuha may be the perfect symbol for the heroine's labyrinth—circular, inward, asymmetrical, multidirectional, nonlinear, beautiful—a journey of great distances that never strays far from the center. After all, a labyrinth is designed to allow freedom of movement while also keeping inhabitants confined within the structure. The maze provides avenues and intersections, traps and hidden doors, riddles and fiercely guarded secrets. Labyrinths are also architectural constructions of geometric and mathematical precision, and, like culture itself, a labyrinth is a design born of human ingenuity. Brute force is rarely the attribute that resolves conflicts. Even reason and logic are hard to trust because a labyrinth misleads and confuses the inhabitants by design. Therefore, a heightened intuition plays a more central role in the heroine's narrative journey. And in terms of storytelling, the heroine's labyrinth is constructed of real or perceived walls and dead ends, such as social norms, cultural traditions, legal boundaries, family duties, gender roles, and unwritten rules. The heroine's labyrinth is both a physical place within the native culture and a psychological system of rules baked right into the sacred geometry of the maze. These rules are uniquely human and uniquely suited to whatever society existed at any given time, real-world or fantasy.

The heroine's journey can be intense and dangerous without a single roundhouse kick, gunshot, or clash of swords. So, you see, the overarching structure of the story itself had to be reconsidered *independently* of the well-established hero's journey. The adventure comes not from the exotic aspects of a distant land but from the secrets, conflicts, and illusions of one's home culture. In conversations, the heroine's journey has been understood and described as an inner exploration, a complex social navigation, or even a jailbreak. And despite many recurring themes, heroine-centric stories do not consistently reinforce gender roles because most heroines regularly challenge gender roles, traditions, rules, and boundaries.

Once I understood the different nature of the heroine's fundamental conflict, I perceived differences across the board in terms of story. The villains of the heroine's labyrinth had attributes that differed significantly from the villains of the hero's journey. For example, villains in the labyrinth are usually members of the heroine's native culture, often social apex characters, half benevolent, half tyrannical. Furthermore, the pattern of events for the heroine's labyrinth didn't always follow the same linear progression as the hero's journey. The archetypal power didn't come from a series of themes for a warrior-oriented hero but came across more like the turning of tarot cards—archetypal forces that entered the heroine's life, each with their own significance and secret meanings.

To finally see the heroine's labyrinth narrative model, I had to let go of all I knew about the hero's journey, which I loved so much and had studied for so long.

And so, I'm asking you to let go of the hero's journey too—not permanently, not out of disregard or disrespect. We simply need to set the hero's journey aside and look with fresh eyes and great empathy at the struggles of our heroines. Like the hero's journey, the feminine monomyth is universal. The heroine's labyrinth has many themes that I believe are both feminine in their dynamism and transcendent to gender altogether. Remember, in the most famous labyrinth story of all time, that of Minos and the Minotaur, although Theseus slays the Minotaur, it is the heroine, Ariadne, who solves the maze.

TAROT – ARCHETYPAL DESIGNS AND STORY

tudying heroines taught me a lot about trusting your intuition and keeping a healthy skepticism about fixed patterns. To honor this wisdom, *The Heroine's Labyrinth* will unleash the interpretive power of tarot cards as our gateway into each of the heroine's archetypal designs. Our approach to narrative structure comes from arranging archetypes into various patterns that make sense to our stories. We'll free ourselves from the suffocating limits of a formulaic approach to story structure.

There are many similarities between storytelling and fortune-telling anyway. We are "telling" something based on images from either an archetypal image on a card or an archetypal image from our psyches. Both processes are loaded with symbolism, creativity, interpretation, themes, improvisation, and meaning. The tarot reader synthesizes a narrative understanding of each card in the sequence that should resonate with the target audience. Other details also come into play, such as the order in which the card is drawn, which theme variation makes the most sense, and whether the card is upside down or right-side up. Therefore, the card reader masters each card's meaning and interpretations while following the arrangement's simple rules. Once mastered and internalized, we can let structure fade into the background. The tarot reader can then optimize their intuitive and creative powers with *the telling* as their focus. And that, dear writers, is what we want most— to *tell* a great story.

This approach moves us away from grids, formulas, numbered lists, and rigid rules, focusing each writer on creative interpretations mindful of story progression and character arcs. We can also have great faith that the archetypal designs will resonate with our readers. They are timeless constructions of the human psyche, reinforced by human experience for thousands of years or more. We'll explore each theme of the heroine's labyrinth as if drawing a card from the celestial deck. We'll then behold the card and unpack all the archetypal power encoded within the design.

Dear writers, we've shuffled our tarot deck and arranged the first spread. We're prepared to draw cards. Our first card is in the Present Position, which carries significant psychic information because it tells us where the heroine's story begins.

ACT I

ORIENTATION (IMMERSION)

The Labyrinth

THE LABYRINTH

Welcome, dear writers, to the mysterious entrance of the heroine's labyrinth. Laid before your eyes is a gateway, a clear passageway into a place where getting lost is part of discovery. The meaning of the labyrinth carries profound archetypal power, for we intuitively perceive both confusion and wonder, mystery and enchantment, dream and nightmare. The heroine's passage through the labyrinth is a distinctive journey that often occurs right within the native culture itself. Notice how the experience and nature of the conflict vary from the hero's journey in significant ways.

Like the hero, the heroine begins on familiar grounds, at home, or in a home-like environment. She quickly learns that although she can move freely, there are special rules for her to follow, like game theory in cultural terms. Many stories, fairy tales, and myths feature a game or game-like scenario for the heroine, and I think this is because the native culture feels like a rule-based reality to the heroine. She's often confronted with a world where her elders and peers insist that she can "win" or "lose." Play by the rules, and you'll live happily ever after. Break the rules, and you'll be an outcast or worse. So, when we encounter Katniss Everdeen in a novel or on the big screen, we see the archetypal heroine cast before our eyes in full color for all to witness—a woman on a gameboard—engaged in a tremendous cultural struggle against a system of rules and hidden dangers. "Every game has its rules," says Maeve Millay in the first season of *Westworld.* "You just need to know how to break them."

The heroine in the labyrinth travels in calculating circles as she attempts to discover the passages and boundaries. She passes beneath the symbols of her native culture, objects of virtue and wisdom. Yet, the heroine may feel disconnected from her duties and obligations—as if such virtues are meant for women of another time but not for her. And no matter how many miles she may travel inside the labyrinth, she never gets far from the center.

The heroine must be cautious in the labyrinth, for she learns that monsters come disguised as friends, family members, authority figures, mentors, and cultural elites. Her enemies are not far away but nearby, passing close to her, sometimes masked, sometimes aligned with her in a fragile state of truce. She worries that even trusted friends may switch allegiances or that her native culture may suddenly turn against her if she disturbs the order.

As the heroine advances, she experiences a constant tension between a sense of restriction and her assertion of free will. She instinctively knows that staying inside the labyrinth risks stifling her identity beneath a predetermined set of cultural expectations. Therefore, the labyrinth is simultaneously a type of elaborate captivity *and* a path forward to freedom.

The heroine sees that others, too, dwell within the maze. These other beings may consciously or unconsciously try to trick the heroine, resist her passage, or thwart her notions of escape. She knows she intrigues the inhabitants of the labyrinth. She knows she is watched. She often learns to wear the social mask of conformity so that she may pass through the corridors of her native culture to pursue her own interests. Heroines face socially acceptable monsters or even beloved beings, villains who are not so easily defeated. Her fear is not death but conversion or capture, and she must devise wards against traps, seduction, unfairness, or trickery.

The heroine typically places less emphasis on brute force or combat, and so she cultivates a highly tuned intuition. She observes with the double mind of the spy, and so she values caution and secrecy. She is a collector of secrets. And because she often discovers the true world hidden by secrets, she learns the nature of deception. She understands the power of facades and perceives hidden realities that others may not see or do not wish to see. As a result, our heroines value authenticity and sincerity since these are the opposing forces to deception. As Anna Karenina says, "Anything's better than lying and deceit."

The above scenario is my best effort at summarizing the basic "feel" of the heroine-centric journey. It's nothing like the hero's journey, and it gets better. But how do mazes and game boards appear in stories? And what can we learn about them?

Fantastic Mazes Hidden at Home

Alice in Wonderland depicts an exotic fantasy journey where the entrance to the maze is in a rabbit hole just outside her house. Once she tumbles into the rabbit hole, all sorts of dreamlike scenarios and bizarre people confront Alice. Indeed, the archetypal power of Alice's rabbit hole spawned a new definition based entirely on our heroine's experiences in the story. According to the current-day Oxford English Dictionary, "rabbit hole" is defined as "a bizarre, confusing, or nonsensical situation or environment, typically one from which it is difficult to extricate oneself." Alice's rabbit hole is one of countless expressions of a fictional labyrinth.

The tension between the heroine and her native culture is so persistent in mythology, literature, and film that labyrinthine imagery is projected right into the settings. Look for it, and you'll see it—confining passageways, claustrophobic chambers, imposing walls, interconnecting tunnels, zig-zagging stairwells, accessways, and hidden or locked doors. The entrance to the fantastical labyrinth is often disguised as an ordinary object or an unremarkable nook hidden in plain sight.

Just for fun, let's glance at two films with the word "labyrinth" baked right into the title. In the David Bowie film *Labyrinth*, Sarah discovers a physical labyrinth just beyond her window. In *Pan's Labyrinth*, the young heroine, Ofelia, finds a dangerous maze hidden beside the military barracks where she and her mother live like hostages. Both films have heroines as their lead characters, and both feature a magical maze hidden beside the residence.

But keep looking, and you'll see what I saw—labyrinths are *everywhere* in heroine-led stories.

Countless heroine-centric stories *appear* to be fantastical outward journeys. However, the adventure is an illusion in which the heroine is still at home, perhaps the subconscious materialization of a daydream. Dorothy Gale must follow a yellow brick road, which is a two-dimensional maze that twists and turns and splits off in multiple directions in *The Wizard of Oz*. Lucy Pevensie discovers the entrance to the magical world of Narnia in a forgotten old wardrobe. Claire Randall finds the exotic world of eighteenth-century Scotland in a forest glen close to home in *Outlander*, while Christine Daae discovers a secret labyrinth just below the Paris Opera House in *The Phantom of the Opera*. Or what about the spectacular maze in *Everything Everywhere All at Once*? Evelyn Wang's labyrinth is a multiverse of every possible "what if" in her life. She navigates each bizarre and haunting dimension using a handheld device that shows the webwork of infinite pathways, and yet, the heroine never really leaves home.

In these overt manifestations, we see heroines immersed in wonderous worlds just beyond the mundane and familiar. There is a narrative tension between confusion and wonder unique to these stories. All this drama and conflict, and the heroine never even left her native culture, or in some cases, she never left her literal home.

In *Foundation* Season 1, Episode 6, "Death and the Maiden," the female android Demerzel states, "The goddesses guide us at every step toward service and truth as though toward the center of a great spiral." Even sci-fi or real-world settings confine the heroine in dark, maze-like environments filled with dangerous side chambers and traps. *The Descent* and *Annihilation* show heroines moving through the claustrophobic passages of nightmarish labyrinths. But who can forget Clarice Starling advancing through the maze in Buffalo Bill's residential basement? Or the android, Ava, trapped inside a sleek and high-tech labyrinth in *Ex Machina*? Nathan, the villain, even describes Ava as "a rat in a maze."

In the critically acclaimed novel *Gideon the Ninth*, a pair of heroines arrive on a distant planet where necromancers and cavaliers gather at the ominous First House. Gideon and Harrow enter a quintessential labyrinth that embodies mysteries, puzzle-solving, psychological tests, and secrecy. Likewise, after decades of cryosleep, Gaal Dornick wakes up alone in an abandoned space station full of empty corridors and hidden mysteries in *Foundation*. And let us not forget the child heroine, Newt, who led the battle-hardened Colonial Marines through a maze of air ducts and ventilation shafts during a desperate escape in *Aliens*.

Whether we are watching Wendy Torrance fleeing through the halls of the Overlook Hotel in *The Shining*, Trinity racing through hallways, alleys, and intersections to find a phone booth in *The Matrix*, or Katniss Everdeen navigating a war-torn urban gameboard in *The Hunger Games*, we are witnessing a heroine in a maze. And she's trying—desperately trying—to find a way out.

The imagery is so powerful because it reflects the fundamental conflict between heroines and the worlds they navigate. These heroines aren't heading out far from home to encounter exotic dangers. They face the threats hidden in plain sight, right within the native culture itself. There seems to be a symbolic search for hidden truths, elusive answers, and ethical fallacies in the places heroines call home.

Dear writers, these are unique tropes and story designs that differ from the hero's journey. Period. And we're just getting warmed up. The archetypal labyrinth often extends beyond a physical or fantastical gameboard.

The Socio-Cultural Labyrinth

We've cast a light on the recurrence of fantastical labyrinths in heroine-centric stories. However, the visual maze is a powerful projection of a more resonant psychological metaphor that becomes more complex in literature and TV shows, where the storytellers have time to flesh out the maze. Other stories like *Orange Is the New Black*, *WandaVision*, *The Room*, and *The Handmaid's Tale* all depict settings where our heroines are held captive in a literal sense by their native culture. But we also see the same dynamic in expanded miniseries that feature heroines such as *Chernobyl*, *The Queen's Gambit*, and *The Crown*.

But nowhere do we see the mighty socio-cultural labyrinth more than in literature. Literature is flush with conflicts and settings, with each story like a snapshot in time. Each heroine faces a culturally unique socio-cultural labyrinth that must be navigated and solved. These psychological restrictions are more nuanced. The labyrinth theme grows in complexity because the vast and intricate maze is no longer conspicuous but camouflaged in the very settings and norms of the native culture.

In *Pride and Prejudice* and *Jane Eyre*, we see heroines trapped in a highly structured society that functions like a labyrinth, only invisible, often more confining than any brick wall. Elizabeth Bennett and Jane Eyre are not held in check by jail cells or the state's law enforcement arm. Instead, they are penned in by the invisible social rules of courtship, marriage, and conduct in polite English society. There is a constant sense of being watched or monitored, in which the heroines learn to parry various social and judgmental attitudes meant to influence their decisions. Anna Karenina grapples with complicated social rules in Imperial Russia just as Mulan does in Imperial China.

Many heroines are often trapped inside a socio-cultural labyrinth where places that should represent a sanctuary, such as the home, are occupied by the story's villain. In *The Color Purple* (1985), we witness a more brutal labyrinth where pregnancy, racism, and abuse surround the heroine, Celie Johnson, at all times. Celie is trapped in a hostile native culture, where the home itself is the most dangerous place.

In *The Henna Artist* by Alka Joshi, Lakshmi encounters the rigid caste structure of India, while Sayuri becomes an indentured servant in the stifling native culture of Japan in *Memoirs of a Geisha*. Many of Lisa See's novels revolve around a central heroine in China who tries to navigate the deadly socio-cultural labyrinths of their home culture. Regardless of the culture or the historical setting, our heroines are often choked off by tight corsets, painful foot bindings, and heavy veils meant to present them as decorative objects or prize-like brides with servile status.

In *One Thousand and One Nights*, the heroine, Scheherazade, doesn't take a linear voyage outward either. She's confined to the opulent palace of the Arabian ruler, Shahryar, and rarely moves away from this singular setting. And again, Scheherazade must survive night to night while entertaining the ruler with her 1,001 tales. The heroine's labyrinth is deadly, the villain is close by, and opulent walls are dead ends. The heroine's cunning keeps her alive rather than her combat skill. I like this example, too, because *One Thousand and One Nights* reinforces the notion that storytelling is a primal survival mechanism.

From Lisbeth Salander in *The Girl with the Dragon Tattoo* to Kamala Khan in *Ms. Marvel*, from Scarlett O'Hara in *Gone with the Wind* to Dagny Taggart in *Atlas Shrugged*, from Hester Prynne in *The Scarlet Letter* to Taraji, Octavia, and Janelle in *Hidden Figures*—our heroines face uncompromising cultural expectations and prejudices. All these heroines possess the capacity to contribute to the world in meaningful ways, but society isn't always looking to them for answers. They meet resistance from friendly faces and combat monsters in the quietude of social decency. Repeatedly, we see the heroine's personal goals subordinated to cultural duties, her sexual desires hidden and repressed, and her curious explorations disguised behind the appearance of conformity. These are not small concepts or minor conflicts. These are expansive and deeply psychological aspects of human culture. They are mythical in their stunning recurrences throughout time and seem universal in their psychic messages. The feminine monomyth is as relatable today as it was a thousand years ago. The labyrinth may change, but our heroine is constant.

Many of these stories also feature a character who serves as the voice of non-conformity to the game rules of the labyrinth. These counter voices include Jolene in *The Queen's Gambit*, Gramma in *Moana*, and Weird Barbie in *Barbie*. The voices of non-conformity help nudge the heroine toward her goals.

The labyrinth is a fundamentally unique design to story structure. The emphasis in the heroine's conflict lies squarely within the native culture. From this **one core difference**, the themes throughout the story fan out and grow into a scintillating and archetypally distinctive narrative model.

Anatomy of an Archetype - The Labyrinth

◊ A set of restrictions or rules based on cultural expectations

◊ The heroine has aspirations that conflict with these rules.

◊ The labyrinth often appears to be game-like with a win-or-lose scenario.

◊ Includes perceived rewards for following the rules and punishments for breaking them

◊ The rules are conveyed by an authority figure or an individual the heroine trusts.

◊ A secondary character usually represents the voice and wisdom of non-conformity to the native culture.

◊ Fantasy mazes are usually in, at, or near the home and have a secret entrance.

◊ Usually includes settings with labyrinthine imagery

Exercises

This book will provide some exercises to better harness your ability to translate the archetypal concepts into your writing. The goal is to see how real stories express the themes in real-time. As many of you already know, there is a big difference between screenwriting and narrative fiction writing. So, these exercises will help develop an instinct for themes in writing.

1. Focus on *The Hunger Games* by Suzanne Collins, the first novel or film (either one). Write down a list of the rules she had to follow. Think of all the advice and guidance she received before, during, and after the Hunger Games. Afterward, take a good long look at those rules. Which characters told Katniss the rules? Who advised her? Did she trust them? Use this as a basic model for designing the rule-based world that your heroine occupies.

2. Now, do the same thing for *Jane Eyre*. The rules are much more subtle since she's in a socio-cultural labyrinth. But

think about it. What are the rules and warnings given to Jane throughout the tale? Again, who relays all these unwritten rules to Jane throughout the story? Which rules does Jane follow, and which ones does she break?

3. Can you spot the symbolic breadcrumbs in the early part of *Moana*? What symbolic object did the storytellers choose for breadcrumbs? Does this symbol ever reappear in the film? What do you think this symbol means?

4. Now, let's take a quick peek at the film *Inception*. Who designs the dream mazes? Why do you think the screenwriter gave this character the name he gave her?

Tarot

Now that we have drawn and explored the meaning of the labyrinth together, we turn one of the most dangerous cards in the tarot reading. The next card reveals a new source of conflict for the heroine, something more direct and often more terrifying than the labyrinth itself.

The Masked Minotaur

THE MASKED MINOTAUR

We have drawn The Masked Minotaur, one of the most powerful Major Arcana cards in the heroine's deck.

The powerful archetype of the Minotaur dates to antiquity, and its origin is inseparable from the labyrinth. According to Greek mythology, Minotaur was the proper name of the unholy offspring of a prized white bull and Queen Pasiphaë. The name Minotaur translates to "Bull of Minos." The abomination grew and became so terrible that King Minos had a sophisticated labyrinth designed to trap the creature within. Therefore, the Minotaur archetype is cursed by evil, possessing the head and tail of a beast and the torso and body of a man. The dual fusion of instinctive animal savagery and intelligent human purpose bequeath upon the Minotaur gifts from both parents. From his queen mother, he gains his noble humanity—love, compassion, social prestige, individualism, and skill mastery. From his father, though, he gains all the savagery of the animal world, which corrupts his human virtues. Love becomes possession, compassion becomes obsession, social prestige becomes raw ambition, individualism becomes ego, and skill mastery becomes a means to tyrannize. The dualism and duplicity of the Minotaur are uniquely suited to the heroine's labyrinth.

By contrast, the hero's journey features the villain archetype of the "Distant Dragon." The main structural difference is that Distant Dragons come from *outside* the hero's native culture and threaten to destroy or subjugate the home society. The warrior-oriented hero must leave the native culture and confront the Distant Dragon in single combat. Therefore, the foreign nature of the Distant Dragon carries the themes of military conquest, brute force, and mass cultural destruction. Thanos, Sauron, Darth Vader, Hela, Grendel, the Night King, Smaug, Voldemort, the Borg Queen, the Queen Alien, Agent Smith, and Khan Noonien Singh are all examples of Distant Dragon archetypes. They are wicked, alien, soulless, machine-like, reptilian, or foreign.

In addition to their overtly intimidating appearance, Distant Dragons often feature a mass destruction ability. Like the dragon archetype, each villain can breathe a stream of fire that flows outward to consume or annihilate the safe havens of humanity. The symbolic dragon's fire comes to life when Smaug sweeps over the laketown of Dale in *The Hobbit*. But annihilating destructive breath comes, too, in the form of the green, planet-killing laser of the Death Star, the atomic breath of Godzilla, the god-like destructive powers of the Genesis torpedo, the Snap from an Infinity Gauntlet, the winter apocalypse of the White Walkers, or the armies of Mordor. Distant Dragons are militant culture destroyers.

You see? Villains are *not* all the same. They are outgrowths of the story's structural conflict and manifestations of the story-world's reality. Villains are made *possible* by their ability to exist in opposition to the established values and morals of the hero's world. The opposing value system comes from an aggressive rival culture in the hero's journey. In the heroine's labyrinth, the value system comes from a corruption of the so-called "good" native culture. The villain reflects the reality of the specific narrative structure.

Heroine-centric stories rarely feature such an obviously menacing villain as a Distant Dragon. The labyrinth is a manifestation of the heroine's home culture, so the villain is **homegrown** and has mastered the ruled-based gameboard upon which the heroine stands. Therefore, the heroine reminds us of the monsters near or inside the home, standing next to us, camouflaged in familiar places, or disguised behind a socially elite mask. The danger is local. The heroine's objective is not to slay a Distant Dragon in single combat but to unmask a Minotaur at the center of the labyrinth.

The Better to See You With

Little Red Riding Hood is a cautionary tale about the danger of masks. The young girl slowly spots the Big Bad Wolf's disguise, but by then, it's too late. Her mistake? She underestimated the danger that the wolf presented. Coraline, too, is deceived by the mask of her Other Mother for a good part of the story. It takes the first half of the story for Coraline to unmask the Other Mother and the second half to defeat her. Identifying a deception is merely the first step toward the heroine's ultimate resolution in the story, but it is not the final step. Coraline must unmask the Minotaur *before* the system of deception can come crashing down.

Time and time again, I noticed the striking duplicity of Masked Minotaurs in heroine-centric stories. The villains were sometimes friendly, helpful, benevolent, and even admired in the native culture. In *Frozen*, Prince Hans appeared to be the heroine's dashing and handsome love interest. And in *Wonder Woman* (2017), Ares, the God of War, was disguised as the brittle old politician who wanted peace and armistice. The Masked Minotaur archetype characterizes this very duplicity in the Minotaur's inherent dual nature—half-man, half-animal. As such, the Minotaur wears a deceptive mask that hides its true face. But the true face of the Minotaur is that of the animal tyrant and brute oppressor who will stop at nothing to get what they want. The mask is publicly conforming, elite, or even seen as a positive force within the labyrinth. Therefore, the Masked Minotaur exhibits both an impulsive, instinctive animal eros and a human need for purpose and social prestige.

The competing desires of the Minotaur lead to a structural nuance within heroine-centric stories. The villain often has a special relationship with the heroine in which the dual forces of **love and tyranny** coexist—and it's worth a deeper look.

Possessive Love

Again, we must reconsider our understanding of combat and conflict between the main character and the villain. Gone are the warrior tropes of single combat out in the open, where the death of the villain (or hero) usually signals victory or defeat. But if we recognize that the Masked Minotaur is a different type of villain, as writers, we must understand how this creates a different structural conflict for our heroine.

Rather than destroy the heroine, the Minotaur usually seeks to convert, capture, or possess the heroine. The militant persona is replaced by expressions of love, generosity, and benevolence one minute, followed by anger, manipulation, or seduction the next. The changes make the Minotaur exceedingly challenging to defeat. The villain can come up close to the heroine, invade her space, and sometimes evoke feelings of closeness. Possessive love gives and takes, creating a villain who seems to phase in and out of villainy. But this back and forth must be seen as a tactic rather than genuine inner conflict within the Minotaur. The human side is cursed, so whatever humanity the Minotaur displays, he does so in the service of his dominant animal self.

We'll explore the role of possessive love more in the next chapter, but this theme is a key component to the nature of the Minotaur. In the end, the possessive love of the Minotaur, however disorienting to the heroine, can develop the story's conflict. Therefore, the heroine's ability to defeat the Minotaur will rarely be based solely on her proficiency in combat unless she's also a trained warrior. She'll often have to break the power of possessive love for herself and other inhabitants of the labyrinth. And bear in mind that possessive love is not limited to a romantic relationship.

I never realized how many expressions of possessive love exist in stories. At first, I thought only of the overbearing husband or groom, such as Cal Hockley in *Titanic* or Immortan Joe in *Mad Max: Fury*

Road, both of whom are perfect examples of Masked Minotaurs. Both villains are members of the heroine's native culture and are social apex characters. Both exhibit possessive love in multiple ways. Immortan Joe possesses several wives whom he treats like a harem of breeding stock. The heroine, Furiosa, not only attempts to escape her home culture but also tries to rescue several other captive wives. On the other hand, Cal lures Rose with the Hope Diamond in one scene and then assaults the heroine a few scenes later, issuing a harsh speech about her role as his wife.

These Minotaurs profess love for the heroines, but their love is tied entirely to the tyrant ego of their animal selves. Lastly, the tell-tale sign of possessive love always occurs when the heroine attempts to leave— both Masked Minotaurs pursue the heroine in a furious rage.

And yet, once I studied heroine-led stories in greater depth, I noticed possessive love in all its forms and relationships. Mother Gothel keeps Rapunzel in a tower through a seemingly "loving" system of lies in *Tangled*. Lady Tremaine is the literal evil stepmother in *Cinderella*, while the evil stepfather, Alphonso, abuses Celie Johnson in *The Color Purple* (1985). Possessive love can strike a mentor figure, such as Jade Fox in *Crouching Tiger Hidden Dragon*, just as it struck the childish simpleton Noah Percy in *The Village*. Ava is held captive by her technological creator in *Ex Machina*, and Princess Fiona is locked in a tower by her loving parents in *Shrek*. Possessive love is a shockingly pervasive theme in heroine-centric stories, and it can corrupt a wide prism of relationships in the heroine's life.

Anatomy of an Archetype – The Masked Minotaur

◊ The villain is a homegrown member of the native culture.

◊ The mask of the Minotaur is often a pleasing human face.

◊ The Minotaur is usually duplicitous, being half benevolent and half tyrannical.

◊ May include an animal totem to symbolize the beast half of its personality

◊ The Minotaur is often disguised as a social apex character within the native culture.

◊ The Minotaur has usually mastered the cultural "game rules" of the labyrinth.

◊ The Minotaur often tries to capture or possess the heroine.

◊ The Minotaur may be hidden in society, wearing the disguise of an ordinary person.

Exercises

1. Identify the Masked Minotaur in the following films: *Everything Everywhere All at Once*, *Captain Marvel*, *Ex Machina*, *The Phantom of the Opera*, and *Black Swan*.

2. In the novel *Their Eyes Were Watching God*, the heroine experiences two Masked Minotaurs. Can you name them? Secondly, there emerges a third Masked Minotaur near the end. What makes the third Minotaur so unique?

3. Just for fun, let's identify the Masked Minotaur of films that have male leads but follow the heroine's labyrinth story model: *The Dark Knight*, *The Godfather*, *Amadeus*, *Fight Club*, *Rambo: First Blood*, *John Wick*, and *The Game*.

Tarot

We see the labyrinth and Masked Minotaur cards on the table. Already, we sense frustration and dread. The Minotaur stares at us with black animal eyes, and we perceive his unwavering will toward possession and tyranny. Now, let's approach one of the great mysteries within the heroine's labyrinth by asking a mystical question. Why does the Masked Minotaur seek to possess the heroine in the first place? The answer to *that* question shall now be unveiled. Let's flip the next card in our tarot deck and behold the archetypal source of the heroine's internal power.

The Sacred Fire

THE SACRED FIRE

n the Charlotte Brontë novel *Jane Eyre*, the heroine exclaims, "I have an inward treasure born with me, which can keep me alive if all extraneous delights should be withheld or offered only at a price I cannot afford to give." Jane Eyre describes her Sacred Fire beautifully, breathing life into the archetype with such rich language. Of all the archetypal designs in the heroine's labyrinth, the Sacred Fire is perhaps the most dynamic and complex.

Fire is energy—impossible to hold physically in the hand, destructive if unattended, creative and life-giving if respected, a source of luminance, and intricately linked to human mythology. In the days of pagan Rome, priestesses of the order of Vestal Virgins tended the Sacred Fire of the goddess, Vesta. Maintaining a continuous flame proved that Vesta watched over and protected the Roman capital. The "eternal flame" is a metaphor for the **continuity** of something precious and vital. We see eternal flames at synagogues, war memorials, gravesites, the Olympics, and other places of solemn sanctity.

Sacred fires and fire worship have been around since the Stone Age. In the novel *The Quest for Fire*, prehistoric human tribes compete against each other to control fire, sometimes traveling great distances with a fragile flame or stealing fire from enlightened tribes and fighting to the death to keep a flame ever-burning. Whoever has the fire survives. In these more literal tales, the Sacred Fire is a vital cultural resource, and some people will stop at nothing to capture it.

Such is the power of the heroine's Sacred Fire in a story.

The Sacred Fire ties the feminine monomyth together because it explains the peculiar patterns of conflict and character motivations that surround our heroines in the story. As writers, the idea of the Sacred Fire is so nuanced and kaleidoscopic that we must take our time to grasp the full power of the ancient archetype. The symbolism of a divine fire that burns bright within the heroine explains a lot. Throughout the storytelling landscape, heroines often wield unique creative powers that draw others to them for better or worse. The heroine's use of the Sacred Fire may be the ultimate boon and moral core of her story. The archetype contains two powerful dimensions—an **attractive force** and a **unique creative power**—both active simultaneously, working together to draw other characters into the heroine's life and stirring the strongest passions of the heroine herself.

The twin concepts of an attractive force and a unique creative power within our heroines should be easy to understand. Both dimensions are relatable on a pure archetypal and subconscious level. Older stories expressed the attractive force as feminine beauty and the unique creative power as the ability to create life, but archetypal designs are surprisingly flexible. Portrayals of the Sacred Fire archetype in older stories may have meant one thing, but today, we can design more evolved and complex versions. The Sacred Fire will always symbolize a beautiful force and a unique creative power, but we, the storytellers, can invent dynamic new expressions. An attractive force can reflect *anything* beautiful about a person, and creative power can be anything **creative**, such as artistry, crafts, superpowers, healing powers, constructive skill sets, causes, a source of passion, or core virtues. And we can trust that the core components will continue to resonate.

The heroine's Sacred Fire is an attractive force since the flame holds our attention. A small but beautiful flame perfectly symbolizes the many expressions of this ancient archetype. Others will claim the heroine's Sacred Fire or even try to steal it, which establishes a familiar conflict dynamic for many heroines in countless stories. Let's examine the nuances of each claim to the heroine's Sacred Fire and how you can use them in storytelling.

The Heroine's Claim - "Individuation"

In stories worldwide, heroines are fully aware of their Sacred Fire and let us know when it's burning hot and burning brightly. Writers, pay attention! You must value your heroine's Sacred Fire as if it were your own. Describe the feeling and dynamics behind this yearning and desire, whether she's extraverted or introverted, and write it down. Let the reader know our heroine is making her claim. Give it a language all its own.

The heroine is often depicted as inexperienced or immature at the beginning of a story. She's becoming more aware of her personal desires and interests and soon seeks greater freedom and agency to pursue them. In other words, the heroine is discovering her Sacred Fire. The heroine must claim her Sacred Fire by expressing some move toward greater freedom and showing interest in the outside world. Our heroine has aspirations that exceed her current reality. The colorful and exotic native culture is just outside her window, and the heroine intends to merge with that world. She senses her potential and relies upon her imagination to compensate for her lack of experience. This vital pulse of the human spirit is relatable to all of us. We are stirred to the core when the heroine claims her Sacred Fire in fiction.

Therefore, the heroine's Sacred Fire symbolizes her vast, untapped, untested, and unrealized creative human potential. Her claim is for freedom and agency to follow her passions.

The Sacred Fire moment in the story shows the audience or reader that the heroine is ready for growth and change. If done correctly, the heroine's Sacred Fire moment can be incredibly powerful in a story.

Musicals provide excellent examples of Sacred Fire moments because they're so brazen and memorable. Whatever forces have kept the heroine in her immature state, she's ready to take a chance on herself and face the world. Elsa vows boldly to let it go. Moana declares her intent to see how far she'll go. And poor Belle wants so much more than her provincial life. And that's just Disney. Sacred Fire songs are standard fare in countless musicals, such as Dorothy Gale's desire to go somewhere over the rainbow in *The Wizard of Oz*, Roxy Hart's dream to be the name on everybody's lips in *Chicago*, or Tracy Turnblad's declaration that Baltimore's going to wake up and see her in *Hairspray*. These opening numbers are splendid examples of a heroine's inner desire for self-actualization. The Sacred Fire moment tells us what the heroine cares about the most in the story.

Author Charlotte Brontë found a brilliant way to demonstrate Jane Eyre's Sacred Fire through literary prose. Jane reveals her Sacred Fire through her language, a perfect expression in rigid English society. She follows the social conventions of her time, yet when she sits and speaks with Mr. Rochester, she expresses her inner thoughts and countercultural opinions through precise and articulate language. The author goes out of her way to remind us that Jane is plain in appearance, which forces the reader to downgrade the impact of her beauty and eros. This is perfect because Jane's plainness allows us all to experience the luminance of her language and subtle self-expression every time she speaks.

The Sacred Fire may be symbolic and magical, such as the ability to spin straw into gold as in *Rumpelstiltskin*, the creative genius of Beth Harmon in *Queen's Gambit*, the creative artistry of Margaret Keane in *Big Eyes*, or the red chaos magic of the Scarlet Witch in *WandaVision*. All four heroines deal with the same problems. They have a seemingly divine creative power that other characters too often seek to capture and monopolize. Understanding the Sacred Fire allows writers to understand the potent conflict dynamics in the feminine monomyth.

Writers can symbolize the heroine's unique creative powers in so many forms. Artistic ability, intellectual innovation, political cause, moral sensibility, intuition, beauty, eros, knowledge, supernatural powers, healing ability, motherhood, love, sexual desire, noble birthright, claim to the throne, or her ability to create life itself—any of these can represent the heroine's Sacred Fire and can be the driving force in the story.

As readers or viewers, we *feel* the heroine's first attempt at empowerment whenever the heroine claims her Sacred Fire. All that unrealized potential is bubbling up and meeting us at a conscious and subconscious level. The heroine is building her will to act on her aspirations because she found the words or actions to give force to the feeling. But while the heroine's Sacred Fire moment throws a gauntlet at the world, trust me: the world responds to the challenge.

The Native Culture's Claim - "Continuity"

Whereas the heroine's claim to her Sacred Fire is the most important, the native culture's is the most powerful. In fact, the native culture's claim upon the heroine's Sacred Fire is the root source of the labyrinth's existence. A continuously burning flame symbolizes continuity in mythological, practical, and cultural terms. Keeping the flame going is the whole point. So, whereas the heroine seeks to assert her passion and agency, the native culture claims the heroine's unique creative powers for the continuity of the family, its traditions, values, and native culture itself.

The heroine understands that her native culture's claim has been staked out long in advance. The heroine's Sacred Fire didn't come from nothing, remember, but came down to her from the much larger, much brighter communal fire of the native culture. The heroine is a member of a family and society, after all. This "source flame" of the heroine's Sacred Fire shapes some part of the heroine's identity, a fact she will struggle mightily to accept and resolve. **So, when the heroine claims her Sacred Fire early in the story by announcing her aspirations, she triggers the native culture's defense of its preexisting claim.**

We've discussed the symbolism of the labyrinth and the conflicts between the heroine and the native culture in countless stories, but here, we must zero in on the source of the conflict. If the heroine rejects the native culture's claim, she risks disrupting the vital continuity of family lineage, cultural tradition, social order, or reputation. Cultures worldwide take their claim *very* seriously.

Therefore, the Sacred Fire also represents the continuous flame of the communal fire, passed down to the heroine through her parentage. This is a long-standing and highly developed claim that society places upon the heroine to use her creative powers for the continuity of family and culture.

An eternal flame symbolizes a continuous link from the present moment to the distant past when the flame had been first lit. If the flame goes out, the continuity breaks, and whatever the flame represents—a culture, family lineage, cause, secret, way of life, skill set, knowledge, or values—is diminished or lost to the world. All too often in heroine-centric stories, the native culture typically interprets continuity very narrowly as marriage and children. That's why so many stories feature a socio-cultural labyrinth designed to steer the heroine toward the archetypes of the innocent virgin, the fertile bride, and the chaste mother—the three archetypes so prized by cultures worldwide. These three roles ensure cultural continuity and family lineage.

As writers, seeing this conflict through the structural and archetypal lens helps to build out the dimensions of your story's conflict. Older stories, namely folk tales or fairy tales, usually favored the native culture's claim to the heroine's Sacred Fire and showed the dangers of the heroine's aspirations. The message in *The Wizard of Oz* is that while you, dear heroine, *think* you want adventure and individual agency, there's really no place like home. In the end, the story favors the native culture's ideals for the heroine. As an interesting modern-day response to the message of *The Wizard of Oz*, singer/songwriter Judy Collins wrote a song in 1979 called "Dorothy," in which the singer depicts the heroine as sullen and regretful for ever leaving the colorful world of Oz. She ends up lamenting the black-and-white world of Kansas.

Luckily, *your* story can favor the heroine's claim to her Sacred Fire and show the dangers of the native culture's rigid rules. "Culture" does not always have to mean ethnic, national, or religious traditions either. "Culture" may also be corporate, professional, institutional, local, family, an interest group, or even a friendship circle, anything that seeks continuity of something valuable to the group.

Daenerys Targaryen in *Game of Thrones* provides an excellent example of the relationship between the heroine's individuation and her preset identity passed down from the native culture. First, she is a descendant of the Targaryen bloodline, so she inherits a title, a great house, a history, and the blood of the dragon, which means fire cannot burn her. The three dragons are literal fire symbols that represent Daenerys' Sacred Fire. Throughout the story, we see Daenerys struggle with moral decisions regularly. She demonstrates an incredible individual will and directs several events in the story on her rise to power. She's as sovereign as they come. But we must not forget that her mission, vision, and orientation toward the world still stem from the "source fire" passed on to her from her family bloodline and native culture. Despite all her personal goals, Daenerys never forgets the Targaryen worldview.

So, we understand the heroine's Sacred Fire, her claim, her hopes and dreams, and now, we see that the native culture defends its original claim and expectations. Already, structural conflict emerges from these two competing claims. Many stories focus on these two claims alone. And yet, there is often a third and more dangerous claimant to the heroine's Sacred Fire.

The Minotaur's Claim - "Possession"

Many heroine stories feature a Masked Minotaur as the villain. The more you familiarize yourself with this unique archetype, the more you'll see it. As writers, we know instinctively that the Masked Minotaur seeks to possess the heroine. We see it all the time and never even question the phenomenon. But *why*? *Why* does the Minotaur want to possess the heroine? We asked this question in the last chapter and will now explore it more fully.

Hinduism may have an answer for us. Kundalini is a powerful concept in Hinduism, which describes divine feminine energy within the body and mind. The Kundalini often uses a healing snake as a symbol because the energy travels along the spine. Likewise, the feminine essence is associated with vibrant energy. Spiritual creativity infuses the energy with divine consciousness and holistic healing powers. The tantric practices of bliss, pleasure, sexual union, and liberation follow the principles of Kundalini. I believe such an archetypal feminine essence—this attractive force—plays a *crucial* role in understanding the dynamic relationship between the heroine's Sacred Fire and the possessive love of the Masked Minotaur.

While watching *The Silence of the Lambs*, I noticed that the relationship between Hannibal Lecter and Clarice Starling began as a formal exchange. Clarice offered favors and privileges on behalf of the FBI, while Hannibal provided clues as to the identity of Buffalo Bill. But pay close attention, and you'll realize that this relationship changes. Hannibal eventually forgoes the haggle over "petty privileges" and focuses squarely on Clarice. He establishes his famous *quid pro quo*, which in Latin means "this for that." He offers a psychological profile of Buffalo Bill, and in exchange, Hannibal gets—details about Clarice Starling's private life. I found this to be an odd exchange. What is Hannibal Lecter *really* getting in this exchange?

I concluded that Hannibal Lecter sought the feminine essence of Clarice Starling, the attractive force of her Sacred Fire. I believe this because the details of Clarice's life—her personal tragedies and her moral grief in failing to rescue her lamb—satisfied Hannibal in the exchange. Secondly, capturing the feminine essence is paralleled in the story. What Hannibal gained through *quid pro quo*, Buffalo Bill took by murderous force. He captured the feminine essence by physically abducting women in an attempt to become a woman. Despite all the overtones and themes in the film, neither Hannibal nor Buffalo Bill were motivated by basic attraction or sexual desire. The feminine essence *alone* motivated each character.

Likewise, when Ariel signs the dotted line for Ursula in *The Little Mermaid*, we see yet another quid pro quo. Ariel gets to be human, and the villain gets Ariel's voice. Again, while someone's voice is undoubtedly strange collateral, Ariel's voice satisfied the exchange. Why? How?

Ariel's voice symbolizes the same thing—her distinctive feminine essence, the attractive force behind her Sacred Fire.

This feminine essence and the heroine's unique creative powers form the core of the divine feminine, which is why the archetype is not just a fire, but a *sacred* fire. **Therefore, the Sacred Fire also represents the unique essence of the heroine that the Masked Minotaur seeks to capture, possess, use, dominate, or monopolize for entirely selfish reasons.**

While capturing or possessing someone's soul is an ancient concept, writers will benefit from perceiving the heroine as carrying a sacred flame that others are drawn to and may try to capture. Therefore, the Sacred Fire is a vital new concept for heroine mythologies and stories. The archetypal symbolism helps us understand the unique motivations of the Masked Minotaur and their relentless interest in the heroine. They know only the possessive love of their beast half, ever blind to the heroine's humanity. Remember, the words "captivate" and "captive" share the same Latin root, meaning "to hold." The cursed Minotaur is devoid of creative powers. And so, I believe the Masked Minotaur covets the heroine's feminine essence.

In *Tangled*, the Sacred Fire is Rapunzel's hair. Her long, glowing hair symbolizes her creative powers to heal, restore youth, and extend life. The Masked Minotaur is Mother Gothel because she holds Rapunzel captive and hordes this power to satisfy the vanity of eternal beauty. Locking Rapunzel in a tower perfectly demonstrates the self-serving mentality of the Minotaur's claim to the heroine's Sacred Fire.

Another perfect but brutal example of the stolen Sacred Fire is in Neil Gaiman's *The Sandman: Dream Country*. In the story, the Greek goddess Calliope carries the attractive force and creative powers of artistic genius and divine inspiration. She's one of the nine Muses in Greek mythology, from which the word *muse* means the personification of creative inspiration. Erasmus is the first Masked Minotaur of the story. He captures Calliope and holds her hostage. He then rapes the goddess over many years, stealing the unique creative powers of the Muse to become an author of great renown.

In the 2014 film *Maleficent*, the heroine's wings symbolize her freedom and uniqueness in the magical kingdom. However, the Masked Minotaur of the story, Stefan, steals the heroine's Sacred Fire, which turns her toward villainy. Driven by his egoistic desire to be king, Stefan cuts off Maleficent's wings and keeps them for himself.

In *Crouching Tiger, Hidden Dragon*, the troubled heroine, Jen Yu, learns the very secrets of Wudang Kung Fu. She is brilliant but self-taught through a stolen martial arts manual. However, she has been captured by a Masked Minotaur named Jade Fox, a rogue female warrior. Once again, we see the expression of Jen Yu's white-hot Sacred Fire through Kung Fu and the alluring effect on all who witness it, for good or ill.

The Three Claimants

The heroine's Sacred Fire creates a unique archetypal conflict for the feminine monomyth. The illustration below shows the basic dynamics and driving forces behind each claim.

The root source of this three-way archetypal struggle likely stems from the tension that builds around the feminine ability to create life. Therefore, the Sacred Fire expresses itself symbolically in our stories. Mythology often features a captive queen or goddess pressed into a marital union or held captive. The native culture and the Masked Minotaur may even form a common cause in heroine-centric stories, such as an "evil suitor" whom the family or culture approves. However, although our stories have certainly evolved and expanded far beyond the betrothal scenario, the fundamental conflict between the heroine, the Masked Minotaur, and the native culture remains surprisingly intact.

Beauty and the Beast provides a perfect example of all three characters making their claim to the heroine's Sacred Fire simultaneously. During the opening number, Belle claims her Sacred Fire by expressing her deep desires for more than her provincial life. The townsfolk, on the other hand, press their claim on Belle by gossiping about her "strangeness" or non-conformity to the native culture. And finally,

The Heroine Conflict Triangle

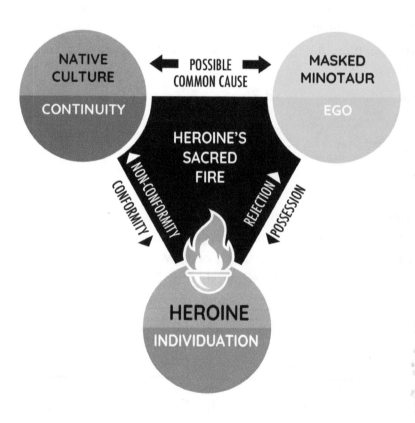

Gaston, who is the Masked Minotaur of the story, arrogantly claims Belle as his future wife without *any* preexisting relationship. He thinks he's in love with Belle but seeks only to possess her. The three claimants have spoken. The story quickly establishes our heroine's classic conflict. By understanding the archetypal significance of the Sacred Fire, writers can skillfully build out the conflicts of our favorite heroines.

One unique solution to the three claims comes from ancient Greek mythology. The goddess Artemis blocked all competing claims to her Sacred Fire by vowing to remain a maiden for all time, choosing instead to master archery and hunting while also assisting women. She symbolizes feminine independence and competency, unpossessed by any Minotaur and unbeholden to the native culture.

Protecting the Sacred Fire

With an understanding of what the Sacred Fire symbolizes, let's take an entirely fresh look at the opening scene of *Star Wars: A New Hope*. We know that the Star Wars original trilogy is a hallmark example of the hero's journey for Luke Skywalker. But, the film doesn't bother introducing Luke until nearly 17 minutes in. Why? Because the opening of the film jumps right into the middle of a heroine story.

Princess Leia is desperately fleeing with the stolen plans to the dreaded Death Star. We're witnessing the full power of the archetypal heroine trying to escape her native culture. But the Masked Minotaur to *her story*, Darth Vader, is bearing down on our heroine's ship. (The head of the star destroyer even looks like a Minotaur's head).

On the surface, Vader is after the Death Star plans. But in archetypal and symbolic terms, he's after the heroine's Sacred Fire, which is Princess Leia's personal cause. The Death Star plans are not just a technical readout of a battle station but the continued survival and, therefore, the *continuity* of the Rebel Alliance. If Darth Vader captures those plans, the Sacred Fire of freedom shall be extinguished across the galaxy. Trillions of lives are at stake in Princess Leia's urgent flight. Subconsciously, we recognize that the fragile flame—the continuation of the rebellion and the lives of trillions—are in the hands of a lone heroine, fleeing and in danger, just out of Vader's reach. The film's imagery strikes at the very heart of our human subconscious.

Funny enough, another classic hero's journey story, *The Matrix*, also begins with a heroine. The film opens not with Neo, but with Trinity, who's talking with Cipher, the Masked Minotaur of the story. The call is a setup. Like Princess Leia, Trinity also battles the law enforcement agents of her native culture and then follows specific directions to navigate an escape from a deadly maze. Ultimately, the Sacred Fire of the human revolution is in Trinity's hands.

The same is true of Sarah Connor in the first two Terminator films. On the surface, Sarah is trying to survive because her unborn son, John Connor, is the future leader of the human resistance. So much criticism has been directed at the idea that Sarah Connor plays a secondary role to John Connor, or that her entire value is reduced to giving birth to a man who will save the world. But once again, we must look deeper into the symbolism. As a heroine, Sarah's value goes *way* beyond motherhood. Think about it. Sarah would protect John's life even if his destiny was to become a tax accountant. But Sarah isn't just protecting one unborn child. When she flees from the Terminator, she's protecting three billion human lives from a future nuclear holocaust.

Therefore, Sarah carries the sacred flame of humanity itself in her hand. And Sarah is haunted by the Sacred Fire she carries. When Sarah sleeps, her nightmares are not of John's death, but of Judgement Day and the nuclear holocaust that obliterates billions of human beings. From my point of view, the story was never really about John. The first two Terminator films are heroine-centric and have always been about Sarah. That might be why subsequent films centered on Schwarzenegger's Terminator or John Connor failed, while Sarah Connor's legacy has withstood the test of time.

In the hit show *The Last of Us*, the heroine, Ellie, is not affected by the fungal infection that's destroying the human race. She must travel great distances and face countless dangers to protect the fragile flame of humanity's continued existence.

We see the same thing in *Children of Men*, where human beings lose the ability to create children. We're fooled into thinking the story is about Theo Faron (Clive Owen). In reality, the story is about the heroine, Kee (Clare-Hope Ashitey), who suddenly becomes pregnant and offers the thinnest hope that humanity might endure. Once again, the heroine holds the flame of humanity's continued existence in her hand. She's also escaping the hostile forces of her native culture to protect this Sacred Fire. Like Princess Leia, like Sarah Connor, if Kee fails, we all die. Protecting the fragile flame becomes the entire driving force of the story.

Taking a step back, I believe the potential to create new life is likely the root source behind the archetype of the divine feminine and Sacred Fire. Likewise, the drive to perpetuate life is encoded within all nature on a rudimentary level. It's a unique and unusual force in an otherwise barren and infinite universe. The continuity of life represents the cold and primal logic behind life's continuity. However, a heroine transcends the primal logic of nature in our stories because she humanizes creation in all its possible forms and expressions. As a writer or storyteller, you will get the chance to design the Sacred Fire of your heroine in new and creative ways.

Anatomy of an Archetype – The Sacred Fire

◊ The Sacred Fire is both a creative power and an attractive force.

◊ From a narrative standpoint the Sacred Fire answers the question: "Why this heroine?"

◊ Consider an object or symbol for the heroine's Sacred Fire throughout your story.

◊ The heroine's Sacred Fire is linked to whatever is most important to her.

◊ There are often three claims to the heroine's Sacred Fire.

◊ The Heroine's Claim: "Individuation"—passion, agency, free will, desire, creativity, magical ability, mastered skills

◊ The Native Culture's Claim: "Continuity"—family, heritage, tradition, wisdom, legacy, cultural values, knowledge

◊ The Minotaur's Claim: "Possession"—tyranny, dominance, power, ego, possessive love, monopoly, injustice, obsession

◊ The competing claims to the Sacred Fire must all be reconciled by the story's conclusion.

Exercises

1. In *The Hunger Games*, what unforgettable way does author Suzanne Collins symbolize and showcase Katniss Everdeen's Sacred Fire?

2. Let's return to *Moana*. Structurally, two heroines in the story have a Sacred Fire, both Moana and Te Fiti. Can you identify the symbols used in the film to symbolize the Sacred Fire of Te Fiti? And what would you pick if you had to choose a symbol for Moana, based on the imagery in the film?

3. In the novel *Their Eyes Were Watching God*, what did author Zora Neale Hurston use to symbolize Janie's Sacred Fire? Why did this work as a Sacred Fire symbol, and how did it tie the heroine's journey together?

4. In the 1986 action film *Aliens*, we see fire symbolism in the flame thrower that Ripley carries with her. Indeed, the image of Ripley, Newt, and the flamethrower is now iconic. I don't think it's an accident that this symbolism appears during the film's final segment. What is Ripley's Sacred Fire?

Tarot

We've explored the labyrinth, beheld the dreaded Minotaur, and laid eyes upon the heroine's mesmerizing Sacred Fire. As writers, we've established our setting, our villain, and our heroine's layered conflicts. As readers of archetypal designs, we must unleash the next recurrent theme. So, how does the heroine attempt to reconcile all these forces in her life? The next card in the deck reveals the First Fate position, which is the heroine's first attempt to reconcile the competing claims to her Sacred Fire.

Captivity Bargain

THE CAPTIVITY
BARGAIN

he captive heroine is so pervasive in storytelling that we either accept the scenario or we reject it wholesale. Once again, the primal precepts are already in place. We can easily conjure up images of the virgin chained to a mountain, her wrists shackled overhead, or the beautiful princess on the balcony of a tall tower, inspired by the world below yet barred from participation. We see a visual symbol of one possible fate for the heroine in the story. Without being told, we perceive the heroine's desire for freedom and worldly experience just as we perceive her lonely, caged condition.

Stories that feature a trapped heroine are everywhere. Many of the great works of literature feature a heroine held captive by her native culture—*One Thousand and One Nights*, *Jane Eyre*, *Pride and Prejudice*, *Wuthering Heights*, *Memoirs of a Geisha*, *Gone with the Wind*, and *Anna Karenina*. The Greek goddesses Persephone and Aphrodite are captured by an arranged marriage, while Ann Darrow stays forever clutched in the massive hand of King Kong. And Beatrix Kiddo, like Sleeping Beauty, lies in the deep sleep of a coma. Bollywood films are rife with plot lines that revolve around a heroine and an arranged marriage. Lastly, the maiden in the tower looms large in medieval folklore with Rapunzel, Juliet, and Cinderella, just as in the modern day with Wanda Maximoff (*Wanda Vision*), Piper Chapman (*Orange Is the New Black)*, and June Osborne (*The Handmaid's Tale*).

But why?

Why are so many heroines captured in the first place? In the hero's journey, the villain often treats the warrior-oriented hero as a physical threat to be destroyed. Once again, we see the tropes of a warrior story, where the hero is physically expendable unless he masters vital skills. But in most of our feminine mythologies, it's nearly the exact opposite—the heroine is often treated as physically essential, almost too precious to risk. Locking the heroine away is to protect the heroine from harm or the temptations of the outer world. Perhaps the sentiment is best reflected in the long-standing cultural command, "Women and children first!" But despite the guarded and protective attitude toward heroines, their free will is so often overruled.

All true. But as writers, we must honor the second rule of the feminine monomyth: **The heroine's labyrinth <u>always</u> regards the heroine as a sovereign individual, regardless of portrayal, historical period, or restrictive circumstance.**

Therefore, even under the most oppressive, worst-case scenarios, we must see the heroine as the sovereign being. If she is forced into captivity, she will come to know the nature of one of humanity's least desirable states of existence, and in so doing, she will model for us a pathway outward, away from captivity. The heroine becomes a symbol not of suppression but of freedom. Captivity is not the state to which the heroine aspires, and we all know this instinctively.

In *I Know Why the Caged Bird Sings*, poet and writer Maya Angelou tells us that a caged bird's song is the secret song of freedom. This is the striking counterintuitive meaning behind all symbols of captivity.

In *The Two Towers*, Éowyn sums it up nicely when Aragorn asks, "What do you fear, my lady?" Éowyn quickly replies, "A cage. To stay behind bars until use and old age accept them, and all chance of valor has gone beyond recall or desire."

From the perspective of the heroine's labyrinth monomyth, the captive maiden represents the unrealized heroine. She is at an early stage in her growth arc. Many heroines actually choose the Captivity Bargain of their own free will in the early part of the story. They agree to it.

We must recognize that the fledgling heroine is actively attempting to reconcile the competing claims to her Sacred Fire. The native culture views the heroine through the lens of communal and family continuity; the Masked Minotaur seeks to monopolize her unique creative powers, while the heroine feels the weight of all her unrealized potential. The three claims upon the heroine's Sacred Fire rarely align, so she must reconcile all three to prevent serious disruption in her life and the lives of others. Therefore, our heroine chooses a compromise—a Captivity Bargain.

The Bargain Made

In storytelling, the Captivity Bargain arrives soon after our heroine claims her Sacred Fire. Members of the native culture recognize the heroine's independence and usually view it as disruptive to the social order, a threat to continuity.

For the Captivity Bargain to work, an established member of the native culture must explain the game rules. The heroine learns what she must do at all costs and what she must *never* do. Or else. Furthermore, the heroine may not fully understand the consequences of those mysterious and forbidden choices. Violating the rules risks stigma, isolation, magical entrapment, physical transformation, physical threat, or banishment. Most importantly, the heroine is often warned that her bad choices may extend to people that the heroine does not want to see harmed.

The message is clear. The heroine's task is *not* to disrupt the social order. She'll pay a price, and others will pay a price with her. Remember, the motives for the native culture are not always anti-heroine but often stem from a view that the heroine lacks the necessary maturity levels or experience to be fully independent. The story world determines the reasons for and degree to which society demands the bargain.

Therefore, heroines who accept the Captivity Bargain are not weak. They accept the Captivity Bargain on unsteady grounds, against convincing pressure, and usually without the necessary experience to counter the demands. The heroine sincerely tries to honor at least one, if not several, external claims to her Sacred Fire. Keep in mind that the heroine almost always agrees to the Captivity Bargain because she *trusts* the person or people who insist upon compliance. At a minimum, the heroine will recognize the logic of conformity and trust that everyone is right. Her response is a natural human response to such pressure.

From a psychological standpoint, our mythologies and collective stories reveal that our mythical heroines have desires and aspirations that they believe are quite valuable and important, while members of the native culture suggest otherwise. **The early internal consequence, therefore, is guilt—guilt at knowing that she aspires to something that her native culture regards as secondary, guilt at a sense of selfishness and guilt at knowing that her aspirations are a source of conflict.** Guilt forces the heroine to stare into the abyss of a pending social stigma, a dreaded scarlet letter.

When the heroine accepts the Captivity Bargain, your readers will feel sympathy and frustration; they'll invest more deeply into the heroine's plight. The audience understands the persuasion, manipulation, or intimidation when the heroine surrenders.

Never mistake the heroine's submission to captivity as a flaw in her sense of self-worth. When a heroine submits herself, she offers her Sacred Fire to others she trusts. She's bestowing a gift of immense value. Our heroines are actively learning the importance of their creative powers, and the Captivity Bargain is an early means to protect their personal claim while trying to honor other seemingly legitimate claims. She is us. We have all done this, and so we understand that the bargains made in our youth are rife with inexperience.

We also intuitively know the heroine will change her mind, but for now, we must stay with her as she makes an unfavorable deal. Writers must remember that their heroine cannot model the behavior for gaining personal empowerment unless the story models the conflicts that deny her that very same empowerment. We must know the tower before we learn how to avoid the fate of that tower.

In the 2023 cultural phenomenon *Barbie*, there's a nearly perfect depiction of a Captivity Bargain. The heroine, Stereotypical Barbie, confronts the CEO of Mattel to try and restore the order of her native culture, Barbieland. To solve the problem, the CEO suggests that Barbie return to her box, and everything will go back to normal. Again, the heroine initially agrees to the Captivity Bargain of her own free will. But as she steps into the pink box, just as the twisty ties are about to shackle her at the wrists symbolically, Barbie changes her mind.

In *Tangled*, Mother Gothel's song "Mother Knows Best" is a brash and funny song that serves as a Captivity Bargain. Mother Gothel recounts all the reasons why Rapunzel should stay captive in the tower. The melody is playful and entertaining but comes to a chilling halt when Mother Gothel reestablishes the Captivity Bargain.

"Don't ever ask to leave this tower again."

Rapunzel then drops her head. "Yes, Mother."

Our heart breaks *because* we know Rapunzel voluntarily accepted a bargain with a Masked Minotaur. We understand that she lacks real-world experience to push back successfully against the pressure.

She offers conformity or subservience in exchange for social cohesion and other perceived benefits. **As storytellers, we must respect this genuine dynamic. Suppose we skip it out of fear of a negative portrayal. In that case, we deny our readers or viewers a chance to understand a Captivity Bargain and how to model the behavior to avoid such bargains in the future.** We must recognize that the heroine's negotiation in the Captivity Bargain is a counterintuitive step toward *freedom*. Though repressed, the heroine's claim to her Sacred Fire is very much intact at this stage of the story.

The Allure of the Bargain

In *Jackie Brown*, the heroine spends most of the movie actively negotiating her Captivity Bargain. The story centers squarely on this theme. Jackie works all sides as she tries to devise a plan that grants her freedom on her own terms. Although the heroine seems to be at the mercy of characters with greater powers than hers, we are always aware that the heroine is sovereign. She's active and independent despite all her severe limitations and dangers. Jackie has a seat at the table. **Therefore, part of the Captivity Bargain's allure is the heroine's sense of negotiating the terms of her desired freedom in the future.**

The possessive love of the Minotaur is a seductive force because the Minotaur usually leverages or offers something of value to the heroine in exchange for her willing subordination to the Minotaur's claim upon her Sacred Fire. In some cases, the Masked Minotaur appears to be the solution to the heroine's struggles against the native culture at home. Therefore, the heroine escapes the confines of the native culture only to become possessed by the Minotaur.

As villains, Minotaurs have established themselves within the labyrinth of the native culture by assuming certain responsibilities for others, usually in the form of stability and security. The Minotaur's physical prowess, vast wealth, and social influence are highly prized in the native culture and make for an alluring exchange. But if the heroine surrenders too much of her personal responsibility, she risks capture or possession by the Minotaur. Therefore, early in the story, the immature or less experienced heroine may find the possessive love of the Minotaur intriguing, desirable, or even in her best interest.

For now, it's essential to recognize the seductive power of possessive love. The Minotaur is skillful and powerful in the labyrinth in ways that the heroine may not yet be. The Minotaur's apparent mastery and power in the labyrinth are two things that the heroine seeks in the early part of the story. A romanticized idea of surrendering personal sovereignty for a real or perceived external benefit should be given the proper respect. As the Captivity Bargain changes or degrades, the heroine will eventually choose freedom over any bargained state of semi-dependence.

Again, the Captivity Bargain should not be viewed as evidence of weakness so much as proof of inexperience. When Katniss Everdeen volunteers as tribute in *The Hunger Games*, she's knowingly subjecting herself to a dangerous Captivity Bargain. She's getting something she wants out of the bargain, even if it's not the best possible outcome. That's why the heroine's labyrinth usually features a Captivity Bargain at the beginning of the story rather than at the end. Therefore, the heroine's bad bargain allows her to gain the vital experience necessary to make fulfilling and mutually beneficial bargains in the future.

To Conform or Not to Conform

That is the question that preoccupies the minds of so many heroines. With the Captivity Bargain established, the heroine must follow the truce willingly or defy it secretly. In many cases, the heroine merely disguises her desire for independence and takes extra care to project an appearance of conformity. All her desires are still in place but must be suppressed or hidden for the perceived greater good. Once the agents of the native culture turn their back, though, our heroines reveal that they are still very much connected to their innermost desires and have no genuine plans to abandon them. In storytelling terms, the contrast between feigned conformity and secret non-conformity adds quite a bit of tension.

The veneer of conformity, however, cannot be sustained. Therefore, the Captivity Bargain is vital to the story because it provides a baseline, a starting point from which the heroine can gain the necessary experience and wisdom to achieve true individuation later.

The Disney Princess

As we discussed earlier, perhaps nowhere is the captive princess more recognized and celebrated in Western culture than in the Disney princess. I polled several women about whether they thought the Disney princess sent the wrong message to young girls. The majority of women agreed that, yes, the messaging in Disney princess films could be counterproductive. Only a handful of women voiced outright hostility toward Disney princesses, but they were a pronounced minority. The primary complaint is that Disney princesses perpetuated the idea that an external individual, often a man, will enter the heroine's life, fix her problems, and make her happy.

Many women felt that the films didn't properly orient them to the real world, which left them with distorted expectations of romantic relationships and/or solving problems on their own. And yet, despite the palpable frustration with the messaging, nearly all the women polled or interviewed still admitted that they had a favorite Disney princess. Belle, Moana, and Elsa rounded out the top three. To be fair, the oldest of the Disney princesses, such as Cinderella, Aurora, and Snow White, seem to be the primary sources of frustration and criticism. However, despite the general aversion to the captive princess archetype, something positive still resonated with many modern women. I found this a bit confusing at first, but through the heroine's labyrinth narrative model, a fresh analysis is available to me, and now I believe the old and the new can be reconciled.

The heroine's labyrinth provides an entirely different context with which to view the persistent theme of the captive princess. And when considered through the lens of monomyth, the captive princess will continue to resonate because she represents a specific stage in the arc of the heroine—one step *toward* the heroine's individuation, *not* a fully realized or final state. From the perspective of the feminine monomyth, the captive princess expresses how our heroines feel at an early stage in their lives. **We honor that stage, even if we've outgrown it.** Therefore, we can see the captive princess *not* as an unwanted archetype that sends the wrong message but as a heroine actively attempting to reconcile competing forces in her early life. Under this perspective, we can honor our heroine's plight and allow the story to progress.

Yes, many stories from earlier eras reinforced the native culture's claim to the heroine's Sacred Fire at the expense of the heroine's claim. But our modern stories are compensating by focusing on the heroine's claim at the expense of the native culture. At one end, we hear Dorothy Gale conclude, "There's no place like home," and at the other end, we hear Elizabeth Gilbert (*Eat, Pray, Love*) respond with, "Operation Self-Esteem—Day Fucking One."

I believe the Disney princess continues to hold a special place for women (and men too) because she represents a youthful stage in our lives where we all had romanticized notions of love and potential. The captive princess, remember, is a sovereign being who will outgrow her situation through great deeds and evolving choices.

The Knight in Shining Armor

In the movie *Shrek*, our favorite green ogre reads a fairy tale book in an outhouse and says, "She waited in the dragon's keep in the highest room of the tallest tower for her true love and true love's first kiss." Shrek laughs irreverently. "Like that's ever gonna happen." He then rips out the page and uses it for toilet paper.

This scene reflects modern attitudes toward the knight in shining armor and the damsel in distress. We reject the notion of a passive princess who believes that someone else—an external force, a knight in shining armor, will sweep in and solve her problems. It's not a practical message upon which we can depend. Suggesting that a heroine is powerless during her Captivity Bargain is antithetical to the feminine monomyth because it fails to emphasize the heroine's autonomy and growth.

The damsel in distress is a reductive portrayal of heroines. Even Joseph Campbell once said, "In the whole mythological journey, the woman is there. All she has to do is realize that she's the place that people are trying to get to."

Campbell made the statement about the hero's journey monomyth, which emphasizes the *hero* and the *hero's* growth arc, not the so-called damsel. The hero had distinguished himself through the warrior-journey and is now worthy of a mature relationship. The portrayal of the hero's new worthiness sometimes leads to the portrayal of a heroine as a "prize" to be won. While there is certainly apt criticism that "heroine as prize" is reductive or demeaning, we do see the theme echoed in heroine stories as well. For example, in the Jane Austen novel *Persuasion*, the heroine, Anne Elliot, is confronted with a potential suitor in Frederick Wentworth. However, since the man isn't distinguished or remarkable, the parents block the marriage. After the Napoleonic Wars ended and Frederick Wentworth became a war hero, he became *worthy* of the marriage and blessing of the parents. Notice even the word "worth" in the name Wentworth? Romance novels, too, abound in potential romantic partners that usually become worthy of the heroine over time. Therefore, a hero or a knight in shining armor who wins the heart of the princess due to his achievements and overall worthiness as a potential partner isn't unique to the hero's journey.

However, Campbell's answer breaks one key rule of the heroine's labyrinth—that the heroine is always sovereign. She's never just "there." **What we really have is an intersection of *two monomyths*—the hero's journey and the heroine's labyrinth.**

A careful look into these stories with a newly balanced perspective shows us two events occurring simultaneously—the hero's Supreme Ordeal, where he attains social worthiness—and the heroine's Captivity Bargain. One arc is ending, while the other arc is just getting started.

The warrior-oriented hero answered his Call to Adventure long before this moment and traveled a great distance. He now encounters the captive princess and, in my opinion, is *absolutely* acting heroically if the hero attempts to rescue her.

Therefore, I believe the knight in shining armor is how the hero sees *himself* in the hero's journey. A warrior attempting to save another person while facing death requires a positive self-image, and a "knight" wearing armor is appropriately dressed for battle. So, what's the issue?

Monomyth Intersection

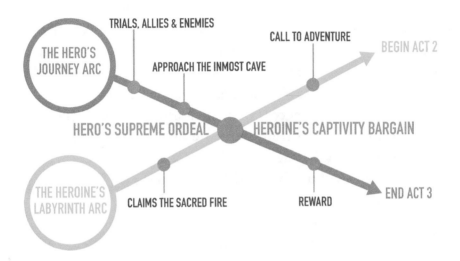

If too many stories are told through a warrior-centric lens, we have an unbalanced perspective.

From the heroine's labyrinth perspective, we also have a heroine in the most dangerous version of the Captivity Bargain. The heroine is living out a terrifying conflict between herself, the native culture, and a Masked Minotaur. The appearance of a potential heroic partner is certainly an interesting development in her life, but such an encounter never solves the underlying problems. The real issue here is that the hero's narrative journey is ending. "And they lived happily ever after" simply skips over the remainder of the heroine's story. We see her in a single snapshot of her life, and her personal resolution to the Captivity Bargain remains incomplete.

Okay, so maybe *that* story wasn't the heroine's story. Maybe *that* story was about the hero. However, if you care about the heroine, as this book does, then we must still make sense of the heroine in the hero's story. We must first recognize the intersection of monomyths, but we'll keep *our* focus on the heroine. We can acknowledge and respect the hero on the journey, and we'll acknowledge and respect the heroine in her labyrinth, even in a singular moment of her arc.

Romance novelist Gail Carriger aptly observed that our heroines spiritually fade when isolated or cut off from family and friends. In the past, we may have viewed such isolation as a negative portrayal more so than an archetypal reality that must be overcome for growth to occur. That was before we had the heroine's labyrinth to use as a parallel model. As storytellers with a feminine monomyth clearly defined and at the ready, we can see her conflict more clearly. **A heroic partner may appear or not. It doesn't really matter to us. So, even if the heroine is rescued at this early stage of her story, she still must resolve the underlying causes of the Captivity Bargain on her own terms in any version of this archetypal event.** In the hero's story, that resolution might get skipped, but in the heroine's story, we're just getting started. Heroic partners entering the heroine's life is another theme we'll explore in a later chapter. For now, let's review the primary aspects of the Captivity Bargain.

Anatomy of an Archetype – The Captivity Bargain

◊ The heroine usually agrees to the Captivity Bargain *willingly*.

◊ Loses some degree of freedom within the native culture

◊ The heroine typically makes the Captivity Bargain to reconcile the competing claims to her Sacred Fire.

◊ Captivity often results in the heroine's isolation.

◊ The Captivity Bargain often appears to be a reasonable solution to the heroine's conflicts.

◊ The characters who demand, recommend, or present the Captivity Bargain are often trusted or in a position of authority.

◊ Often represents a counterintuitive step toward freedom

◊ Associated with inexperience, immaturity, and innocence

Exercises

1. Make a list of your top five or ten favorite heroine stories. How did the heroine enter into a Captivity Bargain early in each story? In what ways did the heroine consent to the bargain, and in what ways did she secretly defy the bargain?

2. In the final episode of *Game of Thrones*, Season 5, "Mother's Mercy," how does Cersei willingly make a Captivity Bargain? Why would a vain and power-hungry character like Cersei agree to such a Captivity Bargain?

3. Like in the follow-up HBO hit series, *House of the Dragon*, how does Rhaenyra Targaryen enter a Captivity Bargain? And in what ways does she follow a path of secret (or not so secret) non-conformity to this bargain?

4. In the show *Squid Game*, which closely follows the story structure of the heroine's labyrinth, when does the male hero agree to the Captivity Bargain? (Hint: There are two instances.)

Tarot

The next card in our arrangement is the most unpredictable of them all, the Wild Card, which may appear in heroine stories at any time and may be helpful or disastrous.

The Black Swan

THE BLACK SWAN

he Wild Card has been drawn. This is the only theme that doesn't apply directly to the heroine's decisions but still shapes her growth in various ways. In this book, we drew the Black Swan in the early segment of the story, but the reality is that this theme may appear at *any time* in the heroine's story. **The Black Swan represents the sudden destabilization of the story world from a disruption of cycles. The disruption is often temporary but severe enough to throw the native culture into disorder.** In most cases, the native culture is at fault due to human error, ignorance, or arrogance.

When Scarlett O'Hara defiantly vows never to go hungry again, she refers to the famine that struck her plantation during the American Civil War, in which starvation, degradation, and death befell the characters in the story. But the sudden destabilization of Scarlett's world from warfare and famine is by no means a rare occurrence.

In the academic book *The Feminization of Famine*, Margaret Kelleher addresses the phenomenon of feminine association with famine—often presented as imagery of gaunt and stoic mothers alongside their gaunt and starving children. Moreover, Margaret explores works of fiction written mainly by women that single out the realities of the Irish and Bengali famines, respectively. She quotes Bulgarian-French philosopher Julia Kristeva, who said literature "represents the ultimate coding of our crises, of our most intimate and most serious apocalypses."

I agree. Apocalyptic scenarios, backdrops, settings, and imagery are encoded within a surprising number of heroine-centric stories. These dangerous themes occurred so regularly that I didn't even notice them until late in my studies. Also, I struggled to know *where* to place the Black Swan since the theme appears randomly—sometimes early, sometimes late, sometimes helpful, sometimes devastating, sometimes small, and sometimes apocalyptic.

Perhaps we see the ominous tornado in the beginning segment of *The Wizard of Oz*, or the mushroom cloud of a nuclear explosion in the middle of *Terminator 2*, or a sudden Florida hurricane near the end of *Their Eyes Were Watching God*.

But why? As a storyteller and writer, I want to know why. What purpose does the Black Swan serve as a narrative pattern? If the heroine's labyrinth is a monomyth, what are the lessons the heroine is trying to teach us?

Again, there are three primary aspects at work simultaneously with the Black Swan. First, these scenarios underscore the unpredictability and full power of natural forces. Secondly, the chaos unleashed reveals the ineffectiveness of human designs. These first two aspects play out effortlessly, with nature in full control. Thirdly, the Black Swan is temporary, with a high ceiling for potential outcomes. Whatever caused the Black Swan, whether it's the regular rhythms of nature or the inevitability of human error (or both), the turbulence will subside.

So, whereas the warning encoded in the hero's journey relates to the inevitable threat of warfare from outside the native culture, the heroine's labyrinth often endures the inevitable disruption of the native culture from the forces of nature.

The spiral, which I regard as a natural symbol for a labyrinth, can also spin wildly and randomly, representing those wild forces of nature to which humanity must contend. Writers should recognize the relationship between the labyrinth—that which is fixed, manufactured, and predictable—and that of the Black Swan—the inevitable upending of human cycles and designs. If the setting for your heroine is more or less among the same native culture, perhaps then we shouldn't be surprised that her story will include a Black Swan. For what pattern is immune to disruption? And what designs of humanity are without their flaws or hubris? With enough time, a Black Swan will visit every setting.

We'll spend additional time covering the heroine and her general distrust of human organization in a later chapter (Cult of Deception), but here, I lay the foundation. Heroines are less trusting in the certainty of human organization, its schedules, and patterns because many are cautiously aware of the Black Swan—the great disruption—and the devastating consequence of miscalculation or unpreparedness. **The lesson seems to be: Do not place all your faith in human systems. The heroine reminds us to stay in tune with all the patterns and rhythms that may not even appear to be patterns and rhythms and so are not as obvious.**

Heroines and Natural Disaster

The labyrinth, though dominated by the powers of the native culture and the Masked Minotaur, is also subject to sudden shocks from both nature and human error. *The Handmaid's Tale* is the result of a global plague that led to a dystopian society predicated on the enslavement of women. There are countless historical fiction stories in which heroines must navigate the sudden Black Swans of war, such as *Sophie's Choice*, *Memoirs of a Geisha*, and *The Nightingale*, just to name a few. In many of these stories, the Black Swan of war unleashes natural disasters such as famine, disease, pandemic, fire, atomic fallout, and the encroachment of nature upon a society unable to maintain itself. And so, it's no surprise that heroine Ellie Sattler confronts John Hammond about the hubris of control in *Jurassic Park*. She clearly states that human control over nature is the illusion that John fails to see.

In *Their Eyes Were Watching God*, Janie experiences the onslaught of a hurricane as it crosses Florida. Not only does she barely survive, but a wild dog bites her beloved husband, Tea Cake. Here, a natural disease plays a more tragic role in her life than the hurricane. The ocean also becomes a deadly spiral for Ariel in *The Little Mermaid* while swallowing up the unsinkable ship with Rose in *Titanic*. That latter film is a hallmark cautionary tale of human overconfidence in their ability to control nature.

In the film *Gravity*, a comet storm destroys the US space shuttle and satellite, which traps the heroine Ryan Stone (Sandra Bullock) in orbit. The film follows Ryan as she deals with the deadly forces of the suborbital atmosphere. Again, plenty of manmade mistakes play a role in her tale of survival. But we also see the forces of gravity at work on Elastigirl when a missile strikes her plane in *The Incredibles*. Flaming wreckage plunges into a dangerous ocean while our heroine saves her two super children. Black Widow endures a similar fall from the atmosphere when the Red Room is destroyed in Marvel's *Black Widow*.

Apocalyptic imagery is present in *Terminator 2: Judgement Day* when Sarah Connor has nightmares about nuclear Armageddon due to misplaced human trust in artificial intelligence. But it's also present in *Star Wars: A New Hope*. When the Galactic Empire destroys the planet of Alderaan, we're not with Luke Skywalker, but with Princess Leia, who's the *only character* in which Alderaan is their native culture. Also, *Coraline* features the unmaking of the Other Mother's world. The heroine must retreat to the alternate house as the world turns gray and disintegrates around her. We see similar apocalyptic images again when Neytiri witnesses the destruction of Hometree in *Avatar*. Here, the world again turns to ash and fire as the native culture is dealt a devasting blow. Scarlett O'Hara, likewise, flees from the inferno of a burning Atlanta, and Ulana Khomyuk investigates a nuclear disaster in the *Chernobyl* miniseries, while Evelyn Wang stares into the all-consuming, nihilistic abyss of the "everything bagel" in *Everything Everywhere All at Once*. Heroines seem to sense and fear the cost of miscalculation and chaotic dangers lying in wait at the periphery. **Therefore, the Black Swan may be an encoded nightmare scenario about unexpected disruptions.**

Even so, not all of nature's intrusions are bad.

Helpful Chaos

The Black Swan is often a force of brutal devastation, but sometimes, the forces of chaos help our heroines. While watching *Moana*, I realized that the heroine's "gramma" perfectly embodies the helpful realm of chaos. In the song "Where You Are" by Lin-Manuel Miranda, the native culture lays out its strategies for survival and happiness, as well as its claim to the heroine's Sacred Fire. But the grandmother enters the song with a different message. She embraces the mischievous and unpredictable nature of the ocean, likening it to her own personality.

Hers is a counter message of non-conformity to the village's expectations and respect for the ocean's unpredictable chaos. Throughout the film, the oceanic spirit of Moana's grandmother plays the role of guardian angel and helpful chaos.

In *Foundation* Season 1, Episode 8, "The Missing Piece," heroine Salvor Hardin discovers the lost ship *Invictus*. She quickly learns that an onboard catastrophe killed the entire crew as the cursed ship continues jumping from one random point in space to another on an endless cycle. Salvor attempts to gain control over the chaos with a strategy described as flipping a coin one thousand times. And she succeeds.

For Rapunzel in *Tangled*, the bad guys unleash a deluge of water into a labyrinth of caves. At first, the surging water threatens to kill our heroine and Flynn Rider. Ultimately, the water helps them to escape while also serving as a reveal for the heroine's creative powers, her hair.

In *A Quiet Place*, a wild barrage of fireworks masks the sound of our heroine giving birth, while Ellen Ripley unleashes the chaotic forces of a space vacuum to defeat the aliens in her first two films.

Furiosa in *Mad Max: Fury Road* and Lady Jessica in *Dune* endure the onslaught of a sandstorm, both of which help the heroines escape. The underlying wisdom of helpful chaos in these two stories seems to be to flow *with* the natural chaos rather than try and control it.

In *Star Trek: Picard* Season 3, Episode 4, "No Win Scenario," the crew of the *Titan* is experiencing a bioelectric storm from inside a chaotic nebula. To make matters worse, their ship is disabled and hunted by a vastly superior enemy vessel. However, heroine Beverly Crusher detects a pattern in the seemingly random bioelectric waves that pulse outward like lightning. She concludes that the bioelectricity waves mirror the contraction patterns found in childbirth. Beverly's insight leads the crew to realize that the nebula is a unique lifeform about to give birth on a cosmic scale. During the final "contraction," the *Titan* rides the bioelectric wave away from danger while witnessing a cosmic birth on the viewscreen. This episode provided a brilliant example of the Black Swan themes of hidden patterns, random danger, natural forces, and a heroine who uses chaos to save the day.

And what of chaos? What of chance and randomness? When heroines are at a loss for options, it's not unusual to see them trust in the chaos of nature. In the Book of Exodus, Moses' mother, Jochebed, famously places her son in a basket and sets him downriver. Once again, the native culture has turned against our heroine by a decree designed to kill the sons of Israelite families. No longer able to hide Moses, she placed her faith in the chaos and randomness of the River Nile. The Pharaoh's wife discovered Moses and raised the infant as her son. As an adult, Moses challenges the very heart of Egyptian power and leads the Israelites out of Egypt. One heroine's decision to trust the randomness of nature resulted in truly epic events.

At first, I struggled to find a direct relationship between the Black Swan and heroines from an archetypal standpoint. Why would a theme centered on random natural events be tied to the heroine at all? And then I remembered the symbolism of Little Red Riding Hood and the connection with budding womanhood, which may be the archetypal source of the Black Swan event.

In *Game of Thrones* Season 2, Episode 7, "A Man Without Honor," Sansa Stark gets married off to Tyrion Lannister as a young maiden. She's against the marriage and enters a Captivity Bargain where the native culture backs off until she comes of age and "flowers." One morning, she awakens only to find the bedsheets stained with blood. The safe and protective truce she'd struck is suddenly over. Frantically, her chambermaids rushed to cover up the evidence, only to be stymied by a passing spy.

Moses and Jochebed by Pedro Américo (1884).

The novel (and film) *Carrie* infamously opens with the Black Swan of menstruation, which scares the heroine. The rest of the story revolves around the event and includes heavy symbolism of blood and womanhood. Once again, the Masked Minotaur of the story is the heroine's mother, who views the Black Swan event as a harbinger of sin.

The Disney animated film *Turning Red* also draws a more subtle allegory for the Black Swan of natural puberty for the heroine. In this case, the heroine magically turns into a red panda bear at random and often inconvenient moments.

The physiological transition from girlhood to womanhood is a physical and definable moment for female characters. A force of nature sweeps in on a random day to change the heroine's world in a big way. The moment marks a non-negotiable change, new potential, and shifting attitudes from the outside world. Perhaps the fickle will of nature reminds our heroines to stay forever guarded about sudden changes. Heroine stories warn us regularly that a Black Swan will arrive again one day to upturn the order of things for good or ill.

Anatomy of an Archetype – The Black Swan

◊ A temporary destabilizing or disrupting event usually caused by nature.

◊ The most common forms of Black Swans are famines, pandemics, fires, floods, or other natural disasters.

◊ A military invasion or foreign occupation of the home space may also serve as a Black Swan.

◊ Often includes apocalyptic imagery or severe damage to the home environment.

◊ The Black Swan reinforces the heroine's distrust of predictable human conventions.

◊ The heroine may place trust in randomness or chaos.

◊ The randomness and chaos of the Black Swan may help or hinder the heroine.

Exercises

1. In *The Mandalorian*, heroine Bo-Katan vies for leadership of planet Mandalore. However, as of this writing, her lifelong quest is yet unfulfilled. What cataclysmic Black Swan event affected her home planet?

2. Now consider the novel *The Other Boleyn Girl*. What is the Black Swan that enters Anne Boleyn's life and has a catastrophic impact on the heroine?

3. In the Torah, or Old Testament of the Bible, Sarah's life is affected by what Black Swan event that forces her (and Abraham) to travel south to Egypt?

Tarot

We have drawn and spent the Wild Card in our deck. We are remind-ed that the mysterious designs of the cosmos are always at work with our stories. The apparent chaos of an ocean can be broken down into hydrodynamic patterns, and even an explosion must follow the rules of chemistry and physics. Remember, forces of chaos are the most com-plex patterns in nature, and they speak their own language. Many her-oines come to learn this cosmic language. However, we have one more card to draw for the opening act. And so, let us turn the next card.

Call to Adventure

THE CALL TO ADVENTURE

ronically, in Joseph Campbell's *The Hero with a Thousand Faces*, he opens "The Call to Adventure" chapter with a heroine tale. He recites a German fairy tale of a king's daughter who liked to play beside a spring in a dark forest. Her favorite plaything was a golden ball she dropped one morning and lost in the gushing spring. During her laments, a frog appeared who offered to retrieve the golden ball in exchange for companionship as an equal in her life. The king's daughter agreed, and the frog retrieved the golden ball. No sooner than the heroine once again had her favorite ball did she flee from the spring and forest, forgetting all about the deal she had made with the frog.

Joseph Campbell uses this mythological story as an example of the Call to Adventure in the hero's journey. The loss of her childhood ball and the arrival of the frog represents the Call to Adventure. While rereading the chapter, I was pleased to see that the story involved a *heroine* who makes a Captivity Bargain that she didn't take seriously. The

Call to Adventure was the appearance of the frog. The heroine's golden ball can also be interpreted as a symbol of the girl's childhood, while the forest spring symbolizes baptismal or transformational change. Of course, later in this tale, the princess kisses the frog, who then turns into a handsome prince.

To Campbell, the Call to Adventure is the moment in a story where the forces of destiny have arrived. There will be a departure from a normal mode of life and toward an environment of an unfamiliar world. And yet, even here, even in this most basic of narrative devices, the Call to Adventure, I found significant differences and, therefore, considerable variance in meaning to such a call in heroine-led stories.

The Refusal to Refuse the Call

When I first began studying heroines in earnest, I did so using the hero's journey rubric. I judged the quality of the writing based on whether the story adhered to the tropes of the hero's journey. At the time, I had no alternative framework to compare stories. Early on, I noticed that many heroine-led stories "skipped" two key steps in the hero's journey—the Refusal of the Call (to Adventure) and the Belly of the Beast.

In the hero's journey, heroes receive the Call to Adventure and then attempt to refuse the adventure. They balk. This seemingly contradictory tandem of events occurred so often in hero tales that Joseph Campbell gave it a name, "The Refusal of the Call." Heroes are reluctant to leave home or suddenly vacillate when the time comes. In *Star Wars: A New* Hope, Obi-Wan Kenobi turns to Luke Skywalker and offers to take the farmboy to Alderaan and teach him the Force. Luke, who'd been pining for adventure the whole movie until then, suddenly grumbles and then refuses Ben's Call to Adventure.

In *The Matrix*, Neo is about to meet Morpheus and discover the secrets of the mysterious Matrix. He gets a literal Call to Adventure on a cell phone that someone mailed to his work cubicle. He follows Morpheus' directions over the phone to escape the office and avoid arrest, but Neo refuses when he's asked to scale down the side of a skyscraper. That's forgivable. But the Call to Adventure occurs again when Neo enters a strange car with potential heroic partners. He's given a choice to discover the secret of the Matrix or get the hell out of the vehicle. Neo initially chooses to leave the car.

In both examples, the hero refuses the Call to Adventure when it comes. Strange, right? But the Refusal of the Call is a defined trope in the hero's journey.

I didn't notice the Refusal of the Call in most heroine-led stories I studied. Not only did most heroines accept the Call to Adventure, but they leaped at it. At first, I thought that this was a flaw in the writing. Diana Prince practically storms off-screen to answer the Call to Adventure in *Wonder Woman* (2017). Moana must be scolded multiple times about attempting to leave her home island, pleading with her elders to let her go. Mulan doesn't need convincing to leave home either; in fact, she needs convincing to *stay* home.

So, a mystery formed before my eyes. In the framework of the hero's journey, why did so many heroines "skip" the Refusal of the Call? And here, understanding the archetypal designs of the hero's journey helped me solve the puzzle.

Let's fast forward.

In *Star Wars: The Magic of Myth*, Mary Henderson outlines another step of the hero's journey called the Belly of the Beast. She says, "The passage of the threshold to spiritual and emotional transformation often requires a form of self-annihilation; in this transition, the physical body of the hero may be slain or even dismembered." She's talking about Luke Skywalker, of course. But she discussed how heroes may be swallowed figuratively or literally by a beast to experience a symbolic death. Pretty horrific stuff, right?

Well, I also noticed that many heroine stories skipped the Belly of the Beast trope as well as the Refusal of the Call. Again, why?

At first, I thought writers skipped the Refusal of the Call on purpose so that heroines didn't come across as afraid or indecisive. Likewise, I assumed that writers skipped the Belly of the Beast theme because they didn't want to show the gruesome destruction of heroines for a symbolic death or disgrace scene. In short, I assumed writers didn't include these unflattering steps as a way to avoid negative or harsh portrayals of heroines.

I was so bothered by these missing steps I even started writing an article called "The Incomplete Heroine," which addressed the missing steps and why I thought it was a mistake. I reasoned that the hero's journey is a monomythic structure that depicts growth and maturation, and these two steps are *vital* to the hero's overall development. But did heroines like Jane Eyre and Moana fail to model growth even though they skipped these two crucial steps in the hero's journey?

I was comparing apples to oranges. In this book, though, we're free of being shackled to the hero's journey, but the contrast helped me better understand the distinctive narrative model for our heroines.

The warrior-oriented roots of the hero's journey contain the archetypal mythos about leaving home to fight and save the native culture. The potential for self-destruction is activated once the hero departs his home sphere. Secondly, the Belly of the Beast delivers the archetypal event we recognize as symbolic death so the hero can overcome their fear of that possible death. This step allows them to develop the courage to face the possibility of their own destruction for real. The hero *should* be scared. The hero doesn't *really* want to leave home to face a fire-breathing, culture-annihilating dragon. By showing us that even heroes are afraid to face dragons, the hero's journey provides a behavior model for dealing with that warrior-oriented fear. The story lets us know that it's okay to be scared.

So, is the Call to Adventure in most heroine-centric stories the *same* thing? Are our stories preparing most of our heroines for a warrior-oriented journey far from home with a probability of personal destruction? I decided that the answer was mostly "no." The heroine's Call to Adventure is different in the labyrinth. And so, what it means to leave home is different.

Home as Comfort or Home as Cage

The meaning and significance of the home represent a massive distinction between the hero on the journey and the heroine in the labyrinth. Our heroic figures are both untested and immature when the Call to Adventure enters their lives. I believe that the meaning and significance of *home* evoke different attitudes about "leaving" home. The labyrinth is a material and cultural world of heavy restrictions that many heroines are actually eager to leave. In many stories, heroines view home as the place where feelings of captivity play out. The Call to Adventure represents that rare opportunity for the heroine to break away and try something unpredictable and new. The heroine *wants* to leave.

By contrast, "home" represents the place of safe returns, a place of comfort and familiarity for the warrior-oriented hero. Home is where the hero returns once their journey into the dangerous hinterlands is complete—the Shire, Starfleet headquarters, the Fortress of Solitude, or the Batcave. In stark terms, home is a vastly more desirable place when compared to the horrors of war in a far-off land. Refusing the Call makes more sense for a warrior-themed story.

The heroine's conflicts and challenges are simply different, as the heroine's labyrinth has established. The archetypal events and the symbolism of "home" are different. As writers, we must respect these differences. We don't have to vilify home but recognize that to our heroines, her desire to leave home is driven by genuine feelings of confinement and predetermined expectations. Many heroines view the home as a place of repetitive rooms, unrewarded puzzles, and monotonous routines. In many stories, home threatens the heroine with feelings of isolation or boredom. Home is the place that *prevents* the heroine from reaching her potential; home obstructs, home confines, and duties at home often stifle her creative spirit.

Therefore, leaving home offers the prospect of discovering or rediscovering a new or unexplored side of the heroine's identity. The search for answers, clarity, and truth drives the adventure and often fulfills our heroines' desires and aspirations. So, the heroine *wants* to leave home and often jumps at the chance when the Call to Adventure comes knocking.

The Call to Adventure is a narrative plot device sometimes confused with an "inciting incident" since such a call may trigger the larger story. However, writers should treat the Call to Adventure as an archetypal event where the heroine encounters a profound opportunity.

Writers may consider including the Refusal of the Call in their story. My advice is to weigh the potential for physical destruction that leaving home presents as well as the degree to which the home is a suppressive environment. The more likely death is imminent from leaving home, the more likely the story will include a Refusal of the Call. The more unreasonable and suppressive the home, the more likely the heroine or hero will leap at the Call to Adventure.

In *Barbie*, we have a heroine who *does* exhibit the Refusal of the Call. Multiple times, Barbie makes it clear that she does not want to go on the adventure to save Barbieland. However, notice that death is indeed on our heroine's mind. Like the hero on the journey, Barbie fears death; therefore, the Refusal of the Call emerges as an appropriate human response on a subconscious and archetypal level to the Call to Adventure.

Either way, the dynamics between the hero's journey and the heroine's labyrinth are different. The motivations are different. The end destinations are different. And so, the monomythic structure of the story is different.

In the heroine's labyrinth model, the heroine will most likely answer the Call to Adventure willingly and enthusiastically. She'll leave the world of predictable home life and enter the more uncensored world of her native culture. Despite the Captivity Bargain, the heroine often believes her entry into the unknown portions of the labyrinth will be temporary or a simple act of curiosity. But she will face the seductive grandeur of the unknown beyond her window, just as she will witness its hidden dark sides and learn its many secrets.

Anatomy of an Archetype – Call to Adventure

◊ The Call to Adventure moves the heroine out of the familiar home sphere and into the mysterious native culture.

◊ The heroine is often motivated by a desire to explore what's hidden and to experience the unpredictable.

◊ The Call to Adventure presents an opportunity for non-conformity within the native culture.

◊ The heroine typically skips the Refusal of the Call (a hero's journey theme).

Exercises

1. Using the above criteria, can you identify the Call to Adventure in *The Little Mermaid* (1989)?

2. In the Hulu original movie *Prey*, what is the event that best serves as a Call to Adventure for the Comanche heroine, Naru? How does her native culture shape Naru's interpretation of the event?

3. What is the Call to Adventure in *Wonder Woman* (2017)?

Tarot

Dear writers, we have come to the end of our story's opening segment. The intense archetypal power of the heroine's multiple conflicts has been established in full. In storytelling terms, we have completed the heroine's orientation to her world, the rules, and the potential consequences. The Call to Adventure has come to her door at last. Our heroine is ready to wander into the darkness of the unknown passageways. She's willing to behold the scintillating wonders behind closed doors and to face dangerous truths around any given corner. With our tarot cards arranged in a precarious pyramid, we now shuffle the deck. Our heroine's story is about to become far more complex as her conflicts evolve, just as she evolves along with them.

ACT II

EXPLORATION
(SELF-REALIZATION)

The Neophyte

THE MIDDLE: EXPLORATION

hen drawing tarot cards, the person drawing the cards may see that the card is either upright (right-side up) or reversed (upside-down). The card's interpretation and psychic content change depending on this basic orientation. For the middle portion of the heroine's labyrinth, we draw the Neophyte card, but she is upside-down, which means the card is "reversed." As we lay the card down on the table, we see that the heroine is uncertain now that she navigates the labyrinth on her own. The Neophyte invites this uncertainty for "the unknown" because it's what fascinates and compels her.

In the opening segment of our story, the structural elements of the heroine and her conflicts have been set in place. The heroine has been oriented to the labyrinth, the Masked Minotaur has been introduced, three claims have been made upon the heroine's Sacred Fire, and the heroine has made a Captivity Bargain—sincerely or insincerely—to resolve the emerging disharmony of the story.

But the story goes on.

Whereas the hero's journey sets our hero on a course away from the native culture, the heroine's labyrinth sends our heroine deeper into the labyrinth than ever before. We draw four more cards—the Stranger, the Trickster, the Thief, and the Shapeshifter. Individually, these archetypal beings serve their own motives. Together, however, these figures generate a natural pattern of misdirection as they attempt to influence or steer the heroine one way or another. Let's draw the next card and see if we can make sense of it.

Cult of Deception

CULT OF DECEPTION

aeve and Dolores in *Westworld*, Rachel in *Blade Runner*, and Ava in *Ex Machina* are robotic heroines with programmable restrictions from "god-like" creators. On the other side of sci-fi, June in *The Handmaid's Tale*, Trinity in *The Matrix*, and Furiosa in *Mad Max: Fury Road* are heroines in a dystopian future where extreme social control creates a dehumanizing society. As such, all seven heroines occupy worlds with distorted reality. The robotic heroines are assigned algorithmic programming, not unlike the cultural programming of their carbon-based counterparts. Either way, these heroines operate under the steady gaze of cameras, sentient programs, and enforcers, so they are watched and monitored. All of these heroines sense flaws in the functioning of their world.

However, regardless of the levels of technology or rigidity of the cultural demands, heroines must also navigate the most precarious aspect of the labyrinth—other people. Many heroines actively search for supporters while hiding their independence. Much of the resistance she meets is unconscious, so the heroine learns to mask her motives, feelings, and actions.

Therefore, the Cult of Deception is the pattern of behavior that emerges from other characters that resist, redirect, or obstruct the heroine to maintain the status quo.

I noticed that in numerous stories, regular people with little, if any, vested interest in the heroine will nevertheless harry or attempt to slow her down. It is as if random individuals sense the heroine's request for clarity, so they instinctively deny it. The Cult of Deception is portrayed in dialogue and interactions between the heroine and other story characters. The heroine undergoes a process of discovering or experiencing various types of misdirection, redirection, deception, persuasion, influence, coercion, and manipulation from other characters.

Heroine-centric stories teach us quite a bit about the nature and scope of human deception—the social manifestations and cultural expressions. At the story's beginning, the heroine takes inventory of her material limitations and learns the labyrinth's hard rules. In the middle portion of the story, she must now experience firsthand how the labyrinth and the Cult of Deception work in real-time. The heroine comes face to face with the mysterious beings who inhabit the labyrinth. These strangers or friends aren't always who they appear to be, and various motives lay the groundwork for the Cult of Deception. Resistance comes with a smile, while help arrives in riddles.

My initial name for this archetypal design was "The Masquerade" due to the blend of social forces within the native culture and the numerous facades the heroine experiences. One can almost imagine the heroine moving from one dancing partner to another in the story, trying to assess their true identity and intentions. Like Sarah in *Labyrinth*, the heroine enters the masquerade with guarded fascination, clearly spellbound, yet convinced that truth exists behind all the masks and pageantry.

"The Matrix isn't real," Trinity says. But although she knew the maze was an illusion, she failed to see her friend Cipher's willingness to betray the group. Human deceit often turns out to be the most consequential. I'm not surprised that Wonder Woman's primary weapon is a Lasso of Truth, a golden lariat that compels characters to be forthcoming with her. Nor am I surprised that Neytiri's favorite greeting in *Avatar* is "I see you," meaning authentically and spiritually, *not* physically. We'll explore how other characters often redirect, obstruct, or mislead our heroines in the story. Some deceptions are conscious efforts by characters with ulterior motives, some are unconscious acts by trusted or neutral characters, and others are manifestations of the labyrinth itself. **Either way, the heroine encounters these illusions for the first time as she confronts a preexisting world that others sustain.**

Fiercely Guarded Secrets

Napoleon Bonaparte famously said that "History is a set of lies agreed upon." I think the same is true of the story world in the labyrinth. We humans tend to pile up a lot of secrets over the years, so a character who explores a sociocultural labyrinth will inevitably encounter the secrets of that world. Layers of human history permeate the rooms and settings. Heroines have the time and curiosity to learn about their increasingly familiar world and to explore the nooks and crannies. She may observe an exchange between people not meant for her eyes, find a hidden object, or uncover a major secret.

Heroines quickly learn that secrets are powerful forms of knowledge. Exposing a secret can destroy social order and sever relationships. Therefore, for those in the know, protecting these secrets may become part of the local culture. The heroine's passage through a given space in the story threatens to scatter certain secrets like a small flock of spooked birds. The heroine's natural curiosity may be seen as dangerous, which accounts for some of the natural resistance she receives. Heroines tend to point out irregularities only to be met with indifference, hostility, or denial. These reactions by others to secretive information only confirm to the heroine that a Cult of Deception exists, and an informal group within the native culture may be distorting reality.

In the HBO miniseries *Chernobyl*, the lead heroine, Ulana Khomyuk, tries to solve what went wrong with the ill-fated nuclear reactor. However, she quickly learns that the Communist party doctrine is concealment and denial. She realizes that the Soviet Union is willing to pretend that nothing is wrong, thereby exposing countless citizens to lethal doses of radiation to maintain the appearance of normalcy. The Cult of Deception prioritized lies over lives.

In the Amazon show *The Expanse,* heroine Bobbie Draper uncovers a black market for powerful Martian weapons. Worse, her nephew is caught up in underground activity. When she goes to the police, she's shocked to discover that the chief of police is coordinating the black market.

A comedic version of the Cult of Deception appears in the 1996 film *Fargo.* Heroine Marge Gunderson simply *shows up* to investigate irregular occurrences, and the Cult of Deception implodes on cue.

Fiercely guarded secrets, ulterior motives, and high stakes are the hallmarks of a Cult of Deception. Native cultures tend to have many scandals and secrets as a natural consequence of human relationships, human foibles, and the long slog of time.

Feminine Eros

The heroine's eros often plays a role in heroine-centric stories. While I make a serious effort not to sexualize heroines, we writers must address the impact of sexual attraction as it relates to story and conflict. The author and story determine when, if, and how the heroine's eros affects the scenes in the story. It can be a casual nuisance or play a central role, as in the romance genre, while the heroine's exploration of her eros drives erotica. Some stories omit any evidence of the heroine's eros or the effects of her eros upon the inhabitants of the labyrinth. Most stories, however, include the heroine's eros as a natural reality, and I believe it contributes to the Cult of Deception.

A common redirection occurs when other characters meet the heroine and become distracted by her eros. A second ulterior motive comes into play as the otherwise neutral character attempts to shift the conversation or encounter in a different direction. While "being hit on" isn't an overt deception, the introduction of an ulterior motive creates a level of guarded caution or mistrust for the heroine. She must now deal with the emerging redirection while maintaining the original purpose of the interaction.

Mythology underscores the homegrown and likely eternal dangers our heroine may face, even in safe places or from trusted individuals. Therefore, today, as in ancient times, we shouldn't ignore the dark side of eros in the feminine monomyth and the ever-present undercurrent of ulterior motives. The feminine eros takes a dark turn among the gods. Zeus disguises himself as a swan to seduce Queen Leda deceptively. Apollo comes to Dryope disguised as a snake. The Titan goddess Aura, who boasted of her maidenhood, fell drunk one night only for Dionysus to violate her. Or, the deception arrives through members of the native culture, often family members, whom the heroine is supposed to trust. Just sticking with Greek mythology, we see Hades betray his niece, Persephone, and Tereus betray his sister-in-law, Philomela. The dynamic between the Cult of Deception and the heroine's eros is ancient. The persistent and often ubiquitous possibility of nefarious motives sometimes leads to attacks upon the heroine. The worst of these attacks, a sexual assault, can devastate a heroine physically, mentally, spiritually, and socially.

Modern stories highlight the danger of seemingly casual interactions regarding the heroine's eros. Shosanna in *Inglourious Basterds* has to ward off advances from Nazi movie star Fredrick Zoller on numerous occasions, nearly thwarting all her careful planning. Once again, Clarice Starling must ward off multiple passes to get her job done, as does Nina Sayers in *Black Swan*.

Other heroines learn to use ulterior motives to advance their cause effectively, such as Beth Dutton in *Yellowstone*, who cold-reads men, challenges them, and creates strategic chaos everywhere she goes. Natasha Romanoff, a.k.a. Black Widow, regularly uses seduction to extract secret information in the Avenger films.

The relationship between a heroine's eros and her trust is a deep and meaningful theme. In *Frozen*, Princess Elsa falls in love with Prince Hans only to discover he had a secret agenda the whole time. In *Shrek 2*, Princess Fiona is met with a disguised Prince Charming, who thinks he can restore the fairy tale ending where he ends up with the princess. In *Avatar*, Neytiri realizes that Jake Sully initially lied to her about his intentions. She feels betrayed. Although Jake is sincere in helping the Na'vi, he underestimates the heroine's reaction to a deception from a person she trusted.

Therefore, heroines usually learn to remain guarded within the labyrinth of their native culture. Luckily, the feminine monomyth provides an equally powerful response to the Cult of Deception—the heroine's intuition.

The Role of Intuition

Although the heroine's tarot card is reversed upon the table, we now notice the third eye at the top of the card, open and observant. While this book covers the disorienting conflicts that beset our heroine, we finally come upon a significant power within the feminine monomyth. Due to the pervasive presence of façades and distorted truths, many heroines develop a heightened intuition. Raw intelligence isn't always the best tool in heroine-centric stories because deceptions are specifically designed to work *with* our logical perceptions, basic assumptions, and intellectual beliefs. Highly evolved deceptions wouldn't be much good if they couldn't bypass the daily traffic of our common sense and general state of reasoning. Therefore, many heroines learn to rely on their instincts and feelings during events. I believe this intuition is superrational, which means *transcendent* of reason.

Clairvoyancy and knowledge of hidden truths are so commonly linked to feminine archetypes that multiple versions of the archetype exist based on the ethical orientation of the woman. The fairy godmother, the old crone, the witch, the druid, the sorceress, and the fortune teller are timeless psychic archetypes—all based to some degree on the intuitive powers of female characters. Each archetype includes a feminine mysticism that seems to defy conventional logic and everyday human perceptions.

Even the threads of divinity within the "divine" feminine converge on some belief in cosmic forces beyond the material world. Keep in mind, by this point in the story, our heroine has experienced both the labyrinth and the Cult of Deception in a diverse range of ways. The natural result is a heroine who is receptive to intuitive signals that scatter beyond assumptions of knowledge or blind trust in human systems. She cultivates a great awareness, like a lighthouse whose luminous beam circles in continuous cycles. **The heroine may distrust structure and seek to disrupt predictability, for predictable order may camouflage hidden and undesirable things. Falsehood relies on a structure, so the heroine soon relies on unstructured perception.** As the world-renowned classicist and mythologist Edith Hamilton puts it: "Convention, so often a mask for injustice."

In Jane Alison's book *Meander, Spiral, Explode*, she discusses the asymmetrical patterns in nature that appear to be mere chaos but *are patterns* nonetheless. Heroines throughout mythology, culture, and time come to rely on an inner sense of natural patterns more than they trust the corruptible patterns of human organization. How often have we seen the camera close in on the heroine's face, her eyes narrowing as she makes a vital, intuitive assessment of the moment? The heroine breaks an evil scheme in many stories or thwarts a villain with a single intuitive premonition. This intuitive ability, which is an accurate perception *outside* of structured reason, stems from the monomythic Cult of Deception in heroine-centric stories.

We have a near pantheon of heroines who emphasize the role of intuition. Many characters in these stories rely on or trust the heroine's intuitive abilities. In *Avengers: Endgame*, Thor's mother, Frigga, reminds him that "I see with more than eyes, and you know that." But comic books also give us Psylocke, Jean Grey, Mantis, and Emma Frost, just for starters. Even on the starship Enterprise's highly technical and scientifically based bridge, we find Deanna Troi on duty. She's a clairvoyant officer who provides intuitive, psychic consultation to the captain in *Star Trek: The Next Generation*.

Many events in *The Matrix* are directed by the foresight of the Oracle, who perceives each character's potential and role in future events. Even in the uber-manly film *The Northman*, we encounter the Seeress, who wears shells and bells to veil her blind eyes but wears a headdress of barley that fans out like cosmic rays. And, of course, who can forget Galadriel in *The Lord of the Rings*? She is a variant of an Arthurian archetype who peers into the future through a mirror and even provides specific gifts that save each character in critical circumstances—almost as if she *knew* they would need such gifts. Lorraine Warren in *The Conjuring* or Tangina in *Poltergeist* each enter a space and receive psychic information, often along with feelings of empathy and knowledge for the events that transpired in those spaces. In *Foundation*, we find the Luminists who follow the visions of the Triple Goddess, who favors holy cycles, the completion of nature, and reincarnation. In Frank

Herbert's *Dune* saga, the all-female Bene Gesserit orchestrates the entire galaxy, a quasi-religious order of clairvoyant diplomats assigned to all the influential houses. "But our plans are measured in centuries," says the Reverend Mother Mohiam.

A heroine may be more willing to bend or compromise to reason during the Captivity Bargain, but she will harness her intuition through the Cult of Deception, enabling her to push back. Not only does the heroine cultivate her intuition at a high level, but as we'll see, she eventually seeks to disrupt or destroy the Cult of Deception in its entirety.

Anatomy of an Archetype – Cult of Deception

◊ The Cult of Deception is a system of illusions, obstructions, and competing motivations that work against the heroine.

◊ The Minotaur's hidden evil nature is often the central deception.

◊ The heroine is sometimes watched or surveilled, usually by the Minotaur.

◊ Ulterior motives are one of the more persistent forms of deception.

◊ Frequently, neutral characters try to redirect the heroine.

◊ The heroine may discover or disrupt secret truths about the story world.

◊ The Cult of Deception develops a powerful intuition within the heroine.

◊ Other characters may be hiding details about the heroine's true identity.

Exercises

1. In the film *Women Talking*, a Cult of Deception is revealed through several different heroines. How do the women approach the topic, and when do they collectively realize that a Cult of Deception truly exists?

2. In the Disney Plus show *WandaVision*, can you list the series of moments that highlight clues that Wanda is experiencing a massive Cult of Deception? Which characters are in the know and try to redirect Wanda during strange happenings?

3. Think of stories where reality itself is disguised, such as *The Matrix*, *The Truman Show*, *Vanilla Sky*, *Inception*, and *Total Recall*. All of these films feature an omnipotent Cult of Deception while also featuring a male lead. Also, each story follows the heroine's labyrinth narrative model. Given what we know about the feminine monomyth, do *you* think these stories might be more interesting with a heroine as the lead?

Tarot

The Cult of Deception is a pattern of human behavior centered around human power and organization. The next card, though, suggests a place, a specific place somewhere in the labyrinth. The back of the next tarot card appears to us as the back of a closed door. We must now turn the card and open that mysterious door.

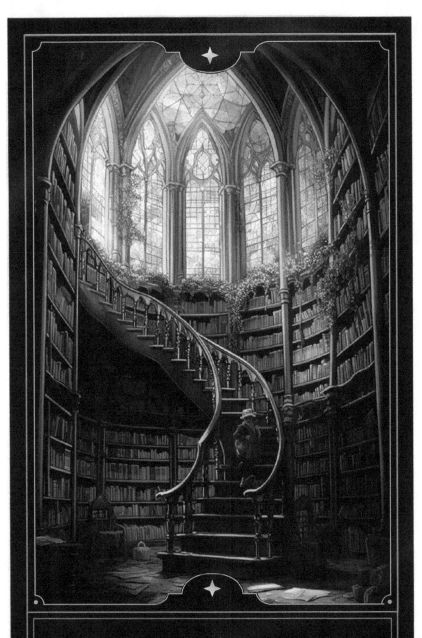

Chambers of Knowledge

THE CHAMBERS OF KNOWLEDGE

he feminine monomyth explores the vast worlds beyond the doors and walls of the native culture. An introspective probe into the physical spaces of the labyrinth creates a unique dynamic to the heroine's journey. She still leaves the "horizon" of her more predictable home life and the symbolic oversight of authority figures. However, she crosses into the fantastical side of the otherwise commonplace world. There is an exotic reality behind a locked door.

Again, we recognize the distinction between a linear outward journey and a circular inward exploration. In the hero's journey, the hero must cross the first threshold by getting past a threshold guardian. The moment is significant because the threshold guardian represents the force preventing the hero's exit from the native culture.

Even though many heroines stay within the realm of the native culture, their journeys are no less fantastic. Indeed, heroine-centric stories have a way of taking a fresh look at familiar places. Gazing into the darkness through innocent eyes is like the beam of light that scans the exotic objects of an attic. Such objects have been fixed in place for a long time, their use and purpose perhaps forgotten. But hidden among the cobwebs and dust are treasures and secrets.

So, in the story, our heroine left home but most likely remains within the native culture. She'll then visit a series of chambers containing a small universe of special knowledge where she may have to pass a social test. **The Chambers of Knowledge are typically indoors, adorned with a pattern of imagery, unique objects, and symbols that all relate to a specific field of worldly knowledge.** These rooms make up the *inner* world of the native culture. And quite often, the chamber comes with a puzzle, game, or riddle to be solved, but more on that in the next chapter.

During an early draft of this book, my mother remarked that the heroine's visit to each worldly Chamber of Knowledge reminded her of her college experience. Like a real-world university experience, gaining cultural knowledge prepares the heroine for future events. Only these chambers are typically less formal.

I think my mother was right. I immediately thought of the Harry Potter series, written by J.K. Rowling. Not only do Harry Potter and the crew visit university-style classrooms, but they also visit many secret chambers throughout the wizarding world. Hogwarts has hidden rooms and many secrets, each one *loaded* with archetypal objects and imagery.

The process of visiting multiple Chambers of Knowledge can last for many chapters or may be the story's entire premise. Rainbow Rowell's *Fangirl*, Richelle Mead's *Vampire Academy*, Netflix's *The Umbrella Academy*, and even the X-Men's secret Xavier's School for Gifted Youngsters all feature a university-style institution where different rooms and chambers hold entire universes of knowledge.

Therefore, the direct training sequences we often see in the hero's journey, where the hero masters a specific set of physical, mental, or combat skills through one-on-one mentorship, are replaced by a system of wonderous interior chambers chock-full of knowledge and secrets.

Compartments of Human Knowledge

In psychology, we're told that human beings compartmentalize their knowledge in the brain. Memories or details are encoded, stored, and recalled through mental processes that occur spatially in our brain space. We recall information consciously, as we do when we try to summon a memory—or unconsciously, as when we dream. And then, of course, all this information exists somewhere in the brain, whether we access it or not, which is our *subconscious*.

In archetypal language, each dark chamber in the story is the physical manifestation of the human mind. **Chambers of Knowledge are material collection points where real-world objects are accumulated, stored, and retrieved. Inside the human brain, knowledge takes the form of abstractions. But in a Chamber of Knowledge, we *see* and *touch* the material version of these abstractions.** The film *Inside Out* is a perfect example of a heroine in a literal brain universe. Next time you watch the movie, you'll immediately notice the labyrinth. You'll also see examples of how each Chamber of Knowledge is a material expression of the human psyche.

In the film, *Tolkien*, the heroine, Edith Bratt, takes a college-aged J.R.R. Tolkien backstage to an opera. There's nothing quite like the backstage of a theater. Physical props to various plays lay about in corners like the strata of a fantasy world—horseheads, giant wooden clocks, Egyptian statues, Victorian umbrellas, candelabras, random segments of a dragon's body, or panels of urban brick walls. Edith and Tolkien stood among the material craftsmanship of the human psyche, facades of the imagination. And yet, the backstage is a lowly place, somewhere between a closet, a hallway, and a warehouse. Of all the places Edith could take her fledgling date, she chose the backstage of a theater, the resting place of countless material archetypes. A Chamber of Knowledge reveals the exotic *interiority* of the human mind and imagination, materialized and scattered before the heroine.

Each chamber contains a collage of worldly knowledge and secret truths buried among the bizarre objects. Chambers are physical spaces containing a niche of reality assembled and fully displayed. The heroine enters the chamber as if submerged in the subconscious mind. Chambers often have a dream-like feeling or appearance because of their fantastical collections and arrangements. Because of the inward nature of the journey, chambers are best depicted as indoor spaces, confined, dimly lit, and often cluttered. However, chambers can be outdoors, depending on the needs and reality of the story. The key is that the heroine is aware she is entering a specific space with defined boundaries and a specific purpose. The chamber may hold a secret, such as the computerized inner sanctum that Ellen Ripley enters, where Mother reveals that the crew is expendable in *Alien*. Or the chamber can be a lighter-hearted display of worldly wares, such as the London fashion shop, where Wonder Woman comically samples a range of women's clothing in *Wonder Woman* (2017).

The heroine enters the chamber and witnesses a wide scope of the human imagination. The combination of a wondrous and unsettling environment underscores the heroine's natural inclination for intuition over logic alone. How else can one navigate a material world born of an abstract human mind without a fresh set of eyes? Chambers are visible proof of the rational and irrational side by side. Some objects and details are hidden, locked away, or lost. Just by observing the items around her, the heroine gains small degrees of enlightenment. Invisible bonds connect the objects of the chamber in mysterious ways and inevitably reveal some truth about the world.

Think of the Warren office in *The Conjuring*, where the Anabelle doll rests among all those other objects. Think, too, of the hidden cavern in *Moana* where Moana discovers the hidden ships that reveal the lost seafaring traditions of her island home culture. Or what about the Your-Self Storage bay that Clarice enters in *The Silence of the Lambs*? Each place has a palette of objects with a unifying theme.

Anatomy of an Archetype – Chambers of Knowledge

◊ Chambers are usually interior spaces within the native culture.

◊ A Chamber of Knowledge is a place that contains a specific subset of worldly knowledge.

◊ The heroine typically gains something useful in each chamber.

◊ The imagery of each chamber should be archetypal and dream-like.

◊ The chamber is a place where an exchange typically takes place.

Exercises

1. In the film *Aliens*, Ellen Ripley returns to the planet LV-426. She knows a derelict spacecraft with alien eggs shares the planet with a human colony. What are the Chambers of Knowledge she visits, and what does she learn in each one?

2. A show with a fantastic set of Chambers is *The Queen's Gambit*, starring Anya Taylor-Joy as chess savant Beth Harmon. Can you name the chambers that Beth enters?

3. Now, let's consider the Charlotte Brontë novel *Jane Eyre*. What are the Chambers of Knowledge for the heroine? What information does she learn about her world in each chamber?

4. Lastly, *The Matrix* follows both the hero's journey as well as the heroine's labyrinth in terms of themes and archetypal structure. For example, the hero doesn't travel further outward away from home but deeper inward into the digital Labyrinth of the Matrix. Can you name three Chambers of Knowledge the hero visits?

Tarot

However, the heroine is rarely alone in a Chamber of Knowledge. Our next card compliments the Chambers of Knowledge and reveals a person who may be helpful or harmful. Let's flip the card and see who our heroine encounters in each chamber.

Chamber Guardians

CHAMBER GUARDIANS

hile reading the screenplay for *The Matrix*, I noticed that Neo follows Morpheus into a building that the script describes as "tenement-like" or "the kind of place where people can disappear." He soon enters the Oracle's apartment, where a "priestess" greets him. The Oracle eventually summons Neo to the kitchen. There, he encounters a woman who looks more like "someone's grandma" baking chocolate chip cookies. The Oracle comes across as pleasant and presents Neo with a social test, which he fails. Before Neo leaves, she provides him with a prophecy that proves vital to the story. She isn't confronting or challenging Neo, nor is she blocking or preventing his passage to a place beyond her kitchen, and her chamber is not a threshold to an outer world.

The Oracle is a Chamber Guardian.

Entering any room for the first time to encounter a warden is an archetypal encounter. We are on someone else's turf. We are visiting and being watched or studied. We may feel guarded, unwelcomed, or curious as we approach the Chamber Guardian. There is a process to be followed here, a ritual rhythm for vetted guests to acquire services, provisions, or information. The Chamber Guardian is the authorized gatekeeper, and they wait patiently for us to announce our intentions.

The Chamber Guardian is both a warden of the physical space and an eccentric master of the worldly knowledge contained within the chamber. The relationship between a heroine/visitor and the guardian/ward of the chamber is an ancient one. Readers will know the feeling. The Chamber Guardian's very purpose is the stewardship of special knowledge. A Chamber of Knowledge is the physical space where a particular sphere of special knowledge is stored for future use or recall. So, when the heroine enters the chamber seeking knowledge, her presence activates the function of the chamber—access to the object or information—while also activating the purpose of the Chamber Guardian—to safeguard the object or information. An exchange of some kind is imminent. However, for the exchange to succeed, the heroine must often pass a test.

We may think of the Arabian Jinn, who occupies the interior of a commonplace lamp. His job is to provide a service, but if the lamp-bearer is not careful with the wording of the wish, the Jinn will issue a cursed or twisted version. Such is the risk of interplay with a Chamber Guardian.

Again, a contrast between the hero's journey and the heroine's labyrinth is helpful. Most writers are familiar with the term "Threshold Guardians," which are powerful archetypal beings in the warrior-oriented hero's journey. We may think of Cerberus, the three-headed wolf that guards the entrance of Hades, or Walrus Man from *A New Hope*, who picks a fight with Luke at Mos Eisley. According to Joseph Campbell, Threshold Guardians stand in the hero's way and block their journey outward to the unknown regions of "desert, jungle, deep sea, alien land, etc." **So, whereas a Threshold Guardian is a belligerent sentry who blocks the hero's *outward* passage to depart the native culture, a Chamber Guardian is an administrative trickster who obstructs the heroine's *inward* exploration of the native culture.**

Whose Chamber Is It Anyway?

One of the more entertaining Chamber Guardians to come along recently is Deirdre Beaubeirdre, played by Jamie Lee Curtis in *Everything Everywhere All At Once*. She's the ultimate warden of a chamber—an IRS agent. The film explores the peculiar relationship between the heroine and a Chamber Guardian. On one end, Evelyn is respectful of the process but resentful of the overwhelming monotony of protocol, sometimes submissive toward the Chamber Guardian's authority and sometimes hostile to the level of an arch-nemesis.

From a structural standpoint, I think the Chamber Guardian is fascinating. Because they are often members of the heroine's home culture, they speak the familiar and nuanced language of the heroine's peers and superiors. They can assume the role of an authority figure, potential suitor, friend of a friend, relative, or official partner. This creates a unique and subtle confrontation between likely strangers that stays within cultural expectations and social etiquette boundaries. Therefore, we must recognize that the puzzle, riddle, or challenge is a *social test* meant to stymie or obstruct the heroine. And while the heroine's encounter with Chamber Guardians may be adversarial, it's not necessarily hostile.

The long tenure of the Chamber Guardian often leads them to assume a false sense of ownership of the chamber. Who but they know the chamber so intimately? Who but they can call themselves a master of the chamber? Instead of a friendly posture of service and safekeeping, the Chamber Guardian maintains an air of territorialism, superiority, and suspicion of visitors. The heroine is usually at a loss, for she is new to the chamber, while the Chamber Guardian commands expertise.

The Chamber Guardian often feigns confusion or misunderstanding, waiting instead for the heroine to utter the "magic words" of a social test. How much does the heroine know? Social tests demonstrate the degree to which the heroine has mastered some cultural protocol or relevant skill set while she continues to assert her request. The social test is the Chamber Guardian's effort to exhibit dominance over "their" chamber. Therefore, the Chamber Guardian attempts to reverse the intended social roles, whereby the visitor must provide a service instead of the Chamber Guardian.

Being social animals ourselves, we immediately recognize the Chamber Guardian's social antagonism. We react to it because, as an audience or a reader, we are like the student bystanders to a schoolyard taunt, and we're eager to see how the heroine responds.

Excellent writing shows instead of tells. The heroine must convincingly counter, dismiss, or bury the challenge. Writers should *never* show the heroine throw a "phantom punch" that lays the challenger to the ground as if the fix was in. If the audience or reader senses a rigged contest in favor of the heroine, then they'll doubt the legitimacy of the heroine on some level, conscious or subconscious. Don't sow doubts on your heroine. As a writer, you must be up to the task. Write the scene so that the heroine overcomes the Chamber Guardian creatively and compellingly. **Keep in mind the heroine doesn't have to establish dominance over the Chamber Guardian; she simply needs to convincingly pass the social test and restore the original function of the chamber, that of service to the visitor.**

In story terms, the function of the Chamber Guardian is to test the heroine, not usually to defeat the heroine. Highly effective Chamber Guardians should present a challenging test so that the scene conveys tension and conflict. In the film *Pan's Labyrinth,* the young heroine, Ofelia, enters a chamber with a long table of banquet food and a sleeping creature at the head of the table. The test is whether Ofelia can cross the chamber without eating from any of the decorative dishes. And the heroine fails this test. Remember that the easier the test and the less formidable the Chamber Guardian, the less impressive the heroine's accomplishment will be.

Why is this important?

The heroine is establishing personal sovereignty in these exchanges. She's gaining vital experience and maturing as a result. Social control over her fades when she learns how to overcome each social test and, by default, the human component in the Cult of Deception. The Chamber Guardians serve as a series of challenges that build up the heroine's abilities and expand her knowledge.

Barbie

The 2023 film *Barbie* has incredible examples of Chamber Guardians. Stereotypical Barbie explores the interiority of the Real World as it relates to her existence. Her search is one of inner meaning, so each chamber becomes successively more profound as she delves deeper into the spaces that reveal truths about her reality.

Barbie's first Chamber is the school cafeteria, where she encounters a Chamber Guardian, Sasha, whom she believes is her real-world counterpart. In classic form, Sasha sits behind a table in a confrontational manner and proceeds to cut Barbie down with the harshest possible take on the doll's influence upon girls. Notice the social contest scenario that Barbie clearly loses since she retreats in tears.

Barbie then enters the lobby of the Mattel headquarters and encounters a Chamber of satirical cubicles (based heavily on Jacques Tati's "Playtime") but quickly gets past the Chamber Guardians.

Barbie then enters the next Chamber of Knowledge, the corporate boardroom. Here, the Chamber Guardian is the Mattel CEO. As covered earlier, the social test is a Captivity Bargain, where Barbie seriously considers going "back in the box" to restore order to Barbieland. Luckily, she passes this test and escapes the Chamber.

And here, the film treats us with a moving and poignant encounter between the heroine and a Chamber Guardian. Although Barbie is in the labyrinth-like hallways of a corporate skyscraper, she opens the door and walks into a 1960s household. Notice the dreamlike quality of the chamber? Barbie encounters Ruth Handler, the inventor of the Barbie doll. Barbie gains insight while listening to her creator in what amounts to an existential encounter. This Chamber contains both knowledge and wisdom.

Coraline

Coraline visits three Chambers of Knowledge, encounters three memorable Chamber Guardians, and solves three riddles. In the first chamber, we meet the former burlesque dancers, Spink and Forcible, eccentric Chamber Guardians who safeguard the worldly knowledge of theater and travel. Angelic Scottie dogs adorn the walls, and old taffy is arranged by year.

The next chamber is the apartment of the Amazing Bobinsky, which conceals a world of circus and carnival. Coraline observes trained mice, cotton candy cannons, and packages of smelly cheese. Phew! The final chamber holds the Masked Minotaur herself, the Other Mother, and depicts an idealized fantasy world for a child. Each chamber exhibits the themes of wonderous illusion and showmanship, and each Chamber Guardian compliments the chamber.

In the movie's final act, Coraline revisits each chamber to solve a puzzle and find a special key. The outlandish elements she witnessed in each chamber now take on a full and bizarre dream-like quality as she tries to thwart each Chamber Guardian.

Beatrix Kiddo

Kill Bill is another heroine-centric saga with elaborate chambers and deadly Chamber Guardians. The entire story emphasizes Beatrix Kiddo's entry into each chamber and her confrontation with the Chamber Guardian. The social test for Beatrix in each chamber is over-the-top combat that few of us will ever forget. But notice how each chamber represents a specific environment with a particular theme and how the Chamber Guardian perfectly suits each chamber.

Anatomy of an Archetype – Chamber Guardian

◊ Chamber Guardians are typically administrative tricksters.

◊ Chamber Guardians are usually the authority figures of the space they occupy.

◊ The confrontation with the Chamber Guardian is based on an exchange of information, services, or favors.

◊ Chamber Guardians are often depicted as a person behind a desk.

◊ Heroines will face a social test from the Chamber Guardian.

◊ The heroine must restore the chamber's purpose, which is access to knowledge or information.

◊ The heroine doesn't have to fight or defeat the Chamber Guardian.

◊ The heroine may even recruit the Chamber Guardian as a heroic partner.

Exercise

1. Can you name at least four Chambers of Knowledge and four Chamber Guardians in *Encanto*, *The Wizard of Oz*, and *The Silence of the Lambs*?

2. As you identify each Chamber of Knowledge, look in the chamber.

3. What are the objects filling the space?

4. How does the Chamber Guardian match the chamber?

5. How is the heroine tested in each encounter? And does the heroine recruit the Chamber Guardians?

6. In the last chapter, you listed three Chambers of Knowledge in *The Matrix*. Now, can you name the three Chamber Guardians of each chamber? What was the puzzle Neo had to solve in each chamber?

Tarot

While the Chamber Guardians help our heroine learn how to break up the Cult of Deception, another more critical encounter awaits her. The heroine is still no match for the Masked Minotaur at the center of the labyrinth. Her future ability to overcome the Masked Minotaur requires a new experience. The next card is in the Growth Position, and so we sense an opportunity brewing for our heroine. Let's turn the next card and see what's in store.

Beast as Ally

THE BEAST AS ALLY

mages of feminine and beastly figures together exist in our minds and psyches so clearly because of a deeply primal relationship. The instant energy of the archetypal image comes with many meanings. The image should convey terror and danger, and yet, we pause. We see the heroine is calm and unafraid. The image could convey the animal allure of sexual desire, the guardianship of a beastly ally, a monster seducing the virgin, or a predator hovering above its prey. I believe all these aspects are true simultaneously based on the trajectory of any given story.

The Beast as Ally theme is perhaps the most pervasive and flexible aspect of the feminine monomyth. Instead of a wolf in sheep's clothing, the heroine encounters a helpful ally in wolf's clothing. In Little Red Riding Hood, we encounter the beast who uses grandma's clothes to disguise himself. In essence, the Minotaur uses the appearance of humanity to disguise his animal self. To my utter surprise, I discovered that an incredible number of heroine stories feature a second Minotaur-like character who uses the appearance of a monster to disguise their humanity.

The Masked Minotaur and the Beast as Ally are both half man, half beast. However, whereas the predatory animal nature is dominant in the Minotaur, the compassionate human nature emerges as central in the Beast archetype. Whereas visiting the Chambers of Knowledge revealed truths about the material world, the Beast as Ally often reveals truths about the nature of humanity. Sometimes, understanding the Beast will unlock secrets about the Masked Minotaur. Such insights will prove vital to the heroine's eventual confrontation with the Masked Minotaur by the end of the story.

The Big Good Wolf

Perhaps the most compelling dynamic of the Beast as Ally theme is that the Beast is nearly a mirror image or doppelganger of the Masked Minotaur. The two characters will exhibit roughly all the same personality traits, flaws, and deplorable behavior; only the Beast becomes a heroic partner of the heroine, while the Masked Minotaur remains the story's villain. They are so close in mannerisms, yet each character plays nearly an opposite role in the story.

The difference between the Beast and the Minotaur is their final ethical orientation, reflected in their respective attitudes toward the heroine and, more specifically, the heroine's Sacred Fire. Whereas the Masked Minotaur is unable to control his inhuman, animal desire to possess the heroine, the Beast's humanity is what shines through. Like the Minotaur, the Beast is also drawn in by the attractive force of the heroine's Sacred Fire, but in the end, **the Beast's defining decision is his rejection of possessive love.** In other words, the Beast honors the heroine's claim to her Sacred Fire. **The Beast as Ally is the heroine's version of the Knight in Shining Armor. The hero isn't the main character of the heroine's story, nor is the hero shiny and overtly valiant. To the heroine, the Beast often appears to be just as dangerous, just as menacing, and often just as unlikable as the Masked Minotaur.** This second, similar character serves a huge role in the story but is often a mirror image in some way of the Masked Minotaur. Strange, right? Yes, but we see it everywhere.

On one side of Sarah Connor, we observe the liquid metal Terminator closing in as it melts through prison bars. On her other side, we see the doppelganger, a second Terminator who moves in to protect her. Both characters follow an uncompromising programmed directive; both are relentless, and both are terminators. In this case, the Beast as Ally is quite literally an identical version of the Masked Minotaur of the first film.

In the movie *Tangled*, Rapunzel meets Flynn Rider, who represents the beast archetype of the story. He shares many of the same traits as the Masked Minotaur. Mother Gothel and Flynn Rider are both introduced in the movie by robbing the king and queen's castle for self-serving purposes. They are both rogues who use other people for personal gain, and both characters exhibit vanity when they admire themselves in a mirror or on a "wanted" poster. However, Flynn surrenders his claim upon the heroine's Sacred Fire, whereas Mother Gothel does not.

And what about *The Silence of the Lambs*? On one side of Clarice Starling, we see the serial killer Buffalo Bill stalking his next victim, while on her other side, we have a second mirror-image serial killer, Hannibal Lecter, providing critical assistance. We have two serial killers, one helpful and one destructive.

When Princess Leia meets the Masked Minotaur, Darth Vader, she experiences him shouting and wagging an accusing finger in her face. Later, we see Han Solo, the Beast as Ally, doing the same thing in another scene. The relationship between both character archetypes is consistent across so many stories.

The incredible range of the Beast as Ally theme, from romance to crime dramas, from fairy tales to fables, is such a powerful archetypal event that we writers need to know the secret ingredients that make up both archetypes. We now know there are two—a Minotaur and a Beast. But how are these two seemingly identical characters so different? From a writing standpoint, what separates these two characters?

Rebels Without a Cause

The beast archetype is usually willing to bend or break the rules of the native culture. In *Gone with the Wind*, Rhett Butler, like Han Solo, is an illegal and roguish smuggler, while in *Shrek*, the Beast as Ally is an ogre openly hostile to Princess Fiona's sophisticated society. To a heroine in a Captivity Bargain, encountering a character who defies the rules of the native culture will intrigue her. Therefore, within the story's context, it is not actually the animal-like behavior of the Beast that the heroine likes but the willingness to defy cultural expectations. For example, Rose enjoyed spitting off the ship's bow in *Titanic* because it was an undisguised act of nonconformity.

Secondly, a defining distinction for the Beast as Ally theme is that the Beast adopts the heroine's cause. Whether it's a rescue or a chance meeting, the heroine usually encounters a Beast archetype, and the Beast takes up *her* mission. In *Star Wars: A New Hope*, Han enters Princess Leia's life as an argumentative mercenary, but even the self-centered Han Solo returns in the critical final hour to take up the heroine's cause. Remember, Leia opened the story to deliver the stolen Death Star plans in hopes of destroying the Death Star. The opening scene of the movie establishes the heroine's goal of destroying the Death Star and saving the Rebel Alliance. Han's goal was to pay off Jabba the Hutt and get rich. But the Beast adopted the heroine's cause.

Gideon the Ninth is a story where the main character is the Beast as Ally. The tale centers on two women where Gideon fulfills the Beast as Ally role, and Harrow becomes her heroine. The two characters do not start on the right foot. Indeed, Gideon is in bondage to Harrow throughout the story, establishing a relationship full of bitter resentment at first. As the story progresses, though, the Beast as Ally pattern takes form, and by the end, Gideon heroically adopts Harrow's cause. She allows herself to be absorbed into Harrow to grant otherwise unattainable powers during the climactic final fight.

In *Tangled*, Flynn is similar to Han Solo because he is a self-centered rogue who eventually takes up Rapunzel's cause. But the film drives the point home with a memorable musical number. When Rapunzel enters the woodland tavern, The Snuggly Duckling, she encounters a veritable den of beasts. Each patron menaces and intimidates our heroine as she passes through their space. And yet, during the song "I Have a Dream," each beastly figure reveals a creative side passion they hid from the world. These misfits align with the heroine's cause during the finale.

Bucking the native culture and joining the heroine's quest are no small things. In the opening segment of the story, members of the native culture redirected the heroine's goal in whole or in part because the heroine had to play by the game rules. But here, with the Beast as Ally, the heroine's goals are intriguing and profoundly affect other characters, especially characters who break social norms. The heroine's worldview, her ethical sensibility, and her course of action are changing the labyrinth through her personal interactions.

Lastly, many Beasts also have an animal totem to symbolize their beastly half, just like the Masked Minotaur. Han Solo has the "Falcon," Ken from *Barbie* has the horse, and Jon Snow is called "Crow," just to name a few examples.

Laws of Attraction

In Stephenie Meyer's *Twilight* saga, heroine Bella Swan has two Beast as Ally characters, Edward Cullen and Jacob Black. Edward is a vampire, and Jacob is a "big good wolf" who can quite literally turn into a werewolf. Her choice turns into a pop culture phenomenon where readers and audiences must choose between Team Edward or Team Jake. Yet, the imagery is timeless. And although both male characters are indeed heroes, they are not wearing shiny armor. We get a glimpse of the heroine's view of potential heroic partners. Bella remains guarded because she knows that heroes have a darker animal side. She doesn't hate the animal side; she wants to know that the hero can control it.

Archetypes themselves do not have gender roles. The graphic novel *Nimona* presents a compelling expression of the Beast as Ally archetypal design. From a structural standpoint, the male supervillain, Ballister Blackheart, assumes the heroine role, and the female shape-shifter, Nimona, fulfills the role of Beast as Ally. She's chaotic and unbalanced, constantly morphing into monsters and beastly creatures. Therefore, heroines and Beasts form a persistent bond in many story worlds, whether or not their relationship is rooted in sexual attraction.

But why are Beast archetypes attractive to the heroine, while the Masked Minotaur is not? Everyone's heard the moniker that girls don't like nice guys. Oddly, from a storytelling standpoint, there are reasons why this makes sense. Within the context of the feminine monomyth, there are clear reasons why the heroine moves closer to the Beast and why the "nice guy" might be a character to avoid.

First, we outlined the vital importance of authenticity and truth to the heroine based on the labyrinth, the Masked Minotaur, the Captivity Bargain, and the Cult of Deception. By now, the heroine is used to facades and deceptions. So, when she encounters a character who doesn't hide their base impulses, she is not only intrigued but has found an unexpected source of *reliability*. It may be counter-intuitive, but here's a character who will deal straight with the heroine, no matter how off-putting. To the heroine, at least the Beast is transparent, unlike the Minotaur, who wears a mask to hide his animal impulses. In a world of illusions, the Beast is exactly who he appears to be—and that realness and authenticity are what the heroine will find so worthwhile.

Conversely, the so-called "nice guy" often plays by the social rules that the heroine has come to dislike. He's revealing little of his true self, which is cause for concern. To hide oneself is actually a trait of the Masked Minotaur, whom the heroine doesn't trust. The nice guy may even be "nice" only because such behavior is so agreeable, rewarded, and inoffensive. He reads the room. He plays it safe. Overtures of "niceness" or displays of the socially acceptable "good guy" can easily mask a hidden tyrannical side. In many stories, the good guy isn't even aware of his overbearing, possessive love. Secondly, the "good guy" who becomes enraged when his "goodness" fails to win over the heroine reveals a major clue. The mask is slipping, and the animal impulse to possess the heroine is starting to show. Therefore, the "good guy" may not yet face the reality of his dark animal side or even acknowledge it's there. By the middle exploration phase of the story, so-called "good guys" are to be scrutinized by the heroine, not trusted blindly.

So, in story terms, we have two characters drawn in by the attractive force of the heroine's Sacred Fire—the Masked Minotaur and the Beast as Ally. But what draws the heroine to other characters? Heroines often take an interest in certain characters who significantly impact the story. The forces of attraction don't always have to be sexual attraction. In fact, the Beast as Ally theme demonstrates a unique dynamic for the feminine monomyth, an instinct to build a bridge where one didn't exist, and driven by curiosity, a need for clarity, and a willingness to mete out the compromises necessary to support an interpersonal relationship. Heroines do this in so many stories that I considered the behavior unique. We're not just speaking about empathy with another person but an intuitive ability to connect with another person's unfamiliar, disguised, or hidden human qualities. I call this distinctive skill "xenopathy."

Xenopathy

To discuss the phenomenon of the innocent heroine and the dangerous beast, I'd like to spotlight the concept of *xenopathy*. The Greek word "xeno" means "stranger" or "foreigner," as in xenophobia or xenomorph. And the Greek word "pathos" means "feeling" or "emotion," as in sympathy or empathy.

The heroine almost always forms a "xenopathic bond" with the Beast archetype. We confront this imagery repeatedly, where the heroine loses her fear of a potentially dangerous beast and sincerely attempts to understand the plight of the beast. She may suspend a negative judgment or question a widely believed stigma about the beast. Her effort to understand a person unlike herself often inspires genuine change in herself and the Beast. The heroine gains wisdom about the animal nature of humanity, while the Beast gains an alternative perspective about his usefulness in the world. Quite often, the interaction is confrontational and challenging at first. But slowly, the mutual intrigue between the heroine and the Beast settles into something constructive.

And while the archetypal power of the virgin and a beast may generate sexual overtones, the Beast as Ally theme is absolutely not limited to a sexual relationship. A good writer must recognize the potential of the heroine's xenopathy. The heroine's ability and desire to understand the Beast and perceive the human condition gives her the space to allow for a mutual growth pattern. Despite our human differences, a universal model exists here for a constructive relationship.

In the HBO hit series *The Sopranos*, New Jersey mobster Tony Soprano is a violent, murderous crime boss. But his relationship with psychiatrist Dr. Jennifer Melfi creates genuine change. She engages the mobster without fear. There is a real effort to understand the nature of the Beast, and their relationship is one of the driving forces of the entire series.

Natasha Romanoff, also known as the "Black Widow," handles her business with supervillains despite having no superpowers. But when superhero Bruce Banner loses control, he becomes the ultimate Beast archetype—the Incredible Hulk. He's massive, out of control, violent, and aggressive. But only Natasha can calm the Incredible Hulk. We see the powerful imagery of a composed heroine again as she approaches the dangerous beast without posturing for combat. Her visage is both serene and fearless. When she reaches out, she conveys a recognition of the Beast's common humanity—and the Beast reaches back.

Game of Thrones is loaded with Beast as Ally themes. The murderous Hound is as brutal as they come. But the Hound eventually teams up with Arya Stark, and the two become unsteady but reliable partners. Notice the big bad wolf-like undertones even in the name "Hound." The Queen Consort, Margaery Tyrell, regularly faces the animal sadism of Joffrey Baratheon with a calm and empathetic demeanor. She's one of the only characters who can advise Joffrey or adjust his warped perspective of the world. Lastly, the most dangerous warrior in the show, the Mountain, is eventually brought into the service of protecting Queen

Cersei around the clock. The imagery is consistent with the Beast as Ally theme in many heroine-led stories.

King Kong has perhaps one of the most famous Beast as Ally motifs. While the world views the giant gorilla as a terrifying monster that must be destroyed, the heroine, Ann Darrow, forms a xenopathic bond with Kong. She seems to see an almost human light in the animal's eyes. Although Kong displays the possessive love of the Minotaur, Anne recognizes that King Kong is also a victim of a human society that is quick to destroy whatever it fears. On the second pass, I think they're wrong to say that beauty killed the beast. Man killed the beast, and *beauty tried to save him.*

Regarding narrative structure, I believe the Beast as Ally serves a range of critical functions. The heroine learns that not all that menaces is evil and not everything that roars is dangerous. Heroines often realize that some of the Beast's power comes from a veneer. She learns more about the deceptive nature of human appearances because she, herself, has learned to mask her thoughts and intentions to some degree. The heroine understands that all too often, the native culture wants individuals to be something they are not, and the result is the appearance of conformity. The xenopathic bond generates the slow process of dropping respective veneers and finding common ground and cause.

This bridge-building phenomenon that comes with xenopathy has even wider ramifications in stories and mythologies. The heroine's ability to strike bonds and forge specific networks that foster human understanding and change is a natural catalyst for solving the labyrinth. Beyond the oft-romantic overtones, xenopathy can also lay the groundwork for major cultural changes, shifting allegiances, and even wide-reaching geopolitical events. Let's look deeper at two variants of the Beast-Heroine motifs, where the heroine draws heavily on xenopathy.

Bridal Ambassador

When the Beast as Ally theme emerges in the story through marriage, we have a heroine who becomes the powerful "Bridal Ambassador." In this variant theme, the heroine marries a foreign groom on behalf of the native culture, and the relationship opens a new pathway for an alliance.

We've already established the heroine's tendency to form a xenopathic bond with unlike individuals, usually menacing or dangerous characters. However, the xenopathic bond is an amazing aspect of heroine-led fiction because it represents a non-violent pathway to success. The heroine models and reflects the real-world actions for cooperation between two people, groups, or nations that may otherwise be hostile toward each other. They find the language and perspective necessary for two worldviews to find common ground and coexist. This doesn't mean that heroines never direct malicious or wartime behaviors, but as far as stories go, the Bridal Ambassador is a role many heroines embrace.

In *Game of Thrones*, Daenerys Targaryen is the maiden sister to the heir of the Targaryen throne. Her older brother, Viserys, is an abusive and selfish representative of the native culture, who treats Daenerys like an object commodity to be horse-traded for his benefit. Daenerys is married off to Khal Drogo, who is the perfect example of a beast archetype. He's wild, passionate, brutal, and barbaric, but by Episode 7 of the first season, Drogo makes an intense declaration, adopting the heroine's cause to reclaim the Iron Throne. Despite minimal screen time in just one season, the Drogo-Daenerys relationship is one of the most unforgettable in the entire series, probably because of the familiar archetypal power contained within the Beast as Ally and Bridal Ambassador themes.

In fact, nearly every single heroine character in *Game of Thrones* follows the Bridal Ambassador version of the Beast as Ally. The older characters, such as Cersei Lannister and Lady Olenna, reflect on their experiences encountering their beastly grooms. But Lady Sansa, Margaery Tyrell, and Talisa all marry into foreign cultures and immediately attempt to alter the course of events. But perhaps the most famous example of the Bridal Ambassador (besides Daenerys Targaryen and Khal Drogo) is Ygritte and Jon Snow. The two come from not just different cultures but are ancient and sworn enemies of each other.

Through Ygritte and her relationship with Jon Snow, the Night's Watch and the Wildlings forge a truce and find a common cause that alters the story's course.

The Female Diplomat

Her Excellency, Chrisjen Avasarala, steals the spotlight in the Amazon Prime show, *The Expanse*. She breaks all the "delicate lady" conventions with a constant spate of obscenities and ruthless political maneuvers. The archetypal prowess of feminine diplomacy has become so recognizable that in 2014, Helen McCarthy wrote a book called *Women of the World: The Rise of the Female Diplomat*. She aptly notes that many women throughout history comprised a corps of "unofficial envoys" before officially being admitted into the diplomatic corps. Yet, from a storytelling standpoint, we writers view the Female Diplomat as a heroine who has long asserted great power and, therefore, hails from an ancient tradition.

Modern stories seem to repurpose the Bridal Ambassador archetype through diplomatic heroines. Female ambassadors are all over contemporary stories, and they resonate due to our familiarity with the Beast as Ally theme. I believe that both the Bridal Ambassador and the Female Diplomat are natural outgrowths of the heroine's xenopathy. The ability to form intellectual and emotional connections to those who are unfamiliar, alien, or foreign is a unique skill set that transcends mere empathy. The ability to shape events through interpersonal influence and bridge-building is right in the heroine's wheelhouse. She usually does so to mitigate or reduce potentially destructive courses of action or temper warrior spirits.

Tensions are high in *Crouching Tiger, Hidden Dragon* when a thief steals the Green Destiny sword from the governor's mansion. Reputations will be ruined if the wrong accusations are allowed to spread. The heroine, Shu Lien, has the foresight, ability, and plan to solve the mystery without disturbing the delicate waters—the Female Diplomat in action. Her methods rely on her ability to mask her agenda during social interactions and careful observations. "Calligraphy is so similar to fencing," she says while watching the wrist articulations of an aristocratic girl as she closes in on the disguised thief. She then devises a discreet social trick to out the thief in private without alerting a soul.

Princess Leia and Padme Amidala are iconic ambassador roles for *Star Wars*, but did you know that heroines utterly dominate this role in the critically acclaimed animated series *The Clone Wars*? Through seven seasons of the popular show, heroines direct numerous events within the Star Wars galaxy as Jedi, Sith, diplomats, ambassadors, and heads of state.

One of the most memorable groups of diplomatic women is the Bene Gesserit in the Dune saga. The Bene Gesserit are an all-female order of priestess-diplomats spread across the galaxy. However, one of the reasons I think these women are so memorable is due to a potent double archetype. They have the archetypal power of the clairvoyant crossed with the influential machinations of the Female Diplomat. Lady Jessica is also a Bridal Ambassador through her relationship with Duke Leto Atreides.

In *Star Trek: The Motion Picture*, we get another example of the Female Diplomat with the underappreciated heroine, Ilia. I wasn't surprised to see that the alien power of V'Ger chose Lieutenant Ilia as its ambassador to humanity. Ilia is abducted and returned as an advanced robotic replica of the female Deltan navigator. The Distant Dragon archetype, V'Ger, views humanity as a "carbon infestation" with little value and plans to wipe out all life on Earth. However, the pure machine logic that replicated Ilia accidentally replicated her Sacred Fire and private emotions. Through Ilia, the hostile machine mind of V'Ger forms a xenopathic bond with humans, particularly Commander Decker. This singular ability ends up saving the world. The film concludes with an epic melding of machine sentience with humanity, which creates a new lifeform in the universe. Talk about building a bridge between two worlds.

Anatomy of an Archetype – Beast as Ally

◊ The Beast as Ally often exhibits as anti-social or noncomformist attitude toward the native culture.

◊ The Beast is usually protective of the heroine.

◊ The Beast is often a doppelganger or mirror image of the Masked Minotaur.

◊ The Beast as Ally rejects possessive love.

◊ The Beast is also drawn to the attractive force of the heroine's Sacred Fire and may even attempt to capture it.

◊ Like the Minotaur, the Beast may also have an animal totem, but it's usually more of a menacing façade.

◊ The Beast almost always adopts the heroine's cause.

◊ The Beast as Ally signals the heroine's growing mastery of the labyrinth.

◊ Many heroines form xenopathic bonds with the Beast to build new bridges.

Exercises

1. Following the Bridal Ambassador variant of the Beast as Ally theme, structurally, who is the heroine of the movie *Braveheart*?

2. Greek mythology features many stories where a goddess, queen, or princess is seduced by a male figure disguised as an animal. Make a list of all the variations of the animal appearances masculine gods assume in mythology.

3. Who is the Beast as Ally in *Maleficent*? What animal does the storyteller primarily use to symbolize this heroic partner?

4. Let's explore the doppelganger phenomenon with *Everything Everywhere All at Once*. Identify the Masked Minotaur and the Beast as Ally. What traits and aspects do both of these characters have in common with each other?

Tarot

The heroine encountered the Beast, which seemed to be yet another dangerous being within the labyrinth. Instead, she gains a heroic partner. But we must advance deeper into our reading. The next card signals another potential heroic partner, but it's in the Trust Position. Trust is a rare and precious commodity in the heroine's labyrinth, so this next card bodes well for the heroine. Let's flip it over and unleash the positive energy.

The Fragile Power

THE FRAGILE POWER

On the Eve of the Battle of Pelennor Fields, Lady Éowyn rejects the notion that Meriadoc Brandybuck isn't skilled or powerful enough to join the battle. She understands more than anyone the slight of being overlooked and undervalued. Against the king's wishes, Éowyn brings Merry onto the brutal battlefield. Merry is overmatched to an extreme when he comes face to face with the Witch-king of Angmar. And yet, Merry's sword and well-timed attack allow Éowyn to strike down the Nazgûl. Merry was indeed fragile, "just a Hobbit," yet his small contribution proved critical during a decisive moment of the battle.

We all understand the concept. Aesop's fables present the tale of the lion and the mouse, where a tiny thorn brings the king of beasts to an agonizing full stop. His roar penetrates the jungle. However, a little mouse removes the painful thorn from the lion's paw. Depending on the version of the tale, the lion rewards the mouse in various ways. The moral of the story is that a Fragile Power can be the most vital heroic partner of them all.

The Fragile Power is usually a physically smaller character, stigmatized, weakened, overlooked, or childlike. Whereas other characters often dismiss, ignore, or reject the Fragile Power when encoun-

tered, heroines often show skepticism toward negative assumptions based on an outward appearance. Heroines defend the Fragile Power in their story world and entrust them with critical responsibilities.

By now, the heroine learns to trust her instincts and recognizes that a vital ingredient might exist below the surface. Due to her experiences with the native culture, heroines have also developed a healthy distrust of social stigmas and dismissive attitudes. So, when others overlook or underestimate a fragile creature, the heroine often takes time to dig deeper and ante up with that rare gift—trust.

And as we'll soon see, the Fragile Power often reveals itself as a deciding factor in the story's entire conflict when certain conditions align. Put simply, heroines tend to push back against harsh judgments. The Fragile Power may even be a hazy reflection of the heroine's younger or less mature self, and the heroine realizes that she has the power to flip the script by *not* undervaluing seemingly minor characters. She can offer the Fragile Power a chance that other characters in the story failed to offer to her.

The heroine's faith infuses the Fragile Power with confidence and bravery, and we often witness these smaller characters perform incredible feats.

Princess Leia entrusts the critical Death Star plans to Artoo-Detoo in *A New Hope*. In *Return of the Jedi*, Leia befriends a child-like Ewok in the forests of Endor. Both Fragile Powers prove to be essential in the struggle against the Empire. *A New Hope* is very nearly the story about how a Fragile Power, Artoo-Detoo, completed the impossible mission his heroine, Princess Leia, assigned him. And the inroads Leia forged with the Ewok tribe led to a counterattack against the imperial forces. The hopeless situation on the forest moon turned into a fighting chance, which allowed the Rebel Alliance to regroup and destroy the shield generator and, ultimately, the second Death Star. Thank you, Princess Leia!

When the Colonial Marines discover Newt on LV-426, they dismiss the girl due to her detachment and silence. Newt wears tattered clothing and clutches a plastic doll's head like a security blanket. To the Marines, the girl is clearly traumatized and of little value. But Ripley sees a Fragile Power and takes the time to befriend Newt. It sure pays off. With countless xenomorphs breaking through the door, the Marines gear up for a final last stand. Recognizing the situation's futility, the Fragile Power activates. Newt reveals an entrance to an air duct, and she *alone* leads the embattled soldiers out of a deadly labyrinth.

Even in the iconic *Superman* movie, Superman is weakened with Kryptonite around his neck while two missiles speed toward their targets. An unlikely heroine, Ms. Teschmacher, comes to his rescue. In an apparent role reversal, the heroine saw Superman as a Fragile Power in that moment and defied Lex Luthor by removing the Kryptonite.

Hidden Victims

The Fragile Power and the Masked Minotaur sometimes share a critical link in the story structure. The Minotaur is the cause, and the Fragile Power is the effect. Quite often, the Fragile Power has been proximate to the Minotaur or knows something about the inner workings of the labyrinth. The seemingly innocuous knowledge may provide the key to defeating the Minotaur later in the story.

By engaging the Fragile Power, the heroine sometimes also learns that there are *other* hidden victims. The heroine comprehends the danger and scope of the Masked Minotaur's destructive operations. The heroine may even begin to question an ethical premise, tradition, or cultural norm of her native culture. Therefore, the heroine's labyrinth is a natural narrative structure that models the behavior for constructive or needed changes. Remember that the heroine usually challenges the native culture to improve it, and the Fragile Power may be proof positive that change is necessary.

In *Ex Machina*, Ava discovers a fragile power when she meets the android Kyoto, a mute servant woman. After an inaudible exchange, Ava inspires Kyoto to turn against the Masked Minotaur (Nathan) at the center of the labyrinth. Only after the heroine slays the Minotaur does she uncover a central room where the hidden victims are powered off and hang like objects in lockers. Ava confirms that Nathan had been building multiple android women for mainly servile or sexual purposes—high-tech objects rather than sentient beings.

In *Coraline*, the heroine encounters the ghosts of the Other Mother's former victims, just as Fragile Powers surround Belle in *Beauty and the Beast*. Most of the characters she meets are under a transformative spell, most notably Lumiere and Cogsworth.

One of my favorite subversions of the Fragile Power theme is in *Arcane: League of Legends*. The badass heroine, Vi, spends the opening episodes as a protective guardian to her younger sister, Powder. The sisters go on many underworld thieving adventures within the crime-ridden labyrinth known as Zaun. Powder is famous for her mistakes and knack for bad luck. In a pivotal scene, Powder tries to save the heroic group. Her bombs misfire and end up killing some of her friends. This time, the deadly blunder is too much for Vi, and she abandons the Fragile Power, calling her younger sister a jinx. Devastated and traumatized, Powder adopts the name "Jinx" and joins the bad guys.

Therefore, writers may choose the Fragile Power to be one of the hidden victims of the Masked Minotaur. By engaging the Fragile Power, the heroine binds herself to a much larger area of effect. The Fragile Power is the character that shifts the heroine's sense of purpose away from herself and onto someone else. Hidden victims establish a moral imperative that the heroine cannot ignore.

The exploration phase of our story began with the heroine struggling against deception, redirection, and resistance. But as this phase draws to a close, we see the heroine flanked now by two heroic partners, the Beast as Ally and the Fragile Power. The heroine has forged these relationships on a personal and sometimes intimate level. She may not realize it yet, but the heroine and her heroic partners are capable of incredible feats together.

The Feminine Triad

One of the strongest shapes in the world of engineering is the triangle. Likewise, one of the most potent forces in storytelling is the Feminine Triad—the heroine, the Beast as Ally, and the Fragile Power. These three characters seem to operate independently and perhaps awkwardly through much of the story. Still, under certain conditions, the Feminine Triad fuses into a committed force that's very difficult to defeat. Suddenly, the heroine moves to the forefront, aided by the powerful Beast on one side and the Fragile Power on the other. The heroine saw the humane value in the Beast and recruited his fighting prowess to her cause. She also refused to undervalue the Fragile Power and gained unexpected or magical assistance. The heroine has unlocked one of the

Left: Replica of Athena Parthenos statue by Alan LeQuire in Nashville's Centennial Park. Right: Statue of Lady Justice.

strongest and most effective battle formations in the heroine's labyrinth. It's worth noting that archetypal imagery is everywhere. Look for it, and you'll see it.

At the end of *Aliens*, we see Ripley flanked by Hicks, the Beast as Ally, and Newt, the Fragile Power. At the end of *Terminator 2*, we see Sarah Connor flanked by the Terminator and John Connor. In Moana, we see Maui and Hei Hei. In *Mad Max: Fury Road*, Furiosa is flanked by Mad Max and the brides.

But the Feminine Triad transcends story and moves into the realm of a pure symbol. Behold the great golden statue of Athena in the Parthenon, which depicts a beastly serpent and spear on her left side and a child-like Fragile Power on her right side.

Lady Justice, too, emanates with the same primal, archetypal power. She holds the sword in one hand, symbolizing the Beast's use of force and strength. In her other hand, she holds up the scales of justice, a symbolic recognition of Fragile Powers. Both images (and many others) show the heroine holding the Fragile Power power symbol higher than the sword, a subtle clue as to her priorities. Although she clutches the blade in an unthreatening and idle position, she still recognizes the sword's importance. The heroine generates cultural power and wisdom through the combined forces of compassion and restrained force, as conveyed in the Feminine Triad.

The Pivot Toward Confrontation

The heroine is prepared to address the conflicts of the labyrinth from a more experienced perspective. She's also moving into a natural leadership position. By engaging a Fragile Power, the heroine is reaching a stage of self-actualization. She's aware of specific beliefs developed through her experiences within the story and must now take a side. The heroine believes that the human spirit should not be stifled, that judgments of inadequacy may be wrong, and that people can change.

Therefore, the Fragile Power may be a shadowy reflection of the heroine's once fragile self-image and a contrasting character for readers or audiences to measure her growth. She's come a long way, baby! We see for ourselves that the heroine is stronger and more experienced. We see the looming conflict through her eyes. And now we see her surrounded by characters who follow her judgment.

Anatomy of an Archetype – The Fragile Power

◊ The heroine befriends a seemingly insignificant or powerless character.

◊ The Fragile Power often appears in the story as small or child-like.

◊ This character appears to be unnecessary or even a burden to other characters.

◊ The heroine eventually entrusts the Fragile Power with something important to the story.

◊ The Fragile Power possesses secret knowledge or a secret ability vital to the heroine's success.

◊ The Fragile Power may subtly reflect the heroine from an earlier part of the story.

◊ The Fragile Power often legitimizes the heroine's autonomy and authority.

Exercises

1. In the classic American novel *Gone with the Wind*, who is the Fragile Power Scarlett O'Hara entrusts and later saves? How does the Fragile Power legitimize the heroine?

2. Who is the Fragile Power in the movie *Barbie*? Does the Fragile Power indicate any hidden victims? Does Barbie ever entrust the Fragile Power with any key responsibilities?

3. In the Jane Austen novel *Emma*, who is the Fragile Power that Emma Woodhouse befriends? Although there is plenty of friction between the characters later in the novel, what key role does the Fragile Power play for Emma?

4. Let's look at the animated film *Zootopia*. Who is the ironically named Fragile Power who helps Judy Hopps? Now, identify the Beast as Ally in the movie, and you'll uncover the heroine's Feminine Triad.

Tarot

We look down at our arrangement on the table and already perceive a great story. We see the Beast as Ally card beside the Fragile Power. The humanity and compassionate strength of the Beast add energy to the untapped potential hidden within the Fragile Power. This energy strengthens our heroine and equips her to confront her fears in the coming events. The next card is in the Crisis Position, so we know that the heroine will be tested as fortunes turn against her.

The Broken Truce

THE BROKEN TRUCE

eason 5 of *The Clone Wars* animated series concludes with an incredible storyline for the heroine Ahsoka Tano. She's the capable and worthy apprentice of Anakin Skywalker, and the two make an excellent, heroic team during this Star Wars era. Despite her long years commanding clone legions to save the Galactic Republic, earning the clone troopers' trust on the battlefield, and forging several deep relationships, the native culture turns against Ahsoka. Framed for a crime she didn't commit, Ahsoka must escape the dragnet of the clone army. We see all the imagery of the heroine's labyrinth at work as Ahsoka Tano races through a deadly maze of tunnels, ventilation shafts, sewers, and alleyways in the Star Wars underworld. The clones now relentlessly pursue Ahsoka, eventually capturing the fugitive Jedi and jailing her. However, the worst manifestation of the ordeal is when the Jedi Council also turns against her. "It is the Council's opinion that padawan Ahsoka Tano has committed sedition against the Republic," says Mace Windu. "And thus, she will be expelled from the Jedi Order."

Feelings of isolation, a sense of betrayal, and a stigma within the public sphere are the basis of the dreaded Broken Truce. The heroine sees that the native culture is not infallible or indisputably ethical. Like

Ahsoka and the Jedi Council, the heroine suspects that her independent judgment on a specific matter may be *correct*, even though this judgment might fly in the face of all the most powerful forces in the labyrinth. The heroine has reached a point of no return.

As the heroine's exploration phase draws to a close, the heroine knows full well that the Cult of Deception will move to redirect her. She knows that feelings of guilt and shame will intensify and cause doubt by breaking the Captivity Bargain. She knows that the Chamber Guardians will resist her. She knows that the Masked Minotaur will reject her individual course of action. The heroine knows all these things. She must now decide whether to commit to her personal judgment and beliefs or yield to the labyrinth's forces once more, knowing it could be permanent this time. Her sovereignty has been at odds with the expectations of the native culture or stifled by the possessive love of the Minotaur or both—and now, these forces can no longer coexist.

The heroine breaks the Captivity Bargain.

At this juncture, the Masked Minotaur will rise to full power. The villain often directs the native culture to turn against the heroine, and as a result, the heroine will be outcast, hunted, or stigmatized. The heroine often tries to escape the social forces that pursue her—whether it's the Mattel board of directors chasing Barbie in *Barbie*, the villagers chasing Sarah in *Labyrinth,* Darth Vader pursuing Princess Leia in *A New Hope*, or the whole police force bearing down on Thelma and Louise.

The Broken Truce can be a dramatic and intense segment of the heroine's labyrinth. The moment arrives when the heroine gains clarity on what she wants due to her growing real-world experience. This time, she follows her Sacred Fire without the romantic notions of her younger self and accepts the darker consequences of her actions. Reality is never kind. Some of the heroine's friends or supporters may become neutral or even desert her when she breaks the Captivity Bargain. Some people side with the native culture instead of the heroine, even if they sympathize with her cause. Suddenly, the many confusing corridors of the labyrinth, once puzzles to be solved, become immovable *dead ends* threatening to return the heroine to captivity.

As far as storytelling is concerned, the Broken Truce may be the most decisive moment in the story. The response from the native culture and the Masked Minotaur should be overwhelming and have devastating consequences for the heroine.

She'll experience real material losses. The stronger the effort to stop the heroine and the more damaging the consequences, the more people will sympathize with the heroine. The Minotaur and native culture move in to crush or capture our heroine before our eyes. There should be real doubt about the heroine's ability to overcome this threat, regardless of whether she's right.

For maximum storytelling impact, the Captivity Bargain should seem almost preferable to all the chaos unleashed—*even to the readers or audience.* If a writer can make the Captivity Bargain feel practical and even reasonable, if only to restore the peace, then you help readers and audiences understand the heroine's plight more deeply. We should feel like maybe, just maybe, the heroine is risking too much. If so, then the dramatic impact of the Broken Truce inspires us all the more when our heroine commits to it.

The villagers have grabbed their pitchforks, and the flying monkeys have been deployed. The heroine, the Beast as Ally, and the Fragile Power often retreat or briefly hide in the story. Under these conditions, the heroine must succeed. But will she?

Witch Hunt

In 1692 and 1693, fourteen women and five men were hanged during the Salem Witch Trials. The religiosity generated mass hysteria around the apparent adherence to witchcraft. The judicial process overwhelmingly targeted women for being more susceptible to the temptations of witchcraft, which included fortune telling and the ability to seduce or influence men. These so-called demonic powers were so attractive to some women that they took up witchcraft, or so went the accusations. The terrible events in Salem also occurred in Europe and gave rise to the phrase "witch hunt." And the architecture of a witch hunt is in place now for the heroine of our story.

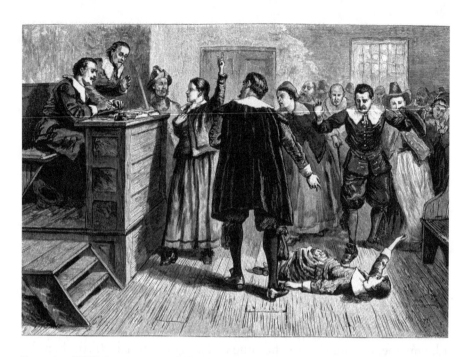

Engraving (1876) depicts a witchcraft trial at Salem Village. The central figure in this illustration of the courtroom is usually identified as Mary Walcott (circa 1692).

One of the most terrifying abilities of the Masked Minotaur is their ability to muster the inhabitants of the labyrinth and set them against the heroine. The decentralized forces behind the Cult of Deception work in the Minotaur's favor and create a coordinated effort to stigmatize, suppress, and capture the heroine. Not all stories have to feature the severity of the Salem trials, but in archetypal terms, some form and degree of the theme are common in heroine-led stories. **I believe a primal fear of mob rule is embedded deep within the dark subconscious of the feminine monomyth.**

Political theorist and philosopher Hannah Arendt addresses the phenomenon of mass hysteria under certain conditions in her book *Eichmann in Jerusalem: A Report on the Banality of Evil.* Hannah analyzes a mid-level bureaucrat named Adolf Eichmann, who coordinated the trains transporting Jews to extermination camps. Late in the war, Eichmann refused to stop the trains, even under *Der Fuhrer's* orders. But why? Hannah struggled to reconcile the man's role in the Holocaust with his ordinary and even unremarkable personality. In one of her conclusions, she says, "Evil comes from a failure to think. It defies thought, for as soon as thought tries to engage itself with evil and examine the premises and principles from which it originates, it is frustrated because it finds nothing there. That is the banality of evil."

This nihilistic banality, or nothingness, seems to be the evil at the heart of the Minotaur's power. The human half may design slogans and ideologies to sway the masses, but at its core, the animal tyrant seeks only power and possession. And in this pursuit, the Minotaur can often marshal the necessary social forces against the heroine.

The Broken Truce can also be random and dangerous, as in Shirley Jackson's short story *The Lottery*, where the townsfolk stone Tessie or impulsive, as in the case of Mary Magdalene. It can be targeted as in the Outlander saga, where a time-traveling Claire Randall's modern knowledge of medicine leads to accusations of witchcraft. Luckily, she survives the ordeal. However, in *King Lear*, the heroine Cordelia does not survive. The heroine is stripped of her birthright and banished when she refuses to lie for her father. She spends most of the play in captivity, and Edmund hangs her when she returns.

The Broken Truce can be the primary premise of a story, such as when the War Boys spend most of the film chasing Furiosa in *Mad Max*, or it can be subtle, as when Fanny Price is sent back to Portsmouth in Jane Austen's novel *Mansfield Park*. The Broken Truce can open a story, such as in *Star Wars: A New Hope* when Princess Leia flees the Galactic Empire or in *Maleficent* when the king comes to invade the Moors.

In *Barbie*, we have a comical but still meaningful example of the Broken Truce. After refusing to get back into the box, Barbie makes a run for it. Mattel's entire board of directors comes chasing after her in manic pursuit. Still being chased, Barbie makes her way back to Barbieland, only to discover that Ken, too, has turned against her. Ken marshaled the social forces of Barbieland against Barbie. The satire of the film provides an excellent snapshot of a Broken Truce. To the heroine, the world feels upside-down, subverted, and hostile.

In the novel *Catching Fire*, heroine Katniss Everdeen says, "At some point, you have to stop running and turn around and face whoever wants you dead." The Hunger Games saga is an overture to the Broken Truce. Katniss is a revolutionary figure who breaks the Captivity Bargain on national television and sparks a greater overarching contest between herself and the native culture. Again and again, Katniss is placed into a life-sized labyrinth, a deadly gameboard, and must survive to reshape public opinion. The Mockingjay whistle and hand signal symbolize the heroine's Broken Truce, which expands into a full-scale revolution.

We get a definitive Broken Truce in the final scene of the last episode of *Arcane: League of Legends,* Season 1. The chaotic heroine, Jinx, launches a missile into the Piltover Council. Her world, the undercity world of Zaun, is a deadly labyrinth of crime, poverty, and Shimmer addicts. Jinx's missile launch is an irreversible strike—a Broken Truce between herself and society.

"I have to do something," says Mulan in the 1998 animated film *Mulan*. She's referring to her looming decision to break the Captivity Bargain with her native culture. Getting caught by an angry mob is replaced by the threat of getting caught wearing a culturally unforgivable disguise.

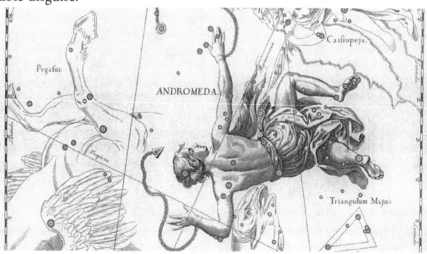

Depiction of Andromeda by Johannes Hevelius (1690).

Even the star constellation Andromeda is an eternal depiction of the mythological Greek princess breaking free of chains at her wrists. She's immortalized in the moment of the Broken Truce.

One example of a Broken Truce where the native culture is notably absent is in *Moana*. Her Broken Truce leads her out to sea, where the native culture does not follow. She recruits the Beast as Ally with Maui, who symbolically transforms into numerous actual beasts. And she entrusts the Fragile Power, Hei Hei, who plays a key role in the story's climax.

But not all heroines survive the Broken Truce. One of the great tragedies of heroine-centric stories is when the Broken Truce leads to the heroine's end. She risked everything to claim her Sacred Fire and to follow her path, and in the end, it resulted in tragic death. Sometimes, after racing through the menacing corridors of the maze, the heroine comes to a decisive dead end. This possibility is real and devastating and serves as a cautionary tale about the darkest powers of the labyrinth and the destructive threat to feminine free will.

Some stories underscore the full danger of the heroine's labyrinth by depicting a heroine who fails to escape or whose efforts come up short. Beyond the hostile witch hunt, there are countless stories in which the heroine doesn't survive.

The Dead End - Tragically Ever After

When a corridor in a labyrinth leads to an impassible wall, we call it a "dead end." The reality behind this term now comes into focus. The inability to change is often a precursor to ill fortunes and symbolizes death. Many stories show us a heroine who zigs and zags only to turn into a formidable dead end, and the heroine realizes the futility of her efforts. The last resort to the Broken Truce occurs when the heroine either takes her own life or goes mad. The suicide may be triumphant or tragic depending on the tale's tone, while madness is usually portrayed as a hellish torment.

From Madame Bovary to Madame Butterfly, from Cleopatra to Juliet, from Odette in *Swan Lake* to Jen Yu in *Crouching Tiger, Hidden Dragon*, we witness heroines at odds with their native culture or who feel so hopelessly possessed by the Masked Minotaur that they see no way out. Suicide symbolizes the most brutal form of individual free will without personal growth or resolution. Change never occurs. Freedom is never attained.

If a heroine cannot defend her claim to her Sacred Fire, she suffers. She suffers mentally, physically, and spiritually, and our stories establish this suffering as a mythic dark side of the human condition. The heroine is sacrificed upon the altar of the native culture, the animal ego, or both. The "dead end" outcome is pervasive in storytelling. Therefore, I believe stories that feature a heroine who commits suicide or goes mad are cautionary tales about the struggles between a heroine and her native culture or the dangers of a Masked Minotaur within our midst.

The Broken Truce is the dominant theme of the 1991 film *Thelma & Louise*. The two heroines decide to break their Captivity Bargains and go on an adventure together. Along the way, their desire for non-conformity and freedom leads to a criminal bank robbery, and the witch hunt begins. Rather than allow the native culture to arrest them for their crimes, the two women refuse to surrender. Thelma, realizing they have reached a dead end in the labyrinth, suggests not getting "caught." The tragic implication is understood, and Louise floors it, sending the car and the two women over the cliff's edge.

In *Avengers: Endgame*, the heroine Nebula comes face to face with her younger self, who is still mentally possessed by her father, Thanos. When older Nebula says, "You can change," the captive version of Nebula says, "He won't let me." The older Nebula then shoots and kills her younger self. The two Nebulas echo a harrowing contrast between the early heroine and the later heroine. By killing her younger self, I believe Nebula is making two statements: one, that she is ashamed of her younger, inexperienced self and wishes to erase that reality, and two, that she wants to release her younger self from the misery of the

Captivity Bargain in the quickest way possible. It's a simultaneous proof of growth and a symbolic suicide.

In *Anna Karenina*, our heroine falls into an adulterous relationship with the dashing military officer Alexei Vronsky. The fallout from the affair doesn't affect Vronsky too much, but it devastates Anna. She is dogged by the social norms throughout imperial Russian society, and we see her steadily lose the battle against the native culture. Anna makes several serious attempts to escape the maddening complexity of the labyrinth but becomes more isolated as the story evolves. She is openly stigmatized before all of St. Petersburg society, which deals a decisive blow to her identity. Facing the impassible dead end of the labyrinth, Anna Karenina throws herself under a speeding train.

Suicide in fiction is a definitive finale to the conflicts found in heroine tales. However, fictional suicides also lead us to a less definitive, but no less tragic alternate outcome. Mental illness provides another harsh outcome in fiction but *doesn't deserve* the negative connotations often associated with such an outcome.

Getting Lost in the Labyrinth

Journalist Vivienne Parry's article, "Were the 'mad' heroines of literature really sane?" —part of the BBC's "Madwomen in the Attic" series also approaches the topic of mental illness in fiction. She, too, sees the archetypal presence of the heroine's struggle behind the social label "madness." That may be how the native culture perceives the heroine's behavior, but she suggests that madness is a sane outcome when all hope is lost. She points to Bertha Rochester (*Jane Eyre*) and *The Woman in White* as examples.

A descent into madness is also an act of individual free will without growth. The heroine becomes a serial fantasist who boldly claims her Sacred Fire through fantasy rather than reality. The well-known short story, *The Yellow Wallpaper*, and the 1990s novels *The Virgin Suicides* and *Veronika Decides to Die* are modern-day mythologies of the captive heroine in a tower that leads to suicide and madness.

Whereas many older fairy tales and fables warn heroines *against* the "dangerous" personal aspirations and individual will, stories with heroine suicides or mental illness warn the native culture against the dangers of suppressing the heroine. When a heroine's bravery and extraordinary effort come up short, we feel that something is unfair. In a subtle way, we feel inspired to pick up where our heroine left off. A tragedy draws attention to an issue that may have been preventable. After experiencing a story where the heroine is destroyed mentally or physically by the labyrinth, we're ready to do something about it. Such a tragic story can inspire change.

The film *Blue Jasmine* depicts a heroine who attempts to navigate an unsolvable labyrinth in her life. Jasmine Francis experiences a Broken Truce on many levels, partly from an unfaithful husband and partly from her husband's illegal activities. The film shows us the damaging power of illusions and deceptions. The heroine's final act is to uphold her own lie, only to wander off alone in the labyrinth, sit on a public bench, and talk aloud to herself.

The 2008 Clint Eastwood film *Changeling* follows the true-life story of Christine Collins, whose son goes missing. The native culture conspires to "find" her son and have the two reunited. Only the boy they found is not her son. When Christine protests, she is forcibly thrown into a mental institution. After an incredible slew of legal battles, Christine Collins eventually succeeded in shining a light on corruption and a broken system. The California State Legislature eventually passed laws that made it illegal for police to place a person into a psychiatric facility without first getting a warrant.

Hester Prynne's decision to wear her scarlet letter defied a social stigma that challenged the Puritan views of the era. Films like *The Snake Pit* (1948), *Streets of Shame* (1956), and *Precious: Based on the Novel Push by Sapphire* (2012) also led to calls for legal changes.

One of the most remarkable aspects of the heroine's labyrinth is the capacity to portray societal problems and inspire change. While certainly capable of reinforcing gender roles or defending societal norms, the monomythic themes and archetypal events of the heroine's labyrinth are entirely suited to *challenge* fixed gender roles, society, and tradition. I believe that most heroine-centric stories do inspire needed cultural changes. The heroine is an insider. She's one of us. She's intimately familiar with our culture and traditions. **Therefore, the heroine is uniquely suited to deliver stories of transformation and change in our home cultures.**

Anatomy of an Archetype – The Broken Truce

◊ The Broken Truce is when the heroine breaks the Captivity Bargain.

◊ The Minotaur usually marshals social forces within the native culture against the heroine.

◊ Often includes some expression of law enforcement from the native culture.

◊ Often accompanies a rapid pursuit of the heroine.

◊ A threat to the Fragile Power may trigger the Broken Truce.

◊ May result in a challenge to the native culture, including changes to traditions, rules, moral authority, or gender roles.

◊ May result in tragedy, such as imprisonment, madness, death, or suicide.

Exercises

1. In the opera *Madame Butterfly*, the Broken Truce occurs off-stage throughout Act II. When does the heroine realize the Broken Truce has occurred, and what is her solution?

2. Let's revisit the film *The Nightmare Before Christmas*. In what way does the heroine, Sally, establish the Broken Truce on her terms?

3. In the novel *The Scarlet Letter*, Hester Prynne's Broken Truce is famously symbolized by what object? Why do you think the heroine wears this symbol proudly rather than feeling ashamed of it?

Tarot

The Broken Truce leaves us feeling anxious and energized. We completed our heroine's exploratory pyramid of cards for Act II of the story. The sensing and discovery that began the arrangement shifted into building alliances and friendships, but ended with a crisis. Therefore, as we look to draw the cards for our final arrangement, we should reflect on the heroine's growth thus far. She's no longer the inexperienced "maiden" of Act I. Her conflict has evolved along with her, but she's gained degrees of empowerment and autonomy through her actions. Our final six cards shall determine the fate of our heroine, so let us proceed with the reading.

ACT III

PERMUTATION
(REARRANGEMENT)

Three of Keys

THE FINAL STRETCH: REARRANGEMENT

We shuffle the deck and arrange the cards in a six-card spread. The harmonic energy of the number six assures us that by turning the final card, the heroine will have achieved *balance* through rearrangement one way or the other. However, the ongoing conflicts with the native culture, the possessive love of the Masked Minotaur, and the competing claims to her Sacred Fire have not yet been resolved. The heroine's tale is entering its final phase, and the heroine's struggle now generates new archetypal themes that converge for a resolution.

The Three of Keys evokes the nightmare of trial and error under pressure. Pursued by danger, we rattle one key after another, praying for the lock to click open. The native culture, the Masked Minotaur, or both close in from all sides. For the heroine has challenged the status quo of the labyrinth, which the Minotaur regards as an unforgivable offense. Whatever the outcome, the labyrinth will likely transform in some way, big or small, hence, the "rearrangement." But how so? In what ways? And who is most affected?

The time has come. And so, we turn the first card of our last deck to see how the Masked Minotaur responds to the Broken Truce.

The Poisoned Apple

THE POISONED APPLE

hile the story of Adam and Eve is thousands of years old, the symbolism of ingested poison, disguised evil, and a heroine is embedded in countless stories. Some stories stay with us effortlessly. Any one of us can conjure up an image of the old crone handing Snow White a beautiful-looking red apple. Like a pleasant object that preoccupies our attention in a dream, that single red apple is a composite of numerous psychological forces, both primal and human. We sense those forces intuitively rather than intellectually. We immediately recognize the appealing appearance as a possible source of nourishment or sweetness but can't shake a nagging awareness of potential danger or sickness. As with Snow White, we perceive the apple as a "good" object, unaware that it has been infused with poison by the villainous queen. However, I believe the symbolism is a thousand times more primordial.

The contrast between the allure of colorful fruit and the danger of poison is among the most primal imprints upon the human psyche. It is passed down to humanity through evolution from earlier primates, who inherited it from earlier mammals, who inherited it from earlier life, and so on, all encoded at a genetic level. Even today, when my kids go on a hike with me, if they see colorful berries on the trail, their first question is "Are they poisonous?" We don't know the outcome unless we take a bite. But whether we're talking about Eve with the fruit in the Book of Genesis or young Sarah with a peach in the David Bowie film *Labyrinth*, heroines who encounter the Poisoned Apple in stories invite serious consequences.

The individual decision to eat a strange fruit is a focused metaphor for *any* decision—one good, like nourishment and survival, and one bad, like sickness or death. Perhaps, then, we shouldn't be surprised to consider that the apple has come to symbolize not only good or bad *outcomes* in animalistic survival terms but good or evil outcomes in human moral terms. Therefore, it may be easy to view the apple as a symbol of the moral dichotomy of good and evil. Even in the book *Signs & Symbols: An Illustrated Guide to Their Origins and Meanings*, the apple "symbolizes temptation and sin."

So goes the thinking.

However, by studying heroines more closely and by recognizing the function of the Poisoned Apple in her stories, the more I reject the notion that the Poisoned Apple is a moral test that the heroine simply fails. After all, the Poisoned Apple is a weaponized gift from a disguised villain. And as we shall see, such a narrative device appears in many other forms throughout countless heroine tales.

The Garden of Eden with the Fall of Man by Peter Paul Rubens and Jan Brueghel the Elder (1615).

As storytellers, we must understand the structural significance, the narrative function, and the meaning behind the Poisoned Apple. Doing so gives us a critical perspective on the Poisoned Apple as an archetypal design with nefarious mythological attributes and hallmarks. And perhaps, once we understand this symbol, we can cut Eve some slack. The theme is recurrent in so many narrative forms that we must return our focus on rule #1 in the heroine's labyrinth—*the heroine is always sovereign*. We writers view her as a woman on a journey and never as an easy mark for a con man or naturally more prone to deceptions than her male counterpart. Let's recognize that the heroine must be deceived and persuaded into a bad decision.

It's time to take a deeper look at all the elements of this archetypal pattern.

By the Pricking of My Thumb

So foretells the witch in Shakespeare's *Macbeth*, but her statement establishes the concept of "pricking"—of something external that enters the heroine's physical being. Whether we're talking about the needle of the spinning wheel in *Sleeping Beauty*, the sedative shot for Sarah Connor in *Terminator 2*, or the tracker jackers for Katniss Everdeen in *The Hunger Games*, the "poison" is something delivered *internally* that puts the heroine in an altered or "poisoned" state. **The heroine isn't killed but rendered unconscious, semi-conscious, or disoriented. Poisoned Apples are usually physical objects with a harmless and sometimes appealing appearance. The disguised poison is consistent with the general themes of illusion found throughout the feminine monomyth and may be its most concentrated expression.**

From a storytelling standpoint, we should immediately recognize that the Poisoned Apple is usually delivered by the Masked Minotaur of the story, which means that the offering is deliberate and in bad faith. The entire purpose behind the Poisoned Apple is to subvert the free will, judgment, or consent of the heroine through deceptive means. This is an indictment of the Masked Minotaur, not the heroine.

Therefore, from a narrative and structural standpoint, we must recognize that the Poisoned Apple is an *attack* upon the heroine, and the apple itself is a weapon.

The symbolism of the Poisoned Apple usually centers on the vulnerable and exposed neck or throat and sometimes on the eyes, whether closed, sleepy, or wide and blank. Katniss Everdeen, whom we just mentioned, is stung on the neck, sending her into a narcotic-like altered state. We see the Poisoned Apple symbol on the throat of Lieutenant Ilia in *Star Trek: The Motion Picture*, where an apple-red sensor serves as a visual symbol of her altered state. Even the cocoon of the death's head moth, the call sign of the hidden Minotaur in *The Silence of the Lambs*, is inserted in the first victim's throat. The mouth and throat are natural focal points for the archetype.

Forced Shutdown

In terms of a confrontation, the Poisoned Apple isn't a face-to-face showdown but an unethical form of coercion, capture, and control. This dynamic differs from the warrior-oriented hero's journey, where the hero fights the villain in single combat. Unfortunately, the Poisoned Apple doesn't give the heroine that chance. Moreover, a Poisoned Apple sets the tone for an *unequal* confrontation, in which the villain will employ highly manipulative means and often muster social forces against the heroine.

The Masked Minotaur wants something they cannot have and do not understand—the heroine's Sacred Fire—and total possession is the only option left to the Masked Minotaur. Therefore, the Poisoned Apple manifests the heroine's greatest fears and anxiety, the final proof that she is to surrender her individual free will rather than merely compromise it through a bargain. The duplicitous Minotaur cannot accept the heroine's claim to her Sacred Fire, so any voluntary agreement for compromise is removed and replaced by a mandate. There will be no Captivity Bargain this time. The heroine must now consider whether to accept the mandate and subsequent authority of the Masked Minotaur.

The heroine's sovereignty, as a reality, exists now solely with the heroine. She's aware of her sovereignty in ways she may not have considered before. Unlike the heroine at the beginning of the story, whose aspirations seem abstract or theoretical, the heroine in the final leg of the story has real-world experiences and allies. The heroine's growing independence is why a Poisoned Apple is necessary.

Once the Minotaur delivers the Poisoned Apple, the "poisoned" heroine often loses momentum in the story. She faces a return to some form of captivity, only this time, *without* her consent. And although the heroine may have taken many steps to protect herself, the Poisoned Apple is explicitly designed to bypass all her proficiencies and render her defenseless.

The Poisoned Apple is like a switch that "shuts down" the heroine without her consent. Science fiction echoes the possessorship dynamic, where sentient female robots serve as symbolic stand-ins for their human counterparts. As android machines, each heroine is programmed with a Poisoned Apple that allows the creator or operator to "switch off" the heroine at will.

In *Westworld*, Season 1, we observe several heroines enduring an interrogation of a kind. They are in an altered state, like a trance, answering questions and often unaware they are unclothed. As the camera moves through the setting, we see multiple characters in rooms like cages, stripped of their free will, clothes, and independence by the Poisoned Apple in their programming. The nudity says something about the operatives' total control over the robotic characters. It's disturbing, and I think the unaware, nude person in the presence of a fully aware, fully clothed person hints at a far darker dynamic in archetypal design.

The Unconscious Heroine and Symbolic Rape

Early in the book, I pointed out how many heroine-centric stories lack the Belly of the Beast theme, which depicts a symbolic death. The themes and function of the symbolic death in the hero's journey are overconfidence, decisive failure, disgrace, loss of confidence, and isolation. I think these themes go hand in hand with the fears of death in combat in a warrior-oriented journey. However, a one-sided attack of deception, succumbing to an altered state, being captured, and a forced extraction of the Sacred Fire are flat-out different archetypal designs. They do not mean the same thing.

Images of an unconscious heroine lying flat on her back, unable to move or resist while the Masked Minotaur hovers nearby, recur in our stories with stunning persistence. This image is a primal echo of deep-seated fear, a pure possessorship dynamic, where the Minotaur has all the power, and the heroine has none. The scenario is what the heroine fears most—to be stripped of her ability to fight back and at the mercy of the Minotaur. In her "poisoned" state, the heroine is defenseless and unable to respond to threats. The possessorship dynamic can be somewhat subtle, such as the nudity we noted in *Westworld*, or aggressive and overt, such as the Facehuggers in *Aliens*.

Facehuggers are perfect examples of Poisoned Apples. Anyone familiar with H.R. Giger knows that the alien concept art was a deliberate metaphor for forced insemination, pregnancy, and rape, in which men and women alike were vulnerable. The creatures forcibly ignore free will, render the victim unconscious, and deliver their "poison" internally. In *Aliens*, they're delivered to the heroine by the Masked Minotaur of the story—Carter Burke. But the Poisoned Apple in many stories remains more suggestive—a psychic echo of the Masked Minotaur's threat to the heroine's identity and her total self.

In *Maleficent*, the Masked Minotaur of the story, Stefan, drugs Maleficent with a version of the Poisoned Apple. We see again the imagery of the Masked Minotaur stealing the heroine's Sacred Fire, symbolized as Maleficent's wings, her freedom, and the heroine cannot defend herself.

Beatrix Kiddo endures the full archetypal spectrum of the Poisoned Apple in *Kill Bill*. We see her unconscious and defenseless at the hospital first against the serial rapist, Buck, whom she later kills. Not long after, the villainous Elle Driver, a.k.a. California Mountain Snake, visits the unconscious heroine. Elle hovers over Beatrix with a syringe, ready for injection, the heroine unable to respond. In *Kill Bill Volume 2*, we see Beatrix in a "transparent" coffin, not unlike the glass coffin of an unconscious Snow White decades earlier. However, the true Poisoned Apple arrives near the end of *Volume 2*. After two films, Beatrix fights to the center of the labyrinth to confront Bill, the Masked Minotaur. Does he fight her in single combat? Nope. Instead, Bill pulls out a gun and fires a tranquilizer dart—a Poisoned Apple—into Beatrix, bypassing the heroine's combat abilities and free will, rendering her unconscious.

When Darth Vader captures Princess Leia in *Star Wars: A New Hope*, we see again the physical captivity of the heroine and a black mind probe aiming a syringe at the heroine. Like all Minotaurs, Vader is attempting to extract the heroine's Sacred Fire—the location of the Rebel's hidden base- the symbolic essence of the heroine's personal cause.

In *Game of Thrones*, the Season 2 finale, "Valar Morghulis," Daenerys visits the House of the Undying. There, she drinks something called Shade of the Evening, a narcotic elixir that disorients her. Finally, another disguised villain, Pyat Pree, reveals himself as a powerful warlock who captures Daenerys in a literal tower. He attempts to steal her dragons for himself. The stolen fire-breathing dragons are overt symbols of the heroine's Sacred Fire.

In *Game of Thrones*, seasons 5 and 6, we follow another heroine, Arya Stark. She enters the House of Black and White, seeking to join a religious order of assassins. The primary rite of passage in the temple is for Arya to surrender her Sacred Fire, her identity as a Stark, so that she can become "no one." As discussed earlier, the Sacred Fire is forever fused to the heroine's core identity, native culture, and personal cause. Arya drinks the poison, slipping into an altered state of temporary blindness. Ultimately, Arya does not surrender her Sacred Fire. Her cause, which is to avenge the massacre of her family, is symbolized in her family sword, Needle. She recovers the sword and resumes her individual quest.

And what about Dorothy Gale in *The Wizard of Oz*? When Dorothy approaches the Emerald City in Act III, the Wicked Witch casts a specific spell, bidding Dorothy to "sleep." She and her heroic partners all fall unconscious in a poppy field.

Captain Marvel features a Poisoned Apple similar to the female androids mentioned earlier. We see Carol Danvers unconscious, upside down, and restrained while a disguised sentient being, the Supreme Intelligence, tries to misdirect and redirect Carol. While she's unconscious, we again see that other characters are trying to extract secret information from her.

Near the end of *Crouching Tiger, Hidden Dragon,* the villainous Jade Fox uses an incense called purple yin to drug Jen Yu, the misguided heroine. We see the disoriented heroine clutching a sword she can barely hold, her sensational fighting skills bypassed and subverted. And when Li Mu Bai shows up, there is again the suggestion of seduction and sexual vulnerability. And although Li's intentions are pure in this case, Jen parts her shawl. "Is it me or the sword you want?" she asks, echoing the dark archetypal symbolism.

In *Shrek 2,* Fiona drinks a potion and falls unconscious. She's in an altered state when she wakes and suffers from confusion. Once again, the Masked Minotaur, the fairy godmother in this case, attempts to garner the heroine's consent through trickery and disguise. As an intriguing aside, the nefarious plan to trick Fiona is hatched inside a tavern called The Poison Apple.

Even in epic mythologies, we see the Poisoned Apple at work. The Hindu goddess Kali was the only one to defeat the demon Raktabīja. Whenever other gods attempted to slay the demon, they failed because a thousand more demons were born when the demon's blood touched the ground. Kali's tongue stretched to the ground to catch the demon's blood, breaking the cycle. But, in defeating Raktabīja, she became "poisoned" by the demon blood and went on a chaotic campaign of destruction. The reverse is true for the Egyptian goddess, Sekhmet, who must be tricked into drinking beer dyed red, like blood, to get her to *stop* a campaign of chaos.

In searching for a universal message here, the ethical failing of the Poisoned Apple is the Minotaur's disregard for individual autonomy and a selfish claim upon another person's Sacred Fire. The Poisoned Apple encapsulates both the circumvention of the heroine's independence and the exploitation of her skills, emotions, time, spirit, passions, attention, love, cause, beliefs, or sexuality. Such a blatant denial of one's freedom elicits our instinctive human hatred of the possessorship dynamic.

How the heroine confronts this primal fear and, more importantly, how she overcomes the Poisoned Apple will model real-world resilience.

Writing a Poisoned Apple Scene

As your heroine gains momentum during the final leg of her story, consider having the Masked Minotaur deliver a Poisoned Apple. The object chosen for the Poisoned Apple should appear harmless and have the capacity to disorient, confuse, or knock out your heroine. Readers and viewers will read or look on with both horror and fascination when they see your heroine succumb to the effects. Remember that the Poisoned Apple's success doesn't make the heroine weak or gullible. On the contrary, the Poisoned Apple shows that the heroine now resists persuasion toward any renewed Captivity Bargain.

Readers and audiences will instinctively fear for the heroine while she's in a "poisoned" state. Show the Masked Minotaur nearby—proximate, perhaps—hovering above the heroine. By using archetypal imagery and themes, you're engaging your audiences at a primal level, where monomythic power grips our subconscious. People from any time and culture will intuitively recognize the Poisoned Apple when they see it and respond in kind.

Remember, the Minotaur usually tries to capture and convert the heroine rather than kill her. What does the heroine possess that the Masked Minotaur seeks to monopolize? Your heroine should have something that symbolizes her Sacred Fire—an idea, a secret, an ability, an essence, knowledge, love, or consent. Whatever physical symbol the heroine has that represents her Sacred Fire, the Masked Minotaur will try to extract or capture it by threat and force.

Anatomy of an Archetype – The Poisoned Apple

◊ Usually delivered by the Masked Minotaur
◊ Delivered through premeditation and in bad faith (often disguised)
◊ Knocks out, disorients, or disables the heroine
◊ The poison is something internal—ingested, injected, implanted, or embedded.
◊ Usually includes a restrained, unconscious, or debilitated heroine
◊ Often depicts a menacing figure hovering above or near the heroine
◊ Usually, it precedes a failed attempt to convert the heroine or persuade her to accept a new Captivity Bargain.
◊ The Minotaur often attempts to extract, steal, diminish, or destroy the heroine's Sacred Fire.
◊ The Poisoned Apple places a special focus on the neck, throat, eyes, or mouth.

Exercises

1. One of the more famous Poisoned Apples is in the story of *Snow White*. While perhaps shallow by modern standards, what quality represents Snow White's Sacred Fire in the story?

2. Can you name the Poisoned Apple symbols of *Women Talking*, *Gravity*, *The Queen's Gambit*, and *Titanic*?

3. The novel *Misery* by Stephen King follows the heroine's labyrinth narrative model perfectly, except the gender roles are reversed. Notice the identical "unconscious heroine" imagery, even though it's a male lead? What is the Poisoned Apple? And what symbolizes Paul Sheldon's Sacred Fire in the story that the Minotaur attempts to extract by force?

Tarot

With the Poisoned Apple card facing up, we recognize that our heroine is in danger. Feelings of anger and powerlessness enter the story, along with a growing need for heroic action. Unconsciousness is not a human state of being; an attack of deception leaves dark clouds over our tarot reading. The next card is in the Moon Position, which can mean many different things. The moon changes in cycles, sometimes bright and watchful, sometimes absent and hidden in darkness, and other times incomplete, like a white scimitar upon black cloth. Let's flip the next card and see how the heroine responds to the Poisoned Apple of the story.

The Unmasking

THE UNMASKING

Humans have been fascinated by masks throughout our short history. We associate masks with social festivities, such as masquerades like Mardi Gras or the Carnival of Venice, where one's social identity is hidden. There's something playful, mysterious, and egalitarian about hidden identities in social settings, as seen on shows ranging from *The Masked Singer* to *Eyes Wide Shut* to *Squid Game*. Concealed human faces seem to go hand in hand with social games and entertainment. In all cases, an unspoken dark side stirs beneath all that color and pageantry, something elusive and even playfully dehumanizing. By covering the face, a person can become a human object without distinction, whether that object is one of fantasy, a faceless cog in a tyrannical machine, or a human symbol.

Since I found numerous examples of masks in stories from both the hero's journey and the heroine's labyrinth, I spent much time looking for definable differences. Did different masks have different meanings? Did the mask say something about the wearer? Do masks play a symbolic role in the nature of the conflict? Well, let's take a look at some of the most famous masks in pop culture. As of this writing, my summary of the top twenty most cited masks are as follows:

1. Darth Vader
2. Batman
3. Hannibal Lecter
4. Spider-Man
5. Jason Vorhees (*Friday the 13ᵗʰ*)
6. Mike Myers (*Halloween*)
7. Ironman
8. Zorro
9. The Phantom of the Opera
10. The Guy Fawkes mask (*V for Vendetta*)
11. Sauron
12. Captain America
13. Predator
14. Boba Fett
15. Ghostface (*Scream*)
16. Dr. Doom
17. The Loki Mask (*The Mask*)
18. Robocop
19. Maximus (*Gladiator*)
20. Jigsaw (*Saw*)

Of these twenty examples, the purpose and function of each mask differed. The reasons for wearing each mask ranged from hiding one's identity to hiding a disfigurement to defensive protection to high-tech functions, like a heads-up display (HUD). Roughly half of the characters on the list were villains, the other half were heroes, and *all were men*. Therefore, like a good masquerade, masks were worn by good and bad guys alike. However, when I considered what a mask meant in stories that focused on a heroine, I did, indeed, discover a massive distinction right away. And none of the Top 20 masks exemplified the Masked Minotaur.

Once again, when I grouped some of the best villains in heroine-centric stories, I noticed that the Masked Minotaur wore a very special kind of mask—*none*—which led me to an important conclusion. **To heroines, the mask that hides a villain is a human face.**

Such a mask is invisible to Google's algorithms, modern AI, and the analytic eyes of journalists who make lists. Therefore, I've put together my own Top 20 masks in heroine-led fiction. The villain's treacherous and tyrannical attitudes hide behind a face that often appears anywhere from plain and commonplace to handsome and socially elite.

1. George Wickham (*Pride and Prejudice*)
2. Nathan (*Ex Machina*)
3. President Snow (*Hunger Games*)
4. Carter Burke (*Aliens*)
5. Black Jack Randall (*Outlander*)
6. Iago (*Othello*)
7. Bill (*Kill Bill*)
8. Alphonso (*The Color Purple*)
9. Mother Gothel (*Tangled*)
10. Cal Hockley (*Titanic*)
11. Dr. Facilier (*The Princess and the Frog*)
12. Buffalo Bill (*The Silence of the Lambs*)
13. The T-1000 (*Terminator 2*)
14. The Other Mother (*Coraline*)
15. Heathcliff (*Wuthering Heights*)
16. Jade Fox (*Crouching Tiger, Hidden Dragon*)
17. Oz (*The Wizard of Oz*)
18. Bertha Mason (*Jane Eyre*)
19. Vidal (*Pan's Labyrinth*)
20. Joe Starks (*Their Eyes Were Watching God*)

I conclude that the perfect mask is no mask at all—such is the wisdom of our numerous heroines. I hope this analogy underscores why unmasking the Minotaur is so difficult for heroines in fiction and why this step is so important. The villainous mask is invisible to outside eyes, yet the heroine must unmask the Masked Minotaur if she is to defeat him (or her).

The Heroine's Growth Arc

At the beginning of the story, the inexperienced heroine acquiesces to the native culture and the Masked Minotaur to reconcile competing demands. In the middle of the story, the heroine circumvented her Captivity Bargain through a series of independent acts. She discovered secrets about her native culture while gaining precious knowledge and experience along the way. This exploration phase ended with a Broken Truce between our heroine and the native culture, which provoked the Masked Minotaur into recapturing her through a Poisoned Apple. The heroine is at a low point because the dark reality of the labyrinth makes escape seem impossible.

The final leg progresses with a heroine in crisis. The crisis captures the reality of the multiple conflicts that converge upon the heroine. *Remember, a heroine in crisis is not a damsel in distress.* She's a complex, three-dimensional character experiencing severe threats from within her native culture, where evil is disguised, and social forces work against her.

However, the heroine at the end of the story is a different woman than the heroine from chapter one. This story segment underscores the importance of including the Captivity Bargain early in our stories rather than skipping it. Some part of the readers or viewers should feel two things simultaneously, which is a sentiment to *accept the bargain and all this goes* away, while also digging in and thinking *time to make a stand once and for all.* The heroine wrestles with these two choices throughout the story, but the villain crosses a line with the Poisoned Apple. The heroine's claim to her Sacred Fire will not be honored. We see that now. **The heroine *must* assert herself or risk destruction.**

However, engaging the villain in the feminine monomyth requires an attack upon the core source of deception. The heroine will discover the true power of human illusions because the mask of the Minotaur can usually withstand several exposures. Bearing witness rarely breaks the illusions that surround the Masked Minotaur. The mask has been so carefully crafted, meticulously maintained, and custom-tailored to the labyrinth that even direct evidence of evil activity can be dismissed. The disguise holds.

Impotent Truth

In her essay "Truth and Politics," Hannah Arendt asks, "Is it of the very essence of truth to be impotent and of the very essence of power to be deceitful?" In this essay, she explores the phenomenon of what she calls "impotent truth," where influential people render vital truths to be of no consequence. And when incriminating truth is inconsequential, then evil propagates. Hannah tried to understand the phenomenon of evil within a culture—in this case, Germany, under the political control of the National Socialist Party. One of her conclusions was the ability of evil to reverse the moral function of truth—incriminating truth is perceived as meaningless lies, a threat to the power base, or simply unimportant.

How many stories depict a heroine giving a dire warning or sharing testimony that ultimately falls on deaf ears? The heroine pleads with other characters to believe her when she describes the evil activity of the Masked Minotaur. But she's often met with blank stares, doubt, or disbelief. Members of the native culture often assure her that there is no villain at the center of the labyrinth. When she insists, others may even question *her* sanity or health. **As the deceptive illusion holds up against the heroine's testimony, and the truth fails to change minds, our heroine recognizes that the source of evil is the mask itself that hides the Minotaur.**

From the psychological standpoint of the heroine, the problem of the Minotaur's mask is a big one. Unlike the hero's journey, whose villain is obvious and out in the open—think Thanos or Emperor Palpatine—the villain in the heroine's story remains hidden and often integrated within the home society. There will be no pitched battlelines where evil is disguised. Therefore, the heroine faces two problems if she is to fight deception.

First, if the heroine attacks the Minotaur while the mask is still up, she risks incriminating herself. Why? **Because the core deception of the Minotaur's mask is that the Minotaur is "good."** A mask of "good" allows the Minotaur to reverse the moral hierarchy. If the native culture perceives the Minotaur as "good," then anyone attacking the Minotaur must be "bad." Therefore, the heroine will be seen through the lens of the Minotaur's inverse morality. Secondly, if the heroine strikes and misses, the heroine has nowhere else to go. The narrative structure of the feminine monomyth doesn't feature a safe return home because the heroine is already home. She'll remain in the native culture alongside those who might condemn her for attacking the Masked Minotaur. Therefore, the mask creates a dangerous trap for the heroine.

If the heroine can rip off the mask to reveal the animal savagery of the Minotaur for a *brief* moment, she opens a precious window of opportunity where defeating the Minotaur becomes possible. Unmasking the Minotaur is not the same as *defeating* the Minotaur. The heroine is well aware that a highly manipulative and duplicitous villain can fully restore their disguise. That means the Unmasking is a critical moment in the story.

The good news is that if our heroine has formed the Feminine Triad, namely, the Beast as Ally and the Fragile Power, she won't be completely alone. Her actions, cause, and moral sensibilities have inspired supporters who come to her defense—and this takes *nothing* away from the heroine's heroic journey. Indeed, inspiring the Beast to her cause and identifying the hidden potential of the Fragile Power are the payoffs of her previous choices in the story. Heroic partners who align themselves publicly with the heroine stand as evidence that the heroine's claim of truth may be correct.

The Unmasking can be direct, like when Wonder Woman unmasks the feeble armistice broker to reveal Ares, the God of War. The Unmasking can be accidental, as when Dorothy's Fragile Power, Toto, pulls back the curtain to unmask the Wizard of Oz. Or, most commonly, the mask comes off during a power struggle between the heroine and the Minotaur late in the story. The benevolent humanity of the Minotaur dissolves, and the possessive animal moves to the forefront. The mask comes off if the heroine can reach this point—where the Minotaur must choose between moral restraint or animal possessiveness.

And the Minotaur always shows their true colors.

The Unmasking of the Minotaur is a fundamental aspect of the feminine monomyth because the mask has become the central object of deception. And writers should remember that the heroine's labyrinth isn't a warrior-oriented narrative model, even if the heroine has some training for self-defense or combat. **Therefore, removing the mask leads to a climactic moment of truth—of hidden evil exposed—and this has greater implications than the fight itself in many cases. The subtle shift in emphasis toward breaking sophisticated illusions may be the ultimate boon of wisdom embedded within the feminine monomyth.**

In *Beauty and the Beast*, Gaston elicits the admiration of tavern men and swoons from women throughout the town. In short, he's a social apex character. Beast, however, is a social outcast; outwardly, he's as beastly as they come. Early on, the Beast exhibits the same possessive love we saw in Gaston, but the Beast later in the story surrenders his possessorship. During the climax, Belle unmasks Gaston as the Minotaur when she declares, "He's no monster, Gaston. You are!" The contrast between the two archetypes, the Beast's unmasked humanity, and the Minotaur's unmasked tyranny, could not be more apparent. Their attitudes toward the heroine and her Sacred Fire separate the two characters.

In *Titanic*, Rose similarly unmasks the Minotaur when she declares, "I'd rather be his whore than your wife." The startling remark immediately contrasts Jack, the Beast as Ally, and Cal, the Masked Minotaur. And like Gaston, the socially beloved Cal Hockley cannot surrender his claim upon the heroine's Sacred Fire when the moment arrives. Instead, he slips into an unmasked murderous rage. "Damn it all to hell," he says, grabbing his bodyguard's pistol and turning to pursue Rose.

In *WandaVision*, Wanda Maximoff suspects a powerful Cult of Deception throughout the series. Not until late in the game does Wanda finally unmask Agatha Harkness, the nosey neighbor, as the Minotaur. Once unmasked, Agatha becomes uncompromising and aggressive. There is a scene where Agatha attempts to steal the Scarlet Witch's red chaos magic by physically pulling it out of Wanda's body. The scene is a perfect visual metaphor for how the Masked Minotaur seeks to steal and possess the Sacred Fire of the heroine.

In *Dangerous Liaisons*, we again begin with two twin characters of comparable values, the Beast and the Masked Minotaur. Vicomte de Valmont and the Marquise de Merteuil are wickedly manipulative aristocrats who use adultery and seduction as tools of power and egoism. The story's heroine is a religiously devoted and incorruptible Madame de Tourvel. After Valmont successfully seduces Tourvel, he slowly evolves and eventually feels inconsolable shame for his actions. Valmont is the Beast archetype because he chooses, in the end, to admit his moral wrongdoing to the heroine, even though he knows he's unforgivable. He commits suicide during a duel, but his final act is to release a bevy of incriminating letters, which unmasks the Marquise de Merteuil as the Minotaur of the story. The film's final scene shows the Marquise removing her mask.

In the Book of Esther, the Hebrew queen Esther is married to a Persian king. The king's primary advisor, Haman, deceives the king into ordering the execution of Jews throughout the kingdom. Before the evil campaign is launched, Esther famously unmasks the hidden Minotaur in their midst, saving countless lives. We should also recognize that had Esther failed to unmask Haman in the court of social power, she could have been executed for the accusation. This trap often hangs like a dark cloud over the heroine during the Unmasking.

While the movie *Coco* has a male lead character, the narrative structure perfectly follows all the beats of the heroine's labyrinth. Coco is at odds with his native culture, and the creative powers of songwriting and music consistently symbolize the Sacred Fire. The Masked Minotaur is the socially beloved idol Ernesto de la Cruz. In the story's climax, Ernes-

Esther Denouncing Haman to King Ahasuerus by Ernest Normand (1888).

to, the beloved king of entertainment in the underworld, is unmasked during the final struggle. The Unmasking created the window of opportunity for the inhabitants of the labyrinth to turn against the Minotaur.

Writers should recognize that an Unmasking can lead to the heroine's tragic death. One of the most famous Masked Minotaurs of all time is Iago in Shakespeare's play, *Othello*. Iago's mask has a renowned reputation for "honesty," which immediately reverses any accusations of dishonesty. When the heroine, Emilia, unmasks the treacherous Iago, the villain quickly kills her. Jafar serves a nearly identical role to Princess Jasmine in *Aladdin*.

Unmasking the Minotaur may be the most climactic event in the story. Although the central conflict is not yet resolved, the heroine must unmask the Minotaur before the Minotaur can be defeated. The heroine is at great risk at this moment in the story, for unmasking the Minotaur forces the villain to choose between their human and animal sides. The Unmasking also contrasts two different types of people in the heroine's life: the Beast as Ally and the Masked Minotaur. One character honors the heroine's claim to her Sacred Fire. The other character does not, and the Unmasking is the moment of truth.

Anatomy of an Archetype – The Unmasking

◊ The heroine unmasks the Minotaur by revealing the hidden forms of tyranny and ego.

◊ The Unmasking breaks the core deception of the story—that the Minotaur is "good."

◊ The pleasing human face of the Minotaur becomes ugly, deformed, tyrannical, or animalistic.

◊ The Unmasking may be the climax of the story.

◊ The Unmasking does not require a combat-style showdown.

◊ May result in a reformed villain

Exercises

1. How and when does Captain Marvel unmask the Minotaur in *Captain Marvel*?

2. In the film *Barbie*, the Kens end up taking over Barbieland. All the Barbies have fallen for a reverse world, where all the Kens are in control. How does Barbie unmask the Kens to restore Barbieland?

3. In the film *Moana*, how is the Unmasking moment a bit different? How does Moana unmask the Minotaur, and what happens as a result?

Tarot

Exposing a hidden evil is an archetypal event that demands resolution. Worse yet, the Unmasking will surely provoke a severe response from the story's most dangerous and treacherous character. The next card is in the Sun Position. Despite the sun's brilliant light that may reveal all that is hidden, the fiery rays may also be a sign of destruction. And so, we look upon the next card atop the deck with great trepidation.

Home as Battleground

HOME AS BATTLEGROUND

e turn the next card and see rampant flames in the beauty and comfort of a domicile. This card, perhaps more so than any other, we fear to behold. Upheaval, betrayal, chaos, and destruction are all implied in the image and are right in the heart of the home. I was stunned to see that so many climactic confrontations took place inside a house for heroine-led fiction. Dear writers, in so many heroine-led stories, the center of the labyrinth is home.

Home.

Home should be a safe place. Our home country is where millions of people live out our shared culture in real-time. Our home city is where we experience one unique cross-section of our native culture up close and well-explored. Our home neighborhood is where we played as children and where our children play now or one day. We eat, pray, celebrate, and socialize here. And our home is where we spend hours with the people we love most—our family and most trusted friends. Home is where we sometimes pass the time in peace and contemplation. Therefore, any story that features a final confrontation *here* brings all the terror and adrenaline of a deadly encounter alongside the emotional shock of ultimate betrayal.

A terrifying scenario forms in our subconscious without guidance—a shared nightmare throughout the animal world, carried over from humanity's most ancient daily life into the current age and likely to go on haunting us long into the future.

We stand in a familiar place. We perceive a trespasser, a malevolent presence that shouldn't be there, a feral predator that passes beyond our window, behind our door, or inside our very bedroom. We feel the paralysis of terror. Our heart quickens. Our breath stills as we hope to stay hidden. As the menacing figure draws closer and closer, we squeeze our eyes shut. In that blackness, we hope that the gaze of yellow eyes or the soft sniff of a bestial snout fails to detect us. And should the trespasser spot us, our primal instincts ignite, for we must freeze, flee, or fight to the death right where we stand.

Grappling with a dark entity inside the home is an archetypal event that's *millions* of years old. The above scenario has auto-populated the minds of each one of us at some point in a dream. The feeling is awful, and we remember it when we wake up. Sometimes, we're so bothered by the residual emotional terror that we tell someone about the dream as quickly as possible.

One of the most overlooked themes in the feminine monomyth revolves around where the dangerous confrontation occurs. Based on the narrative structure of the heroine's labyrinth, where forces within the native culture drive the conflict, we shouldn't be surprised that the final showdown takes place on familiar ground. I think Home as Battleground merits a profound distinction as a storytelling theme.

Home as Battleground moves the heroine into the Minotaur's path, and this time, the heroine cannot or will not retreat. **Our heroines repeatedly experience a story climax *inside* a house or on home turf.** Even famous short stories, such as Charlotte Perkins Gilman's *The Yellow Wallpaper* or Shirley Jackson's *The Lottery*, depict heroines on home turf.

The heroine's journey is a powerful and circular inward journey, so the center of the labyrinth isn't very far from where she started her journey. There, at the heart of a cultural sanctuary, an inner sanctum of regular life, the heroine enters battle with the *unmasked* Minotaur. At a glance, we may tell ourselves, okay, the climax is here, and it makes sense that the setting would be in the home or on home turf. But we shouldn't take the psychology of such a battle so lightly. Home as Battleground is an ancient archetypal nightmare.

I believe these stories and scenarios reflect artistic expressions of primal fear and a residual conflict repeated through time and across any culture.

Whereas the warrior-oriented hero usually travels outward to confront the Distant Dragon upon the *villain's* home turf, our heroines tend to go into battle right in the heart of a household, surrounded by the symbols and objects of her own native culture, and in places where she thought herself safe. **These are environments where everyday life occurs, where the heroine has invested her trust, and where daily rhythms and cycles pass through private spaces. Now, these communal settings are rendered compromised, mere background noise to a struggle.** And there stands the Minotaur. In its unmasked state, the Minotaur is a terrifying monster. Unlike the Poisoned Apple, where the Masked Minotaur attempted to subdue, capture, or convert the heroine, the unmasked Minotaur is willing to harm or kill the heroine by this point.

Consider the heroine-centric film *The Terminator.* The Masked Minotaur not only invades the home of Sarah Connor but continues to break all the rules of expected safe havens within the native culture. Sarah's first instinct is to hide in a crowded public place, such as the Tech Noir nightclub. However, the Terminator attacks the heroine in public anyway. Then, in an iconic and unforgettable scene, the Masked Minotaur of the story brazenly invades one of the *safest* places available to the heroine, a police station. The scene perfectly embodies the primal horror of a hostile force invading an inner sanctum.

No Retreat

As stated in the last chapter, the heroine must be mentally and spiritually prepared for some level of confrontation at this point. Home as Battleground presents us with an unusual dynamic for the heroine in the labyrinth.

There's nowhere else to go.

If the heroine retreats, she'll knowingly abandon her home to evil forces. Therefore, when the heroine unmasks the Minotaur, she instinctively understands that fighting the Minotaur will determine the fate of "home" itself. The heroine has emerged as a legitimate moral alternative within the physical space, and her point of view is incompatible with the views of the Minotaur.

The reason the heroine is unwilling to submit to or compromise with the Minotaur during the final stretch is no longer merely for her independence. The heroine's distinct moral position—now clear, visible, and understood when contrasted to the Minotaur—*requires independence to exist.* She fights because obeying or negotiating with the Minotaur only enables an immoral position that contradicts the heroine's beliefs. Therefore, the final confrontation is less about fighting the Minotaur and more about refusing the moral code of the Minotaur to occupy the home space.

For example, when Ken takes over Barbie's Dreamhouse, Barbie faces the loss of independence and the final surrender of her Sacred Fire. The inner sanctum has been compromised in full. Here, we arrive at the crossroads of competing claims to the heroine's Sacred Fire. There's a sense of irreconcilable worldviews and a contest for autonomy.

Not all systems of ethics can coexist, so the heroine's conflict often reflects contradictions, moral failings, and social abuses right within the home. The meaning and symbolism behind Home as Battleground convinced me that the heroine's labyrinth is not a narrative model that perpetuates old tropes. Instead, it can be a tool for challenging the native culture, harmful traditions, gender roles, or modes of life that allowed the Masked Minotaur to flourish in the first place.

Looking at our modern stories, I found countless examples of hero-ine-centric stories in which the battleground is at home. It's incredible to see so many examples of this pattern, and in some ways, I'm surprised I never noticed it before.

Hunger Games is a classic example of the heroine's labyrinth. The heroine's native culture is Panem's District 12. Once again, home, fam-ily, and friends are not safe. President Snow hides in plain sight with a benevolent outward face and a hidden tyrannical face. Katniss Ever-deen fights on her native soil. Author Susan Collins even states that she modeled the Hunger Games storyline on Greek mythology, where the native culture sacrifices seven boys and seven girls each year to a Minotaur inside a maze. Here again, we see the components of the psyche successfully recycled into new stories in new ways, yet the basic archetypes remain. And we continue to respond to them.

In *The Color Purple* (1985), the story is replete with a world of interconnected labyrinths; home after home has a Minotaur within. Celie's father is the tyrant of her first home; she goes on to marry a widower named "Mister," who is the tyrant of her new home. No place is safe, and battles are often fought—and sometimes lost—right inside the places Celie calls "home." Incredible acts of brutality and violence, including sexual assault, all occur behind the closed doors of private spaces. Home is an ongoing battleground throughout the story, and the heroine never truly escapes the labyrinth.

In *Kill Bill*, Beatrix Kiddo makes her way through two films before finally arriving at the center of the labyrinth—a cozy, affluent, residen-tial household. The Minotaur has been awaiting her. However, the her-oine also encounters her daughter, the Fragile Power, for the first time in this home. The girl wears pajamas and frolics about in pure inno-cence, causing our heroine to suspend the long-awaited battle. Beatrix even assumes the mantle of motherhood as if role-playing in a dream of what could have been. Home is Beatrix Kiddo's final battleground.

For Clarice Starling, the center of the labyrinth is also an innocent-look-ing suburban residence. She sees a familiar commonplace setting—a dusty living room and messy kitchen. But this familiar place transforms as Clarice descends into a menacing underground labyrinth where the heroine stalks the Minotaur. The home is Clarice's final battleground.

A similar scenario occurs in the 2022 film *Barbarian*, where a dangerous maze and dark secrets exist just below a residential home.

Coraline Jones also unmasks a Minotaur in the center of her home, her "Other" Mother. The final battle begins in a replica of Coraline's living room. The pattern in the hardwood floor transforms into a deadly three-dimensional spiderweb, and the furniture pieces suddenly appear as insects caught in the web. The unmasked Minotaur descends upon the heroine, but all within the home.

In *Tangled*, after exploring her native culture, Rapunzel discovers that the center of the labyrinth is the very starting point of the journey—her tower bedroom. There, within the inner sanctum of her private life, our heroine unmasks Mother Gothel once and for all. The looming confrontation occurs on the most personal and familiar ground to Rapunzel.

Ex Machina presents a similar situation. The android Ava is held captive in a high-tech labyrinth, which is actually a residential fortress, the home of the Masked Minotaur. Like Rapunzel, her final battle is against her captor, which takes place in the halls of the only home Ava ever occupied.

Frozen also features two heroine sisters, Anna and Elsa. In one scene, Princess Elsa experiences a full-scale invasion of her ice castle by members of the native culture. In another scene, Princess Anna unmasks Prince Hans, a tyrant disguised in the veneer of a charming suitor prince. The final battle occurs throughout Arendelle, in and around the home of both sisters.

In the final episodes of *The Clone Wars*, seasons 5 and 7, beloved heroine Ahsoka Tano clashes against the forces of her native culture on her home turf as well. The show maximizes the themes of betrayal in familiar places, and the heroine is outnumbered and overmatched. However, the truth remains that the Jedi Order of the Galactic Republic—the place that Ahsoka most trusted and called home for so many years—becomes the battleground for her very survival.

Anatomy of an Archetype – Home as Battleground

◊ The home itself is often at the center of the heroine's labyrinth.

◊ An invasion of the inner sanctum signals that even the safest places have been compromised by the Minotaur.

◊ If a final confrontation occurs, it takes place on familiar ground, within the home, or in a home-like environment.

◊ The symbolic meaning behind Home as Battleground is a contest of the heroine's will against the Minotaur's power.

◊ The confrontation is usually against the *unmasked* Minotaur, who becomes animalistic and tyrannical in full.

Exercises

1. In the Hulu original movie *Prey*, the young Comanche heroine, Naru, confronts a predator on her home turf. In what ways does the story show a threat to the symbols, objects, and animals of the heroine's native culture?

2. Scarlett O'Hara has one deadly confrontation in the novel *Gone with the Wind*. Where does the confrontation occur, and who is the Fragile Power that shares this setting with the heroine?

3. The horror genre centers heavily on the archetypal Home as Battleground. List five to ten of your favorite horror flicks. How many of them feature a heroine and Home as Battleground?

Tarot

The deck can be cruel to our heroine. The ultimate danger the heroine feared most has come to the forefront. The next card calls into force the cosmic need for balance—the heroine's response to overwhelming odds. Confrontation, danger, and the invasion of the heroine's inner sanctum release a frightening cosmic energy, a call for help that will not be answered. And so, we are left with the heroine alone. The next card is in the Warrior Position, signaling previously unknown courage and hidden bravery.

The Shieldmaiden

THE SHIELDMAIDEN

he Shieldmaiden is the most powerful card in the heroine's tarot deck and one of the most extraordinary archetypal events in all storytelling. Perhaps nowhere is heroism more clear and overt, more primal and present, more shocking and inspiring than the heroine's spontaneous transformation into the Shieldmaiden. It's heroism at its purest level and occurs in the blink of an eye.

Structurally, the Shieldmaiden most commonly emerges during the final confrontation with the Minotaur in the third act. It can occur earlier in a story as an emergence moment for a heroine, but the significance of such a transformation has the greatest impact during the climax. **The Shieldmaiden is when the heroine physically interposes herself between the Minotaur and a defenseless character, typically just a few feet away.** The heroine blocks the Minotaur to prevent harm to another. The heroine might be wearing full armor or an evening dress.

It doesn't matter.

Symbolically, the heroine becomes a human shield against power, violence, brutality, and destruction. She stares evil in the eye and stands her ground against a physical force as the first and *only* responder. The more I recognize the Shieldmaiden in stories, the more stirred I am by her decisive action. The Shieldmaiden represents an extraordinary dynamic for confrontation in fiction because it carries a dual role. The heroine must not only stop the fearsome Minotaur, a proximate and physical threat, but she also protects another potential victim who shares the space with her.

The heroine is *not* acting in the manner of self-sacrifice, although it may appear that way—for her goal is to deny the Minotaur's advance, if even by one step. She's drawn a red line in the sand. The heroine often moves suddenly and instinctively into the Minotaur's path as a preventative measure, fully conscious that her act carries all the gravity of a deadly escalation. She rises to this challenge because failure is not an option. If she fails, not only might she be captured or destroyed, but the life she defends might also be captured or destroyed.

The Shieldmaiden moment is both a point of no return and an all-or-nothing gamble.

The very concept of a Shieldmaiden is a powerful archetype because the woman herself acts as a physical barrier, a human shield, to withstand brute aggression in defense of fragile life. The dual purpose of the heroine's confrontation is both dynamic and distinguishable from the pure single combat of the hero. **As viewers or readers, we become the defenseless person observing the battle from behind the heroine. She's our last line of defense.** All of nature, it seems, recognizes this red line when drawn by the heroine. And the more menacing the Minotaur, the more heroic the heroine.

How does the final confrontation of the heroine's labyrinth contrast with the hero's journey?

The warrior-oriented hero typically confronts the Distant Dragon in single combat in the hero's journey. The battle's significance usually emphasizes competency, virtue, and worthiness for the hero, to which the hero has devoted much training. The dark and light archetypes stand in opposition to each other in perfect contrast. Good versus evil. The potent imagery impacts us when we see it. Whether it's Luke Skywalker crossing lightsabers with Darth Vader, Neo turning to face Agent Smith, or a gunslinger staring down the lawless bandit, the archetypal design rings true. The hero has undergone a transformative trial and has the confidence, willingness, and ability to fight a militant villain who never loses. The hero challenges the evil alpha. Like two rams facing off in nature, the recurrent theme tells readers or viewers that we are in the story's final stages. The hero and villain will resolve the central conflict in this battle.

However, inside the heroine's labyrinth, where the battlefield is often at home or upon home turf, the heroine faces off against a different enemy. She frequently faces a villain she once trusted. There is an intimacy to the danger and the risk of disturbing preexisting relationships and general order. The heroine is rarely concerned with worthiness in her final confrontation. Her rush toward danger is a superrational act, not a calculated strategy.

The Shieldmaiden persona emerges whether or not the heroine has training and whether or not she's prepared for the confrontation. The archetypal power of such a moment resonates at such a high level when we contrast it against the heroine's Captivity Bargain at the beginning of the story. We'll be amazed that this is the same character, yet the heroine has earned this moment. Here, the heroine does not yield. We *feel* the evolution of her personality as we witness her actions. We fully understand the danger to the heroine, just as we perceive the threat to the person she defends. Our primal psyches recognize the confrontation on a subconscious level.

While the heroine's labyrinth doesn't stem from the warrior-oriented arc, the Shieldmaiden shows us that a physical threshold still exists, and many heroines, warrior or not, are prepared to cross this threshold.

And what about the feminine warrior? They are widespread in fiction and history. While the heroine's labyrinth tends to veer away from many warrior tropes, it's worth emphasizing that heroines may be a warrior or trained as a warrior nonetheless. I even went so far as to examine the feminine warrior *in story terms* to see if I found any patterns or narrative symbolism unique or distinctive to our heroines. Perhaps now's the time to discuss literary fiction's most common feminine warrior. In searching for recurrent archetypal patterns in the feminine warrior, there does seem to be a *preferred* warrior class. Whereas the Shieldmaiden is a warrior persona that any heroine may assume when the moment arises, perhaps no other warrior type is more espoused by women than that of the Archer-Huntress.

Archer-Huntress

Katniss Everdeen is a great example of a feminine warrior. She did not learn archery for war. She learned it to hunt for food to feed her family. Her skill set is that of a hunter in the traditional sense. However, when applied in the survivalism of the Hunger Games, her bow becomes a deadly weapon of attack. The feminine warrior is a powerful and evocative archetype that spans all cultures. From Joan of Arc to Nakano Takeko to the all-female Dahomey Mino army of West Africa to the vaunted Valkyries of Norway, the heroic warrior woman appears in full regalia, armed and ready for battle. Like her male warrior counterpart, she symbolizes cultural vigilance and vitality. Her valor is unquestionable.

The sword may be a masculine symbol for outward combat, but the bow and arrow are excellent symbols of inner peace and deadly focus. When a heroine draws back on a bowstring, she is harnessing all her innermost powers, holding the pose by stabilizing the body, and using the senses to adjust and readjust before firing the arrow with purpose. The act is not unlike yoga, in which stability, balance, focus, strength, and concentration are paramount. The physical skill set is insanely demanding, as anyone who has attempted high-level yoga can attest. The archer-huntress is nimble, highly mobile, and can strike from afar.

We see timeless Artemis reborn as Katniss Everdeen from *The Hunger Games* or Neytiri from *Avatar*. But the list is a long one. Merida from *Brave*, Susan Pevensie from *The Chronicles of Narnia*, Kate Bishop in *Hawkeye*, the goddess Diana, Lara Croft in *Tomb Raider*, Omega in *The Bad Batch*, and the Grand Huntress herself, Phara Keaen, in *Foundation* all used bows as their preferred weapon. Even the word "Amazon" means "no breast" in Greek because the Amazon warrior women removed one breast to prevent interference with a drawn bowstring.

As writers, we are not confined to the bow but know that the relationship between a heroine and archery is ancient. Something resonates here. The archer-huntress is a powerful feminine archetype, a fighting woman who moves quickly, acts precisely, and knows the hunter's virtues of patience, stillness, sustained strength, control over the body, attention to nature and surroundings, and accuracy of the shot. The archetypal hunter hunts out of necessity to feed and protect the family.

The Shield as a Weapon

While studying goddesses for the heroine's labyrinth, I was struck by the imagery of Durga, the fearsome Hindu goddess of motherhood, strength, and creative destruction. She has multiple arms and carries both the bow of the archer huntress and the shield of the Shieldmaiden. As weapons, the bow is for offense, and the shield is for defense. The shield stays close to the body; it's intimate and personal, protective, and wards off aggressive strikes or incoming arrows. The shield is designed to endure a *sustained* attack in conjunction with a possible counterstrike if necessary. However, I've reconsidered the full scope of the shield's symbolism when viewed through the lens of the heroine's labyrinth.

I originally included a chapter called "Defeating the Minotaur" or "Slaying the Minotaur," but I realized that the heroine's tale is not the same as the hero's warrior-oriented tale. Slaying the Dragon is an essential climactic step in the hero's journey, the final culmination of growth and maturity, where victory demonstrates the hero's self-actualization within the framework of the story's conflicts.

The heroine's confrontation differs from the hero's journey. I think this is important because, in warrior-oriented heroic fights, combat often reflects a military or tactical battle—the hero may engage, withdraw, reengage, or even retreat, if possible. The battle may stretch over long distances and may involve a strategic pursuit. For those who don't know, "withdrawing" in a military sense is not the same as retreating. To retreat is to flee for your life, usually forced upon the retreating member or group by the enemy. To withdraw is to strategically disengage and reposition before resuming an attack. It's a strategic choice. However, for many of the confrontations in heroine-centric stories, the very nature of the conflict doesn't usually follow the same tactical style. **The heroine will not withdraw because to do so would be to abandon the defenseless life and destroy the purpose and motive behind her stand.**

But after studying so many heroine stories, especially novels, I couldn't avoid the reality that showdowns were either much smaller on average or not present in the story's climax at all. I had to remind myself that the heroine's labyrinth is distinctive and that even my preconceived notions of what a "climax" might look like had to be revisited. The Shieldmaiden—her stand, motives, and resolve—made me realize that the shield, while clearly a defensive tool, might be the heroine's greatest weapon.

By enduring the onslaught of the Minotaur, by withstanding and holding firm, the heroine exposes the Masked Minotaur for what they are. This wholly present fortitude in the face of physical or social brutality highlights the ultimate source of control and illusion. The Shieldmaiden's stand breaks the deception that the Minotaur is "good" once and for all. Therefore, the shield protects the heroine but may also become the object against which the Masked Minotaur shatters. For a heroine, standing up to brutality doesn't mean she must match or become brutality.

The consequential confrontation is often less about the physical victory over the Minotaur as it is the disintegration of a mode of life, where something dishonest, destructive, repressive, deceptive, or tyrannical is exposed through the heroic actions and personal convictions of the heroine. The final showdown may indeed include a traditional fight—but not always. I believe it's possible that the hero's journey might have even conditioned writers and readers to expect a showdown or that we believe that showdowns are the most exciting way to resolve the story's conflicts. But as enlightened writers who know of the heroine's labyrinth and the Shieldmaiden, we can allow for a broader range of climax and resolution.

A Physio-Visual Archetype

As readers or viewers, we hold our breath when the heroine suddenly waxes radiant as the Shieldmaiden. So many stories project the confrontation between the heroine and the Minotaur right onto the pages and big screen. I found examples of the Shieldmaiden nearly everywhere I looked, and some heroines became icons during their Shieldmaiden moments.

In *Aliens*, Lieutenant Ellen Ripley, the so-called "fifth wheel" of the marine platoon at the beginning of the story, becomes the Shieldmaiden at the end. When the Queen pursues Ripley back to the orbiting *Sulaco*, Ripley knows she's overmatched. After she distracts the Queen Alien from focusing on Newt, Ripley's next instinct is to retreat. However, while running away is understandable, "retreat" fails to meet the superrational logic of the Shieldmaiden because poor Newt is left undefended. Therefore, Ripley rises to an impossible moment. She must transcend the simple logic of retreat and self-preservation. The heroine reengages the battlespace in a hydraulic loader and confronts the Queen Alien. Ripley stands her ground now as the ultimate Shieldmaiden and her renewed presence assures us that retreating is no longer an option. Newt is in the room with Ripley, just a few feet away, so the red line must be enforced by her alone. Ripley's Shieldmaiden moment is perhaps one of the most famous of all time. But Ripley isn't alone by a long shot.

In *Wonder Woman* (2017), Diana Prince strides across No-Man's Land's barren, war-ravaged landscape. Behind her, the Allied forces hide in the trenches. When the German army opens fire, Wonder Woman raises her shield. There, she endures a blistering hail of machine-gun fire, her legs buckling under the strain, herself the only target on the battlefield. Yet she stands as a singular force against the mechanized might of an entire army.

In the novel *Jane Eyre*, the hidden Minotaur (Bertha) strikes Mr. Rochester by lighting his room on fire. Jane is the first and only responder. The heroine rushes into the blazing room to find Mr. Rochester unconscious and unable to wake. She saves his life by pulling him to safety.

In *Frozen*, we get an incredible visual for the Shieldmaiden. Princess Elsa is about to be struck down by the sword of the villainous Prince Hans. Princess Anna steps in at the last second between her sister and the Minotaur. She transforms into a physical shield, a statue of unbreakable ice with Elsa just behind her. The Minotaur's sword shatters against Anna's hand.

In *Avengers: Infinity War*, Vision collapses on the battlefield and cannot fight. The indestructible Thanos advances upon Vision as a relentless force, battering aside some of the best superheroes in the MCU. However, the last line of defense is a heroine, as we've come to expect, the Scarlet Witch. In a perfect image of the Shieldmaiden, we see the heroine physically in between an advancing brutal force, warding him off, while a weakened Vision lies helpless on the ground behind her.

Another excellent Shieldmaiden moment occurs in *Game of Thrones*, Season 1, Episode 2, "The Kingsroad." Catelyn Stark checks on her recently paralyzed son, Bran, who lies defenselessly asleep in his bedroom. When Catelyn enters her son's room, she sees an assassin with a knife about to strike. When the killer raises his knife, Catelyn doesn't even think about it. She rushes between the assassin and Bran, grabs the blade with her *bare hand*, and staves off the attack.

In *The Return of the King*, the Witch-king of Angmar attacks King Théoden, tossing him to the ground like a ragdoll. When the giant winged beast comes in for the kill, Éowyn steps directly into its path. "You shall not touch him," declares the heroine, sword and shield at the ready. Again, we see the heroine physically interposing herself between overpowering danger and a defenseless person. When the Witch-king declares that "No man can kill me," our Shieldmaiden famously responds, "I am no man."

In *Moana*, Maui falls wounded in the final battle and loses his magic weapon. He's defenseless. The Masked Minotaur of the story, Te Ka, rears back for a fatal blow. But Moana lifts the pounamu stone to the sky, and the green luminance stops the Minotaur in its tracks. Moana then walks right up to the villain, showing no signs of fear or apprehension. Once again, the heroine is both unassisted and clear-minded. With stunning visual impact, Moana returns the stolen Sacred Fire of the goddess before pressing her forehead against the Minotaur in a show of love and understanding.

In the horror film *Poltergeist*, Diane Freeling quietly tends to the laundry when she hears her daughter's alarming scream. She doesn't calculate her chances. Unprepared and wearing only a nightshirt, the heroine charges down the hallway alone to confront whatever demonic power awaits behind the door.

Sarah Connor faces down a nearly invincible T-1000 in *Terminator 2*. In this film, she's fully trained in tactical combat and weaponry. Near the movie's end, Sarah stands her ground as the seemingly invincible villain approaches—John Connor stands behind her. She then repeatedly discharges her shotgun at the Minotaur, blasting holes into the liquid metal and backing the T-1000 up to the platform's edge.

At the end of *A Quiet Place*, a deaf girl named Regan Abbott stands in paralyzed fear as a killer creature approaches. At the last second, Regan's mother, Evelyn, steps in front of the monster, eyeball to eyeball, and empties both shotgun barrels at point-blank range.

In *Ex Machina*, the android heroine, Ava, escapes her imprisonment inside the labyrinth. The Shieldmaiden scenario arises when Nathan, the Masked Minotaur of the story, issues a parental command to "Go back to your room." Once again, the heroine calmly approaches the Minotaur before breaking into a full charge. We further see the imagery of the human shield, the physical object of defense, when Nathan bludgeons Ava's robotic arms into mangled stumps.

In the popular Netflix series *Stranger Things*, the young heroine Eleven regularly steps in front of dangerous creatures to protect her friends. A nosebleed always follows our heroine's Shieldmaiden moments.

In *Star Trek: The Motion Picture*, the Shieldmaiden archetype reappears during the climax. When Commander Decker keys the final sequence by hand to join with V'Ger, Captain Kirk moves to stop him.

But Lieutenant Ilia steps in Kirk's path and shoves him to the ground like a rag doll. The red line will not be crossed.

We get a sad reminder that Shieldmaidens can also fail. In *Conan the Barbarian*, cult warriors sack young Conan's village. When the evil warriors approach young Conan, his mother stands before him, defiantly raising her sword at the enemy. But Thulsa Doom delivers a Poisoned Apple through a spell of hypnosis upon Conan's mother, bypassing her ability to defend herself. While in the altered state, Thulsa slays the mother. However, at the end of the film, Conan is knocked down during the final battle and fails to parry an incoming sword strike. But the ghost of the feminine warrior, Valeria, assumes the role of Shieldmaiden and stops the blow. "You wanna live forever?" she asks.

In *Avatar*, the hero's journey battle between Jake Sully and Colonel Quaritch is underway. The Minotaur is about to deliver a fatal blow. But our heroine, Neytiri, leaps in and interposes herself between Quaritch and a defenseless Jake Sully, hissing a deadly warning.

In *The Fifth Element*, once again, we see the physical body of the heroine as symbolizing a shield. Here's another film that appears to be about a hero, Corbin Dallas (Bruce Willis), when it's actually a heroine-centric story. Leeloo *is* the fifth element. Her mantra, "Protect Life," sums up the primal instinct that drives the Shieldmaiden. At the end of the story, her very essence, her Sacred Fire, becomes the shield that staves off the world's destruction.

Do male characters ever rise to the role of Shieldmaiden? Yes. Gandalf the Grey makes a red line against the Balrog when he famously declares, "You shall not pass!" He didn't go on offense but made a life-or-death defensive show of force with a literal demarcation line. Behind him, the Fellowship stood no chance. And recently, an incredible Shieldmaiden moment occurred in *Spiderman: No Way Home*. During the final confrontation with the masked Green Goblin, Toby McGuire's Spiderman notices that Tom Holland's Spiderman has lost all emotional control during the battle and fully intends to murder the villain. But the villain is under a form of mind control and has a claim to innocence. Right before Holland's Spider-Man enacts his immoral vengeance, McGuire's Spider-Man leaps in front and stops him. The two heroes speak no words, but the imagery is clear: **life behind, brutality in front, and the Shieldmaiden in between.** It's striking. For added symbolism, the battle takes place upon the giant bronze Captain America *shield* that fell from Lady Liberty herself.

So, we've made it to the ending segment of the story, and the heroine is contesting the will of the Masked Minotaur. She's reached a moment of clarity in her quest where the uncompromising villain moves in on someone or something the heroine intends to deny. Consider the physicality of her blocking the path of the Minotaur. Have her stand in the way. Show that she's drawn a demarcation line upon which the Minotaur cannot cross. She's the sole authority of this red line. As a storyteller, you've created a scene that demands split-second resolution. It's a point of no return for your heroine. What does the Minotaur do? What will the heroine endure as a result? What will it cost her? Will she survive a confrontation with raw brutality? What happens to the defenseless character right behind her?

All of these questions generate the height of a dramatic moment in storytelling, and the heroine has her moment. Good and evil come face to face within the heroine's labyrinth.

Anatomy of an Archetype – The Shieldmaiden

◊ The heroine physically interposes herself between the Minotaur and a defenseless person.

◊ The heroine's body symbolizes a physical shield and a red line.

◊ The heroine's primary goal is to block the Minotaur's advance.

◊ A defenseless person shares the room or space with the heroine, usually a few feet away.

◊ The heroine intends to survive the confrontation, not sacrifice herself.

◊ The heroine risks severe physical harm even if she's not trained for combat.

◊ The heroine often withstands any or all retribution.

Exercises

1. In Stephanie Myers' *Twilight* saga, what was Bella Swan's initial power, and how did this expand once she became a vampire?

2. In film, a Shieldmaiden moment is dramatic and easy to spot, whereas in a novel, an author must rely on the reader's imagination. Now, think of a heroine-centric novel that doesn't have a film adaptation yet. Can you spot a moment in a chapter that meets the criteria for the Shieldmaiden?

3. Can you spot two Shieldmaiden moments from two different heroines in *The Incredibles*?

4. Enjoy a watch or rewatch of *Everything Everywhere All at Once*, and as the film moves toward the conclusion, can you spot Evelyn Wang's Shieldmaiden moment?

Tarot

The goddess of power descends, filling our mortal heroine with all the radiance of the divine feminine. We see that the Minotaur cannot withstand the clarity and conviction of the heroine's stance. It is as though the blinding light confuses, disrupts, and shocks the Minotaur, stealing away all the dark energy that fills their heart with the will to dominate. And in that vacated space, the will of the heroine presses forward. The Shieldmaiden archetype transcends time and culture and emerges in our stories with stunning regularity. The next card is in the Outcome Position, and we must turn it to understand the aftermath.

The Broken Spell

THE BROKEN SPELL

inally! We feel relief at seeing a card with greenery, beautiful flowers, life, and a radiant spectral sky. Something
unmistakably *good* has come about. The heroine's story
culminated in a dynamic confrontation, and here, we
have some resolution—harmony, balance, and beauty. In archetypal
terms, the heroine overcomes the evil within the labyrinth. **Therefore,
the Broken Spell is the rapid rearrangement of the native culture
from a dark labyrinth into a restored or idealized world.**

We humans like a bit of magic in our stories, and sometimes, the
end of a story feels magical. Loose ends are suddenly tied up, and the
heroine, who stood her ground against the Minotaur, achieves some
finality. The heroine's story can end in different ways. It can end dra-
matically, where a rapid transformation of the native culture sweeps
through the story, upturning all that was bad with all that is good
again. Her tale can end tragically, or it can end quietly, where the resolution is a more private affair.

Whatever the result, heroine-centric stories have recurrent patterns
in the aftermath of the heroine's clash with the Minotaur. The Broken
Spell is likely a derivative of the fairy tales and folklore of long ago,

where the evils of a story are magically imposed. In modern stories, magic or technology may still be at the center of the Broken Spell. Still, I believe that the "magical transformation" stems from archetypal truths hidden deep within the realm of human reality. Why *would* so much change so quickly, as if by magic?

The Core Deception

As we learned, the core deception stems from the mask of the Minotaur, which is all based on one lie—that the Minotaur is "good." The mask hides the fundamental truth—that the Minotaur is also "evil." The Minotaur's possessive, animal nature is dominant but hidden. Therefore, whenever the Masked Minotaur leaves evidence of his true and evil self in the real world, a lie must be told to cover up the evidence or alter the context of their evil actions. One by one, these smaller lies accumulate and build a system of illusions tied to the original lie—that the Minotaur is "good." The inhabitants of the labyrinth can't believe one lie and reject another. No—the web of lies must be accepted in its entire form, which allows the deception to be maintained. Therefore, structurally, when the heroine unmasks the Minotaur, she breaks the core illusion—the Minotaur is good—and instead exposes the truth—the Minotaur is evil.

Once this truth is exposed, the core deception can no longer exist. All the lies get overturned at the same moment. Reality is accepted, and the Cult of Deception collapses.

Indeed, reflecting upon lies is a psychological form of trauma. One or many different characters can see the world as it is, maybe for the first time. That's why some stories symbolically depict a magical transformation of the native culture. A revelation of truth is a climactic event in the story by itself. It doesn't always require combat against the Minotaur because the damage has already been done. **Truth and the Minotaur cannot coexist.**

Quiet Victories

A magical transformation may not be the appropriate ending for every heroine story. But something true about the world came about through the heroine's actions, and something true always matters.

Literature features numerous stories where the Broken Spell is a quiet affair. Ebbs and flows and the basic rhythms of the native culture feel or seem to be mostly unchanged. In these stories, breaking the power of the Masked Minotaur is most likely a private affair. The Minotaur's tyranny over a household or individual didn't impact the society at large, so when the reign of the Minotaur comes to an end, the native culture continues. In these stories, the heroine has freed herself privately, not publicly, and these quiet victories can often be the most poignant.

Many great works of literature feature a quiet Broken Spell. In *Their Eyes Were Watching God*, the narrator provides examples of all the gossip about Janie. She's cast in a suspicious light over the death of Tea Cake, and the townsfolk all assume the worst about Janie. The Broken Spell occurs once she's acquitted and the truth comes out about her innocence. All the gossiping townsfolk suddenly change their tune about Janie as they align themselves with the truth. Both *Jane Eyre* and *The Scarlet Letter* offer less satisfying resolutions to the heroine, but the Broken Spell occurs at the bitter end when it's too late.

Though less dramatic, these quiet victories are no less important. In fact, the quiet Broken Spell is the most likely version of the archetypal event. Most life changes are of a minor, more intimate nature. The heroine may break the spell of a Minotaur over the household without changing the overarching society. For example, Ma in *Room* escapes hostile captivity with her son but doesn't change the underlying causes of abduction or sexual assault in society. In fact, she doesn't even change her father's outlook on the situation. The quiet victory doesn't render Ma's Broken Spell any less impactful. Remember that stories are about individual characters and what they overcome. The Broken Spell frees our heroine as well as anyone they protect. The reverberations of the Broken Spell may affect a small space or group of people, or they may shake the foundations of the native culture as a whole.

A Return to Light

The death or defeat of the Minotaur represents the end of a tyrannical reign within the native culture. The heroine has simultaneously resolved the Captivity Bargain and the Broken Truce, meaning she has achieved significant autonomy and social power within the labyrinth. A spell has been broken. Light pours into the darkness, the tyrannized are set free, and life returns.

I still found numerous stories featuring the dramatic Broken Spell, in which a rapid return of goodness and luminance swept over the native culture. Such rapid, often magical recoveries for the native culture suggest that the suppression of truth allowed tyrannical realities to exist in the world. The suppression of truth is accompanied by the propagation of lies and explanations that the labyrinth inhabitants are willing to believe. The Cult of Deception has an almost magical power over society, as the heroine has learned. Inhabitants of the native culture are spellbound, conditioned, or made evil by the deceptive efforts of the Masked Minotaur. Once the Minotaur is decisively unmasked, this mysterious and destructive way of thinking vanishes.

Wonder Woman (2017) addresses the idea of a spell when discussing the German army in World War I. She believes that the ongoing world war is a corruption of the Masked Minotaur of the story. She explains, "But Ares is *behind* that corruption. It is Ares who has *these Germans* fighting. And stopping the God of War is our foreordinance." In her statement, Wonder Woman blames the Cult of Deception, the spellbinding spirit of warfare that directs all men to their doom. Break the spell, end the war.

The Broken Spell is most prominent in the fables and fairy tales, where the allegory is more literal. Think of *Swan Lake*, *Cinderella*, and *Beauty and the Beast*. The Broken Spell literally spreads across the screen or stage like a magical wave of color and light. The transformation is the "rearrangement" of the final stretch. Even in modern retellings, such as *Moana*, once the Masked Minotaur is overcome, beautiful, life-filled green earth floods and spirals back into the world in the most satisfying way possible.

However, you'll find the same Broken Spell even in modern, heroine-centric stories. As mentioned, *Wonder Woman* (2017) features a powerful Broken Spell. At the film's end, once Wonder Woman defeats Ares, the spell breaks, and the dark skies turn to a glowing sunrise. The hell-like fire blazing all around her goes out, and the surviving soldiers stop fighting each other and smile over the obvious beauty in the world. In *Mad Max: Fury Road*, the Broken Spell occurs when the inhabitants turn the valves, and life-giving water gushes forth for all. The spirit of celebration overtakes the War Boys and starving citizens alike. In *The Silence of the Lambs*, Clarice Starling is inside a dark and nightmarish labyrinth, the basement of Buffalo Bill. Almost immediately after she shoots the Masked Minotaur, a window is unblocked, and sunlight pours into the basement. The camera focuses on the more pleasant image of a butterfly decoration. *Ex Machina* also features a Broken Spell for the heroine. Ava leaves her claustrophobic and captive labyrinth to enter a bright and open society in a white dress, ready to experience her humanity on her terms. Likewise, in *Barbie*, the Broken Spell is the restoration of Barbieland to a colorful and vibrant feminine play space. And like Ava, Barbie engages the new world of the Broken Spell as an independent real woman, cellulite and all.

The Nature of Evil in Heroine Stories

Evil is a real thing. While there are varying degrees to which some-one may enact evil, the concept of evil is intertwined in our stories. These days, writers and, perhaps, audiences are less comfortable with notions of good and evil characters. Labeling one character as "evil" seems so absolute. Friedrich Nietzsche's *Beyond Good and Evil* grapples with the intellectual concept of good and evil, attempting instead to find an alternative framework to judge human actions. He postulated that human presumptions about good and evil might be the root cause of destructive conflicts. He theorized that human conflicts might be avoided in a future where humanity rejects this bipolar ethical model. So then, to best understand the wisdom of our heroine tales in terms of good and evil, let's contrast it with the hero's journey.

The hero's journey provides a straightforward view of good and evil. Mass subjugation or cultural annihilation is wrong and easy to spot, so we get clear good and bad guys. The militant visiting team is evil, and the militant home team is good. The good overcomes evil, not because of the militancy but because of moral and humanistic values that the bad guys lack, restraining and guiding "good" militancy. Therefore, how and when to use force is at the heart of the hero's journey. The ethical framework of competency in using force and self-control is present on the individual and societal levels. That's why many hero's journey stories include a mentor character that nurtures the discipline and virtues of restraint. *Spider-Man, Lord of the Rings, The Matrix, The Karate Kid,* and *Star Wars* all deal extensively with the consequences of power, responsibility, and force. Individuals and cultures that are quick and reckless in their use of force risk becoming Cobra Kai or the Galactic Empire, while individuals and cultures that embrace virtue and restraint become Miyagi-Do or the New Republic. Therefore, evil stems from corrupt uses of power and force.

The heroine's labyrinth, however, often features a world where evil is hidden, disguised, and hard to perceive. Secondly, we have a more challenging time blaming an "outsider" of evil because evil hides within the native culture, right among the good guys. **Therefore, the Broken Spell is a functional worldview that fails.** The full scope of evil may only be understood once the deception surrounding the Masked Minotaur is exposed. Only then can we behold the true cost of human suffering. The immediate restoration of society suggests that the nature of evil is especially dangerous when it hides in plain sight and operates by disguise. As a member of the native culture, the heroine is uniquely positioned in these stories to recognize many deceptions in the story world, and her journey through the labyrinth builds her ability to destroy a uniquely evolved Cult of Deception.

Therefore, the Broken Spell shows and warns us that the masses can be spellbound. Mass deception leads to groupthink, and groupthink plays a part in the tyrannical labyrinth, where regular people quickly rationalize evil things as good. Are the story's characters thinking as individuals, or were they spellbound by the inverse morality of the Masked Minotaur? From what I can tell, the heroine faces a form of evil that has existed since the beginning of time. How many times have we beheld evil on an incredible scale in human history only to ask ourselves, *How did we not see this? How could human beings be capable of such a thing?* **Therefore, heroine-centric stories warn us that some evil advances in the daylight under false pretenses. We will not recognize it fully until the Broken Spell, and then, only then, will the obvious evil be seen by all.**

The hidden evil of the heroine's labyrinth does not invalidate the militant evil of the hero's journey. Both are dangerous to humanity and need to be explored and understood.

For writers, the Broken Spell should signal the end of a core lie. I believe it's essential to allow the Broken Spell to breathe a bit and allow the readers or audience to deal with the realities of a Cult of Deception. Who was most affected? Who were the victims? What happened to them as a result? Who looked the other way? Who helped willingly? Why were so many lies considered believable? The greater the Broken Spell, the more change our heroine has affected. And whether that change was personal or societal, the heroine's journey through the labyrinth was the catalyst. I prefer the Masked Minotaur to be defeated or overcome in a way where they face the consequences of their animal nature one way or another. Or, if the Masked Minotaur succeeds or evades consequence, then the story should serve as a warning—evil is still out there.

The Reformed Villain

A new trend in storytelling is to have the heroine challenge a reluctant villain, who gives up their cause and joins the heroine. Yay. Now, a villain may change their worldview when confronted with undeniable proof that their behavior is harming others. The villain was misguided, but now they know better. Reform stories can work and have worked, but they don't model growth for the heroine—*they model growth for the villain*. The heroine merely nurtured the villain's change.

While the reformed villain absolutely works for certain stories, I'm mostly against this scenario as the standard or go-to theme. Some writers or critics prefer not to stigmatize a character as a villain. But a reformed villain, or Minotaur as Ally, should be the exception, not the rule. Why? Because the feminine monomyth *already* addresses the basic concept of growth and reform with an unlike individual.

The Beast as Ally explores the everyday miracle of two diverse individuals finding common ground *willingly*. Human desires and interpersonal experiences create a bond that emerges without coercion. The Beast archetype grows, but so too does the heroine. **Therefore, heroines must know the difference between a potential heroic partner and a direct opponent to her sovereignty.** It's essential to understand what makes the Minotaur, well, the Minotaur, and not a target for reform. The heroine's labyrinth models both relationships, so storytellers should keep the distinctions clear. Heroines will inevitably confront "the unchangeable being"—a Minotaur with whom a genuine relationship is impossible. Writers should be aware that each theme carries unique lessons and wisdom, so it may be wise to include both themes instead of duplicating the Beast as Ally for the villain.

If modern stories focus *too* much on reformed villains in heroine-centric tales, they risk sending a weakened message. **Just as the damsel in distress freezes the heroine in her Captivity Bargain stage, the reformed villain freezes the heroine in a Beast as Ally stage. In one trope, the heroine is forever bound to await an outside force to**

save her; in the other trope, she's forever bound to nurture change in someone else.

Follow your story to its natural end. If your villain is destined to reform, such as Te Ka in *Moana* or the Wizard in *The Wizard of Oz,* then so be it. Reformed villains happen. Just know your story and heroine and understand your archetypes and themes.

Anatomy of an Archetype – The Broken Spell

◊ The heroine breaks the core deception of the Minotaur in the story world.

◊ The world or setting often experiences a rapid rearrangement.

◊ The transition moves from darkness to light.

◊ The imagery and symbolism highlight growth, life, color, and creation.

◊ The hidden victims are freed.

◊ The Minotaur is defeated or reformed.

Exercises

1. As the heroine Neytiri fears that the battle against the humans is lost, the spell breaks in the film *Avatar*. How does the Broken Spell demonstrate the humans' failed worldview while reinforcing the Na'vi's worldview?

2. *Wuthering Heights* has a unique Captivity Bargain for the heroine Catherine Earnshaw. How does the author demonstrate that there is indeed a spell of sorts cast upon the star-crossed lovers, and how do we encounter the Broken Spell?

3. At the end of Season 5 of *Cobra Kai*, in an episode called "The Head of the Snake," there is a showdown between rival dojos. While the final confrontation exactly mirrors the hero's journey with single combat between Danny Larusso and Terry Silver, there is first an Unmasking. Which character first confronted Terry Silver about his deceptions? And what happens to Cobra Kai once the Broken Spell occurs?

Tarot

The Broken Spell rearranged the labyrinth in some way, significant or small. We have witnessed an external change in the heroine's world. But what about the internal change in our heroine? What has happened to *her* after the events of the heroine's labyrinth? And here, we press our fingers against the back of the final tarot card. We knew all along that the final card lay in the Heart Position, one final revelation as to the heroine herself. Are you ready to turn this, our last card?

Atonement

ATONEMENT

e turn the card and see a woman facing herself in a mirror. The image upholds a powerful archetypal moment in which the present confronts the past. What have we learned about our heroine, and, more importantly, what has our heroine learned about herself?

As we glance back, we see the many corridors of the labyrinth spiral and fade into the distant darkness, but for the first time, we know what lies in that darkness. We have traveled the labyrinth together; we visited so many nooks and crannies, curves, and hidden doors; we encountered awful dead ends, only to make an about-face and carry on in another direction. We held our breath as the heroine confronted the Minotaur at the center of the labyrinth, and we saw her struggle to break free of the dangerous enchantments. And yet, after all of this, we're still very close to where we started. Let us set our thoughts upon the heroine of the story.

She's changed.

And change is a one-way ticket. The heroine's tale may continue, and other labyrinths may await her entry, but for now, she's grown and matured in a vital way. But what does it all mean in the end? What does the heroine get out of all this?

Self-Actualization

In studying the hero from the hero's journey for decades, I asked myself, what did the hero gain in terms of self-realization? What *specifically* did the hero gain that guided and motivated him, if even on a subconscious level? The answer was revealing. For the warrior-oriented hero, the answer was **worthiness.** You see, the warrior secretly understands and resists the knowledge that his native culture views him as *expendable.* Therefore, at the end of the hero's journey, the hero attains a vision of himself as valuable, competent, disciplined, and ethical—a knight in shining armor. ***I am not expendable* is the hero's urgent declaration of being.** Even the recurrent theme behind the hero winning over the princess or getting a medal serves as evidence in story terms that he is now *worthy* of a relationship or *worthy* of cultural distinction. But that's the hero.

So, here we are in the same place of a different story alongside our heroine. She is us. So, we writers must then ask the existential question. What did the heroine need to realize about herself? What is true about *her* now that our story is at an end? Let's ask: Is the subconscious pursuit of *worthiness* what motivates our heroines? Did she fear the abyss of an expendable life in her journey through the labyrinth?

I don't think so.

Looking over all the heroines in all the stories we've discussed, I didn't see worthiness as the source of self-actualization. In fact, heroines are often treated in the opposite way of the warrior-hero—not as physically expendable, but physically *essential* to the native culture—to the point of protective and overprotective suppression. Therefore, although the story establishes the heroine's importance early on, her identity is buried beneath cultural pressures and a predetermined set of choices. Ultimately, the heroine's free will feels secondary to more significant family or cultural expectations. Other characters claim the heroine and her creative powers while, at the same time, ignoring her plea for alternatives. This silencing is at the heart of the heroine's unfulfilled self-actualization.

As the heroine attempts to take control of all the dimensions of her identity, she is challenged, doubted, dismissed, or overruled.

But, here, at the end of the story, we see that the heroine was *right*. She was right about something that mattered to her and, most likely, mattered to others in the labyrinth as well. The native culture, the Cult of Deception, and the Masked Minotaur denied this critical truth about the heroine for most of the story. Beliefs and attitudes about the heroine were inaccurate, so many characters denied her true identity throughout much of the story. But the truth has been restored. **Therefore, the journey through the labyrinth culminates in the heroine's validation.** She was right about something others denied and failed to see. In a world of illusions and elusive dangers, the external affirmation connects with the internal self-actualization of the heroine.

However, with validation comes larger responsibility. Whenever a person or character is validated, they must adjust their identity. Looking back, they were right under all those doubts and crushing fears. Atonement allows all the characters of the story a chance to reconcile, as well as the reader and audience. We, too, must reconsider our views of the heroine and find meaning in her story. She's a heroine, after all, and fulfilled a vital human role for all of us on the sidelines. She's why we remember so many heroines through the ages and continue to tell their stories.

Atonement with Self

Like worthiness, validation *can* be an external force bestowed upon the heroine from the native culture—but the internal version of validation is the most important. The heroine did not set out consciously to seek validation, just as the hero didn't consciously seek worthiness. But at the end of her journey, the heroine is validated.

As writers, give your heroine a moment to reflect. Looking back, the heroine recognizes the full power of the labyrinth in a way that her unformed self could not. She can appreciate her willingness to press forward. Her instincts on right and wrong, good and evil, proved correct, so she knows now that her intuition is a reliable internal force despite the confusion of the outside world. The heroine broke the Captivity Bargain; she defied many reasoned warnings, yet here she stands. She was right, and the world benefited.

I think of the cover of the novel *The Red Tent* by Anita Diamant. The cover art depicts a woman outdoors in a red robe with her arms uplifted and hands at rest behind her head. Her eyes are closed, and her expression is stoic but serene. The woman appears to be enjoying a private moment of serenity while standing upright. The artwork captures a glimpse of a woman at peace with herself despite the turbulence of an unforgiving world.

Heroines must face themselves now with the frightening knowledge of their undeniable accomplishments. Atonement with Self shifts the heroine's sense of identity. She must come to terms with the opposing forces of doubts and resolve, failings and achievements, shortcomings and clear strengths. Atonement with Self is scarier than one might think. Negative and positive energies are always within us—so they exist side-by-side in our characters. The heroine realizes the negative energies within her *didn't* prevent her success nor suppress her transformative powers in the world. She can forgive herself by letting go of the guilt that may have built up through the heroine's labyrinth.

The heroine may also realize that the Atonement with the Self is a temporary reprieve from the outside world. The negative energies of doubt, anxiety, and anger will likely rise again, and other labyrinths still wait to be entered, but for now, the heroine internalizes her power and sovereignty.

Atonement with Native Culture

In the movie, *Moana*, the heroine's father sings a song about Moana's predetermined path to becoming the leader of her island culture. Her father takes her to the tallest island peak and shows her a stack of stones known as the Place of Chiefs. He tells her that a time will come when she will place a stone upon the mountain in the tradition of all the prior chiefs.

Moana, though, yearns to explore the oceans beyond the reef. These are the two claims upon the heroine's Sacred Fire. The story finds Atonement with these two rival claims rather nicely in two ways. First, Moana's desire for seafaring matches her culture's secret but *original* spirit, which means that her journey recovered a lost cultural value rather than overturning a bad one. And secondly, when we see the stack of stones at the end, Moana's symbolic conch shell sits on top. In other words, Moana took her place as the tribe's leader, which was the native culture's claim to her Sacred Fire, but she did so as the leader of a *seafaring* culture, which honors her claim and restores the native culture.

Atonement with the native culture may be the most psychologically and spiritually gratifying to the heroine. This book has demonstrated that the conflict between heroines and their native culture remains a timeless and persistent theme. Remember, some part of the heroine's Sacred Fire comes directly from the communal fire of the native culture, and this shared bond is hard to break entirely without profound internal consequences.

In the memoir *All You Can Ever Know* by Nicole Chung, the author details her journey to discover her biological parents after being adopted by Americans at a young age. Nicole was adopted, and like many adopted people, the urge to *know* something about their past heritage can be overwhelming. This base need, Nicole's desire to understand who she is and where she came from, drives the entire real-life story. Human beings aren't spontaneous creations. We are a continuation of a burning flame of life, family, and culture, whether we like it or not. Despite all the frustrations, all the angst, and all the conflicts between the heroine and her native culture, she will still likely feel a need to make peace here.

Atonement with Mother

I originally planned on an analysis of the Atonement with Mother scenario since the hero's journey featured the hero's Atonement with Father. I usually resist this urge to match the hero's journey; however,

I cannot ignore this basic resolution. At the end of a heroine's story, what timeless theme echoes our shared realities here? What about the mother-daughter relationship, or, I should say, the heroine-mother figure-dynamic?

Maureen Murdock first introduced me to the notion of the heroine-mother figure dynamic in her book, *The Heroine's Journey: Woman's Quest for Wholeness*. While the book didn't help me pattern my stories, I never forgot Maureen's thoughts on the topic of heroines and their mothers. Maureen says, "The mother/daughter relationship and the separation from the mother are so complex that in most women's literature and fairy tales, the mother remains absent, dead, or villainous."

I think Maureen is right. With the heroine's labyrinth defined, I have returned to this theme. Female or mother versions of a Masked Minotaur are certainly not *more* villainous than masculine Minotaurs. However, I see one specific clash within the feminine monomyth that may relate directly to a heroine and her mother, and because of it, I believe that more and more stories in the future may indeed focus on the Atonement with Mother. The Sacred Fire conflict between the heroine and her native culture, so prevalent in the heroine's labyrinth, may indeed center on the mother or be embodied by the mother.

There is one structurally irreconcilable dynamic early on in the story. Simply by being a mother, the mother character automatically fulfills the native culture's preference to raise a family. The mother is passing the communal fire of family and culture down to the daughter. Therefore, ancient pressure for marriage and children is the exact claim that the heroine most strongly *rejects* early in the story, if not forever. **So, the heroine's individual claim to free expression and independence when set against the mother's role as a parent, which echoes the native culture's claim to the heroine's Sacred Fire, may indeed be irreconcilable for a while. Therefore, by reconciling herself with the native culture, the heroine also lays the groundwork for an Atonement with Mother.** The mother figure must accept the heroine's claim to the Sacred Fire, and the heroine must accept her mother's continuity of culture and family. The mother figure still has a Sacred Fire of her own, so deep down, she understands the heroine's feelings and desires. The two characters are *not* as different as they once believed.

In *Everything Everywhere All at Once*, the Atonement arrives in a mother-daughter relationship. The heroine, Evelyn Wang, has a Beast as Ally through the aptly named "Alpha" Waymond, who is a shadowy doppelganger of the Masked Minotaur, who is her daughter. The Beast and Minotaur are family members who seek to permanently sever their relationship with the heroine, the husband through a divorce, and the daughter through self-annihilation. The final scene shows the heroine reconciling with her daughter. They both first acknowledge the Sacred Fire of the other and agree to honor each other. The film's conclusion? Despite everything that's wrong about everything, everywhere, relationships and love are *still* worthwhile.

In *Barbie*, the Atonement reconciles all three claimants. First, Barbie restores the native culture of Barbieland to its original purpose. Even the real-world pressures from Mattel cease their attempt to put Barbie back in the box. Therefore, the native culture surrenders all claims to Barbie's Sacred Fire. The Beast as Ally in this story is Ken, who attempts to diminish Barbie's Sacred Fire and convert Barbieland to Kendom. True to the Beast as Ally archetype, Ken's humanity wins out. He also surrenders his claim upon the heroine's Sacred Fire. Lastly, Atonement with Mother is quite powerful in the film. Although Barbie has no birth mother, Gloria and Sasha have a mother-daughter dynamic. The two reconcile once they accept each other with all their imperfections, a core theme throughout the film.

In whatever form Atonement assumes in the story, the reconciliation process is vital for the heroine. All three forms of Atonement may be necessary for the most satisfying end: Atonement with Self, Atonement with Native Culture, and Atonement with Mother.

Anatomy of an Archetype – Atonement

◊ The heroine attains validation.

◊ Atonement can be with the self, the native culture, the mother, or all three.

◊ The heroine lets go of the accumulative guilt from The Broken Truce.

◊ Members of her native culture acknowledge the heroine's efforts.

◊ The story world changes in some way, big or small.

◊ The story must reconcile all claims to the heroine's Sacred Fire.

◊ Who's claim won out?

Exercises

1. Now that you, dear writers, fully understand the importance of Atonement and all the forms it may take, can you identify why the character arc for Daenerys Targaryen failed in the end? In what way did the writers avoid the Atonement of the heroine?

2. In the film *Titanic*, how does Rose find Atonement with herself and the native culture? Lastly, how is Rose reconciled with all the passengers of the ill-fated maiden voyage? Which Atonement did the film skip?

3. While writing this book, I struggled to find great examples of Atonement with Mother, which harkens back to Maureen Murdock's observation. Therefore, I'll pass it to you, dear writers. Why do you think stories avoid or even unknowingly skip Atonement with Mother? Lastly, can you name three stories that satisfyingly tackle the mother-daughter Atonement?

Closing a Reading

Only at the end of a tarot reading do we see the face of each card. We glance over the arrangement and should take a moment to appreciate all the energy and concentration that goes into interpreting archetypal images. As writers, we've harnessed the timeless powers of each archetype and fused them with our imaginative storytelling powers. Despite all the dream-like aspects that are open to interpretation, we're not creating gibberish. We're anchoring it all to the recurrences of the human condition. Our writing instincts take over and fuse the concepts into our stories. Fortune-telling is not that different from storytelling when you think about it. Like the fortune-teller, the storyteller conjures up the most intriguing creative ideas using instincts and premonitions and then funnels the ideas through the superstructure of narrative order.

The heroine's labyrinth is a loose story structure for your imagination and creativity. Trust your writing intuition. And like a tarot reading, the cards may come up in a different order; some cards may not be used at all, and some may be the focus of your entire story. You can go through the themes of the heroine's labyrinth multiple times for many different types of stories, and you can use the themes in conjunction with the themes of the hero's journey. Like a psychic reading, there are no hard rules—only good reads and good writing.

The Feminine Monomyth – Some Final Thoughts

The heroine's labyrinth isn't an absolute shape but a flexible pattern that emerges in our stories to varying degrees and in infinite forms. It's a growth arc, both in storytelling and in character. It's a multidimensional *narrative* model that carries numerous recurrent themes, consciously or unconsciously, by the writer of heroine-led fiction. And we learn from these stories *because* of the recurrent patterns, which signal something timeless in our shared humanity.

I believe the heroine's labyrinth is the ancient *dream of the goddess* embedded within all of us, sometimes majestic, sometimes tragic, compassionate and creative, severe and chaotic, waning anxious beneath many doubts, then waxing radiant in the hour of consequence. By following her desires and intuitions, the heroine of our stories aligns herself with all the forces of the psyche that create the constant heroine in the first place—she who stretches back into our collective mythologies, who has lived through all our various histories, who lives now in our memoirs, who reappears in fantasy worlds or stares back at us from a distant human future. The constant heroine is all around us. She'll continue to emerge in the patterns and rhythms of our stories just as she'll be visible at times in your personal life. Perhaps that's why we seek her out in so many stories. She's like a mirage of a living human truth that we understand without language and often with minimal, if any, context. The truth is…beneath all those archetypes, images, and symbols, the timeless and constant heroine is *you*.

APPENDICES

THE GENRES

nce I developed a working model for the heroine's labyrinth, I realized just *how many* of our stories match the labyrinth model over the journey model. So, I'd like to take a few minutes and cover the genres that work well, if not perfectly, for the heroine's labyrinth.

Writers! Pay attention!

If your preferred genres are among the following examples, then the heroine's labyrinth may be particularly useful to you. Most of these genres emphasize specific heroine-centric themes while minimizing or omitting certain other themes altogether. As a simple tool, I cite the prominent themes in each genre.

Horror

Heavy Emphasis on:

◊ **The Masked Minotaur**
◊ **Home as Battleground**
◊ **The Poisoned Apple**

While writing this book, I purposely removed tons of examples that related to the horror genre. Why? Because the horror genre is like the heroine's labyrinth abridged and on freaking steroids. Horror stories take the heroine's labyrinth, strip it down to the bare bones, and focus on a deadly clash between the Minotaur and the heroine inside a home.

First off, many horror films indeed feature a female lead. Second, the battles almost always take place inside a home. Thirdly, from *Friday the 13th* to *The Texas Chainsaw Massacre* to *Scream* to *Halloween*, the villains are masculine Minotaur archetypes who wear literal masks. One difference in the horror genre is that the Masked Minotaur is typically not duplicitous. A traditional heroine's labyrinth will feature a perfectly disguised Minotaur in society, bearing an outward and benevolent "man" face while hiding the animalistic "monster" face. Although the Minotaur often wears a mask in horror, they lack the benevolent veneer. However, in movies like *The Witch* and *Black Swan*, the Minotaur is disguised and unmasked in the end. *Black Swan* is particularly effective. In the finale, viewers watch the film's female lead, Nina Sayers, physically transform herself into the Masked Minotaur—the hedonic and tyrannical black swan—who had mercilessly tormented the heroine throughout the movie.

In the vast multitude of horror films, the drama occurs not only in the native culture but within the heroine's home. *The Babadook* is a particularly frightening story with a Shieldmaiden emphasis. Several films feature both parents and children, such as *The Conjuring*, *A Quiet Place*, and *Poltergeist*, but shift focus to settle on feminine bravery during critical showdowns. Heroine Evelyn Abbott (played by Emily Blunt) has to give birth without making any noise in *A Quiet Place*, for crying out loud. Even secondary characters, such as Jillian Guiler in *Close Encounters of the Third Kind*, endure a scary siege of her house that results in the alien abduction of her son. Clearly, the home itself, the sanctuary of family life and safety, becomes a terrifying battleground where many heroines must fight back.

The labyrinth motifs are also strong in the horror genre, with films like *The Descent*, *The Shining*, *Escape Room*, *Annihilation*, *Barbarian*, *Saw*, *Nightmare on Elm Street*, and *M3GAN*. Nearly all these films feature a female lead who navigates a maze-like world where a deadly Minotaur relentlessly stalks them.

The horror film is a very specific modification of the heroine's labyrinth. The basic model is the same, but several themes are skipped to maximize the effect of a handful of other themes. Namely, the horror genre emphasizes a Masked Minotaur (usually male), with the heroine's own Home as Battleground, a claustrophobic labyrinth, and an evil Cult of Deception.

The Crime Drama

Heavy Emphasis on:

◊ **Unmasking the Minotaur**
◊ **The Cult of Deception**
◊ **The Chambers of Knowledge**
◊ **Chamber Guardians**

When I asked my mother to name some of her favorite heroines growing up, her first answer was Nancy Drew. And she had me promise to include Nancy in this book. Luckily for my mom, Nancy is a perfect heroine to take the spotlight here.

Nancy Drew set the tone decades ago, her stories written by multiple women authors under a pseudonym. She debuted in the 1930s, and at the time, many professionals in the publishing industry seemed shocked that a female detective could compete with or even dethrone the Hardy Boys. However, by studying the heroine's labyrinth, I'm not surprised. The archetypal heroine makes a perfect detective, and the process aligns with a familiar tapestry of conflicts—disguises within the native culture and hidden victims. Nancy Drew is now a globally recognized name who inspired powerful women such as Supreme Court justices, the same as everyday heroines like my mother.

But Nancy Drew kicked open a door for a veritable army of female detectives in fiction—Olivia Benson in *Law & Order: Special Victims Unit*, Eve Polastri in *Killing Eve*, Vivian Johnson in *Without a Trace*, Jessica Jones in *Alias*, Renee Montoya in *Birds of Prey*, Jessica Fletcher in *Murder, She Wrote*, Temperance Brennan in *Bones*, Veronica Mars in *Veronica Mars*, Enola Holmes in *Enola Holmes*, and Dana Scully in *The X-Files*. There are plenty more crime-solving heroines out there, and we'll probably see plenty more in the future.

Like the horror genre, crime dramas also emphasize certain aspects of the heroine's labyrinth while deemphasizing other themes. For example, whereas the horror genre goes all in on the animal side of the Minotaur—who wears a mask but whose identity is not important—the crime drama specializes in the human side of the Minotaur, whose mask has been perfected. The villain is a genuine criminal or murderer hidden within the native culture. *The Silence of the Lambs* is one of the best examples of a complete heroine's labyrinth, with every theme in the story. It's an excellent film to study. However, most crime dramas are streamlined to achieve the psychological effects of mystery and danger.

Detective heroines exhibit the basic disposition of the Shieldmaiden, only more patient and professional. They want to protect the fragile powers of the world and have the skill set to do it. Every time you see a detective flash a badge, they are literally flashing their "shield." The shield symbolism is synonymous with law enforcement and crime shows. The heroic Shieldmaiden who unmasks a menacing Minotaur to protect life is among the most ancient feminine archetypes in history.

Clearly, the crime drama is a classic labyrinth within the native culture. Detectives spend much of their time moving through the labyrinth and encountering dangerous and helpful spirits that either block their passage or aid their hunt for the Minotaur. The detective must move in repetitive circles to close in on the Minotaur. Heroines know that the Minotaur will continue to harm the native culture until unmasked and brought to justice.

The Chambers of Knowledge motif is front and center in the crime drama. Heroines encounter multiple Chamber Guardians, consistent with the heroine's labyrinth. The heroine enters different chambers, each jam-packed with specific symbols and objects from one corner of the world, with hidden secrets or information. Each chamber has an individual who confronts the heroine (or detective) and either obstructs or aids the quest. There is *always* a challenge. Typically, the heroine (or detective) must ask the right questions, prove their sincerity, solve a riddle, or speak the magic charm before the Chamber Guardian provides the next clue. If the heroine (or detective) fails, they will leave the chamber defeated and may have to return later. The Chambers of Knowledge are one of the more magnified themes in crime dramas.

The Cult of Deception is another heavily emphasized theme for obvious reasons. Misdirection and illusions are at the very center of the conflict. Whether the deceptions are from the labyrinth, the uncooperative world where the Minotaur resides, or traps laid by the Minotaur, the Cult of Deception works overtime in the crime drama. Everyone seems to try and throw the detective off the scent. Red herrings are imminent. Nothing is as it seems, and detectives, like most heroines, rely on intuition in deciding who to trust or when measuring the sincerity of advice or assistance.

But here again, the hero's journey is ill-suited to form the basis of organizing a crime drama. The heroine's labyrinth model, however, is a nearly perfect match.

Romance

Heavy Emphasis on:

◊ **The Sacred Fire**
◊ **Beast as Ally**
◊ **The Broken Truce**

As a writer, it behooves you to know that romance is the top-selling genre in the industry. Period. According to the Romance Novel Sales Statistics at the time of this writing, 82 percent of romance readers are women. Most of the top ten bestselling romance novels are also *written* by women. Since much of the romance genre follows the heroine's labyrinth, again, I'm not surprised. *Fifty Shades of Grey* by E. L. James, *Pride and Prejudice* by Jane Austen, *Gone with the Wind* by Margaret Mitchell, *Outlander* by Diana Gabaldon, and *The Time Traveler's Wife* by Audrey Niffenegger round out the top five best-selling romance novels worldwide written by women.

The Beast as Ally is by far the most dominant theme in a romance novel, emphasizing the romantic relationship between the heroine and a Beast archetype. Following closely behind is the archetypal power of the heroine's Sacred Fire, in this case, clearly denoting her feminine eros and passion. The fire burns bright in these stories. There are often several claims made upon the heroine's Sacred Fire, one of which usually bears the possessive love of the Masked Minotaur.

Labyrinths feature prominently in romance novels as well. Often the social rules of the native culture create elaborate barriers between the heroine and the Beast, which simultaneously boosts the rival Masked Minotaur's power.

I won't pretend to be an expert in the romance genre; however, having read *Pride and Prejudice* as part of my study on heroines, I can say that this very romance novel contributed significantly to the heroine's labyrinth. One of the most famous written lines of all time—"It is a truth universally acknowledged, that a single man in possession of a good fortune, must be in want of a wife."—perfectly captures the powerful dynamic between the heroine, the native culture, and the possessive love of a Masked Minotaur. Like Anna Karenina, Elizabeth Bennet taught me how a heroine's public choices provoke strong responses in a story, such as whom the heroine chooses to dance with at a ball. The conflict of an arranged marriage is central to countless stories of countless heroines. The heroine Lakshmi in *The Henna Artist* escaped an arranged marriage, only to be followed by her husband. The social rules and traditions of 1950s India create an elaborate labyrinth for Lakshmi.

Another book for writers that deals with heroines and is written by a female author is *The Heroine's Journey* by Gail Carriger. She's written numerous books, including romance novels, and her advice on writing heroines may prove helpful.

Tropes from the hero's journey can also be highly effective in romance, mainly if the heroine leaves the native culture. For example, the *Outlander* series carries many themes from both the hero's journey and the heroine's labyrinth.

Revolutionary Tales

Emphasized:

◊ **Home as Battleground**
◊ **The Broken Truce**
◊ **The Labyrinth**

You say you want a revolution? Well, find yourself a heroine. You'll find that many women have been involved in revolutions throughout history. Hounaida A. El Jurdi and Nacima Ourahmoune wrote an article in February 2021 with the headline "Revolution is a woman—the feminization of the Arab Spring." Sounds right to me.

From Joan of Arc to Meena Keshwar to Boudicca to Qiu Jin, female leaders and feminine symbolism in revolution seem to be close sisters. After the American Revolution, Lady Liberty raised her torch to the rest of the world for the first time. One of the most famous paintings of the

Liberty Leading the People by Eugène Delacroix (1830).

July Revolution features a woman holding up the French flag and leading the armed revolutionaries behind her.

Since the native culture itself is the problem, and the cultural leader is deemed the enemy, the heroine's labyrinth storytelling model works perfectly for revolutionary tales.

Once referred to as "proto-feminism," the first movements of what we now recognize as a wide-scale and ongoing feminist movement began in the eighteenth century. Coincidentally, this is the exact century that kicked out the Age of Revolution. Author Hannah Arendt noted that the revolution is a relatively modern concept. Feminism began around the same time revolutions did.

In most heroine-led fiction, heroines model behavior for breaking conventions that no longer apply or never should have been in the first place. Rose Dewitt-Buchanan rebels against the English aristocracy in *Titanic*, Katniss Everdeen overturns the society in Panem in *The Hunger Games*, and Zephyr Halima seeks to overturn the Genetic Dynasty in *Foundation*. These heroines are catalysts for real change in society. The narrative monomyth is set up to do this in subtle ways, but a few tweaks of emphasis in the story structure and your heroine might well end up capsizing the social order.

Within the heroine's labyrinth monomyth, a genuine pathway exists to changes in the native culture. As stated earlier, despite familiar and often despised tropes like the Captivity Bargain, the heroine's labyrinth can serve as a model for breaking captivity. This means that the labyrinth's structure must be rearranged by the story's end, and often through the heroine's actions, choices, and convictions. On a small scale, the rearrangement might be an escape from the traditions of a single household, such as the mother, Betty, in *Pleasantville*. Or it may be the revolutionary overturning of society, as in *The Hunger Games*. The heroine's non-conformity to the native culture can be a model for individual empowerment or expanded into a model for revolutionary non-conformity.

In the film *Pan's Labyrinth*, the young heroine, Ofelia, is an innocent girl amidst the revolutionary conflict in Spain. The film's end shows Ofelia attempting to protect her baby brother's life (total Shield-maiden) by wandering into a magical labyrinth just outside. The background imagery depicts fire and revolution as opposing forces clash. The image perfectly matches the Home as Battleground theme in revolutionary tales. The place where the heroine is supposed to feel safe is often where the Masked Minotaur dwells or where the conflict erupts.

If you want to tell a tale of revolution, consider a heroine as your main character. Her instincts to resist the labyrinth of her native culture will be ideally suited to a larger and more widespread civil conflict.

Superheroes & Comic Books

Emphasized:

◊ **The Masked Minotaur**
◊ **Home as Battleground**
◊ **The Shieldmaiden**

The superhero genre is somewhat of a mixed bag. Most of us think of the hero's journey for superheroes. I propose that the hero's journey is particularly effective for superhero origin stories. However, for those who follow superheroes regularly, such as in a TV series or comic book run, you'll find that once the superhero's origin is established, their adventures carry on with a different rhythm. For example, most of Superman's conflicts take place in Metropolis, his adopted native culture, with villains that are masked or hidden within. Batman, likewise, is consistently at war within both the criminal elements of his native culture, Gotham City, as well as the culture itself, which often sees him as a villain.

I believe that the heroine's labyrinth not only deserves to be viewed as the dominant model in superhero storytelling overall but that there may be a correlation between the rise of feminism, the dawn of the nuclear age, and the emergence of the superhero genre. Sound crazy? Maybe.

First, the comic phenomenon began in newspapers as funnies, a.k.a. the comic strip. However, comics evolved, and the true advent of modern superheroes took shape after women's suffrage in 1920, when Western women were asserting themselves in the public consciousness. The Golden Age of Comics followed from 1938 to 1955, encompassing World War II, the rise of the Atomic Age, and the advent of the Cold War.

Superman first appeared in 1938, then Batman in 1939, then Wonder Woman in 1941. Rosie the Riveter first appeared less than two years later, in 1943. Early feminism profoundly influenced Wonder Woman, and some early storylines clearly followed feminist topics at that time. Therefore, Wonder Woman emerged at the very beginning of the superhero genre and had close ties with feminism. Three years after Wonder Woman's first appearance, the world changed.

The use of the first atom bombs to end World War II ushered in the Atomic Age. The nature of warfare fundamentally changed with the proliferation of nuclear weapons among the superpowers. A full-scale war could lead to a nuclear holocaust. Ideas like "mutually assured destruction" and the "Doomsday Clock" came into being. **The warrior-oriented hero on the journey had to be extra careful when setting out to slay the Distant Dragon in the Atomic Age.** The provocation could mean the end of the world, a risk no longer worth taking on either side.

Large-scale military engagements and pitched battles gave way to espionage, geopolitical influence, and subversion abroad and at home. Suddenly, the Cold War adopted a new tactic—Home as Battleground.

Even male superheroes such as Captain America, Batman, Spider-Man, Superman, and Wolverine battled Masked Minotaurs within their own native cultures. More and more, homegrown Masked Minotaurs replaced Distant Dragons, who menaced the native culture from within, such as the Joker, Green Goblin, or Lex Luthor. Most supervillains wear proper masks and have a hidden identity.

Therefore, apart from many **origin stories**, I believe the superhero genre may be more closely rooted in the heroine's labyrinth. Superhero strategies in the home culture align nicely with those of the heroine. *This does not invalidate the hero's journey by any stretch.* Societies will *always* need warriors ready to leave the native culture and defend it from encroaching threats abroad. I think the hero's journey isn't the *only* go-to model anymore.

Even an analysis of the Marvel Cinematic Universe reveals the split. Starting with *Ironman* (2008) and ending with *The Avengers: Endgame* (2019), we see Masked Minotaurs in each superhero's individual story, but then a Distant Dragon (Thanos) comes to threaten Earth itself and eventually, all life in the universe. Even more interesting for Gamora and Nebula, two superheroine sisters, the heroine's labyrinth still comes to life. Thanos is their father. So, even the militant Distant Dragon to the Avengers remains a Masked Minotaur to Gamora and Nebula—an apex tyrant within their family and from among their native culture. Amazing.

In my opinion, the superhero genre *began* from the tradition of the hero's journey but became fertile ground to redefine the heroic role to include the heroine's labyrinth. Perhaps we just didn't know what to call these changes, so we confused the distinctive themes with variations of the hero's journey.

The emergent concept of mutually assured destruction, coupled with the rise of modern feminism alongside the comic book industry, places the heroine's labyrinth well within the superhero genre.

Historical Fiction / Biographical

When I set out to write the early life of Byzantine Empress Theodora, I tried to follow the tropes of the hero's journey. It was all I knew. Anyone who reads *Far Away Bird* will see Campbell's fingerprints in the story. You'll see the Refusal of the Call, the Wise Guide, the Road of Trials, and even the oft-skipped Belly of the Beast theme (symbolic death). And yet, while writing the story, so many problems emerged where the hero's journey had nothing to say and no place in Theodora's story. For one, Theodora had real-life biographical details that I had to follow. This will be true of *all* historical fiction, where events and actions occur that the writer must address and in chronological order. Historical narratives and readers' expectations bind writers to numerous biographical and historical facts. How *did* a prostitute transform into the stuff of empresses? Well, the heroine's labyrinth gave me a way forward that echoed the ancient struggles of a heroine without twisting history. And it worked.

Therefore, dear writers, historical fiction may summon all the themes of the heroine's labyrinth as needed. If any theme comes to the forefront, perhaps it is the labyrinth itself, each maze like a unique artifact of another time and place. Every labyrinth is just as rich and magnificent as it is dangerous and repressive. Historical fiction also places us, the reader or audience, right into the shoes of a past world, giving us a chance to see ourselves in a human system unlike our own, exotic yet oddly familiar.

Today, when I go to a bookstore, the historical fiction section is utterly dominated by historical heroines. Women comprise a massive demographic for book sales and dominate many genres, including historical fiction.

So many historical heroines have conflicts and character arcs that take place within their respective native cultures. The heroine's labyrinth is an excellent narrative format that aligns with numerous historical stories.

Memoirs

Perhaps nowhere has the hero's journey frustrated writers more than the memoirist. Like historical fiction, the memoirist must follow biographical details while finding some narrative structure. The hero's journey didn't always work. In many ways, the memoir is historical fiction since the author recounts autobiographical events from the near past. The Historical Novel Society defines historical fiction as at least fifty years ago. The memoirist, though, relies on personal experience instead of historical research. However, whether from research or memory, writers must rebuild a world of the past while following a narrative form and character arc.

Memoir writers may benefit the most from the feminine monomyth. The process of organizing an entire life's worth of stories and moments into a more concise story structure is hard enough as it is. I've heard from numerous writers who tried to use the hero's journey model to structure their narrative. In so many cases, the monomythic structure didn't apply, or it fit awkwardly with the details of their life.

If you are trying to write a memoir and the hero's journey doesn't work, then try the heroine's labyrinth. You may have left home but likely stayed in your native culture. Or, if you relocated from one culture to another, the immersive process of learning social and cultural rules would still resonate. Also, your villains in life may have been closer to home. Your villains may have had a duplicitous nature, perhaps boasting social status or power while masking a cruel and tyrannical nature. And as my mother pointed out, the Chambers of Knowledge themes closely follow a college experience full of discovery and challenges.

I strongly encourage men and women to consider the heroine's labyrinth when organizing their life into a story. The power of monomyth is likely to work for your life's story. A monomyth is that common thread that goes through the human experience in a narrative form.

Some memoirs have changed the world and shed light on humanity, such as *I Know Why the Caged Bird Sings* by Maya Angelou, the Holocaust trilogy *Night, Dawn,* and *Day* by Elie Wiesel, *Reading Lolita in Tehran* by Azar Nafisi, and *I Am Malala* by an adolescent Malala Yousafzai, who won a Nobel Peace Prize for her brilliant memoir.

Don't underestimate the power of your memoir. You're writing a memoir in the first place because you believe something valuable may be gleaned from your life experiences. And that, dear heroine, is definitely worth writing about.

The Journey Continues...

Well, dear writers, alas, we've come to the end of our journey together. Not only have we explored the treacherous labyrinth, we've taken the time to understand all the archetypal events that come with such an exploration. We've pulled out the patterns found in heroine-centric stories, and as a result, we've come to understand our heroines better and learned quite a bit about storytelling.

However, several people have asked for a shift in focus to a single story, with each theme highlighted and discussed. Therefore, I invite you all to visit **DouglasABurton.com**. There, I have a list of films, shows, and books that break down the themes of each story. Moreover, as writers, we're always in this together. You'll also find an area where *you* can submit your own story breakdown using the heroine's labyrinth for fellow writers to read and share. If we use your submission, you'll receive credit along with any links to your social media pages.

You'll find strategies for applying these archetypal designs to your own stories. I also share my full bibliography for all the books I recommend for further reading and different angles on the general topic. My ultimate goal with this book is to help writers like you!

Thanks for reading.

Visit DouglasABurton.com

ACKNOWLEDGMENTS

The Heroine's Labyrinth would not have been possible without a bevy of heroines and heroes in my life. I want to thank my wife and mother, Crystal and Sharon Burton, for all their time, patience, and insight; my father, Alan Burton, for the hours of discussions about story and meaning; my friend Luci Williams, for her creative genius and feminine perspective; and finally, Kamran Pasha for his time-honored wisdom, mentorship, and professional council.

I'd also like to thank Jeniffer Thompson and her team at Monkey C Media for their hard work in producing this book, Caroline Leavitt for her professional feedback, Christopher Vogler for his veteran expertise and advice, and finally, Heath Robinson, Brianna da Silva, James Bacon, and Davae Breon Jaxon (DBJ) for their early partnership in discussing and exploring the heroine's labyrinth in depth.

For those who are interested in The Heroine's Labyrinth, please join me on the YouTube Table Talk channel where I often appear to discuss pop culture, story structure, and more.

YouTube.com/@Table_Talk_Podcast

AUTHOR BIO

Douglas A. Burton is a novelist and storyteller whose various works emphasize heroic women in fiction. Burton's debut historical novel, *Far Away Bird*, brought Byzantine Empress Theodora to life through an intimate biographical account. The novel collected numerous awards including gold medals for the IBPA's Best New Voice in Fiction, Readers' Favorite Historical Personage, and eLit's Best Historical Fiction eBook. *Far Away Bird* was also a finalist for the Montaigne Medal (Eric Hoffer Book Award) and the ScreenCraft Cinematic Book Competition. Burton's newest book, *The Heroine's Labyrinth*, is a nonfiction writing craft book that offers a paradigm shift for story structure. Presented as a distinctive counterpart to the well-trodden hero's journey, Burton explores the unique narrative arc and archetypal designs that recur in heroine-led fiction. He currently lives in Austin, TX with his wonderful wife, Crystal, and two energetic boys, Jacob and Lucas.

Follow the author and reach out to him with questions about *The Heroine's Labyrinth*, speaker inquiries, and fan love:

DouglasABurton.com

FAR AWAY BIRD

DOUGLAS A BURTON

Also by Douglas A. Burton

Far Away Bird

"...elegantly written historical tale in which [Burton] effortlessly weaves sweeping emotion and fine detail...."
—Kirkus Reviews

"More than just an imagining of Theodora's rise to notoriety and power during the Byzantine Empire, the novel is a vivid tale of survival, healing, and femininity."
—US Review of Books

Multi-award winning novel including gold medals in the Readers' Favorite Historical Personage, IBPA's Best New Voice Fiction, eLit's Best eBook in Historical Fiction, Montaigne Medal finalist (Eric Hoffer Book Award), and the ScreenCraft Cinematic Book Competition.

Inspired by true events, *Far Away Bird* delves into the complex mind of Byzantine Empress Theodora. This intimate biographical account follows the extraordinary transformation of a poor young woman in a rigid medieval society. From the brothels to the bathhouses, from the theaters to the palaces, Theodora learns to let go of the people she loves most and embrace her own exploitation. But when Theodora finally chooses her own personal sovereignty, no matter the cost, her battle leads to an impossible destination—the throne of the empire.

Empress Theodora is one of the most misunderstood women of history. *Far Away Bird* immerses the reader into a corrupt underworld that history classrooms tend to keep at arm's length. Theodora's salacious past has been fertile grounds for historians to defame and diminish her stunning achievements as an empress. And while tales of shamelessness stick to Theodora like a scarlet letter, the story of her troubled youth reveals an all-too-human side to her place in history. Look closer. *Far Away Bird* reconciles one woman's notorious past to the making of an empress.

Available everywhere books are sold.
ISBN: 978-17330221-0-1(paperback)
Support local and buy from your favorite local bookseller.
Check out Doug's favorite in his hometown
of Austin, Texas:

BookPeople.com
https://www.bookpeople.com/book/9781733022101